Quality Short Stories
An Anthology

Edited by
Larry Parr

PublishAmerica
Baltimore

First printing

At the specific preference of the author, PublishAmerica allowed this work to remain exactly as the author intended, verbatim, without editorial input.

ISBN: 1-4241-0843-8
PUBLISHED BY PUBLISHAMERICA, LLLP
www.publishamerica.com
Baltimore

Printed in the United States of America

Contents

William L. Walker is a U.S. Army veteran who served in Vietnam in 1969, returning home in early 70. After a twenty-eight-year career with the Los Angeles Police Department, he retired to the solitude of South Dakota. There, his VFW Post served as volunteers at the Fort Meade Veterans Hospital and as sthe Honor Guard for veteran's funerals at the National Cemetery in Sturgis, SD. He listened to many stories from other veterans, how they felt out of place upon returning home, many never quite fitting in. From their stories and his own experiences, he wrote, "The Sarge" a returning vet's story with a happy ending.

The Sarge
William L. Walker

It was 0215 hours…2:15 AM to most people. Sirens blared, waking the residents of the temporary village, warning them of an impending rocket attack.

It was a common occurrence, harassment fire, not so much intended to destroy anything, just to annoy anyone within the possible impact area and disrupt sleep. Rocket attacks were so common in that part of Vietnam, most soldiers quickly learned how to distinguish between those that were close and those that would pass overhead. If the soldier believed a rocket was coming close, he shouted, "Incoming!" loudly enough to get the attention of anyone within hearing distance.

When soldiers heard, "Incoming!" they crawled under their bunks. Outside the barracks walls was a double row of sandbags stacked four feet high to protect the men inside. Unless a rocket detonated directly on the roof, those inside were relatively safe.

At that hour, normal people in normal places would've been sleeping or arriving home from a night out, but not him. He was as normal as anyone, but his current circumstances were anything but.

A few seconds earlier, he'd been sleeping in a corner bunk in a sixteen-by-thirty-two-foot plywood barracks, known by the residents as a hooch. He stayed in bed. It was almost the safest place to be.

He was the Sarge, although his rank was actually Specialist 5. In that company, little attention was given to the difference between a Sergeant E-5 or a Spec 5, as the Specialist rank was called. The person so designated by the powers that be was the leader, the man in charge, regardless of rank.

It was the same in his case. He was in charge of the group of soldiers living in hooch number one. He was the hooch chief, squad leader, and, in his case, the section chief of a group of soldiers consisting of those living in his hooch and several from two other hooches.

At the moment, the section wasn't his concern. Under tactical conditions, his responsibility was the squad, himself, and ten soldiers, all but two of whom were presently in hooch one. The other two were somewhere in transit, not yet assigned to the company. The soldiers they were to replace rotated home one week earlier.

His squad, section, and nearly everyone in the company called him Sarge, mostly out of respect for his leadership and experience. He had nearly three years in the Army, one more than the next soldier assigned under him. He was the man the younger soldiers looked up to, especially in tactical situations. He was also the oldest man in his squad, having celebrated his twenty-first birthday four months earlier right there in Nam.

If that had been a ground attack, he would've directed his squad to man the portion of the perimeter they were responsible for, but it was a rocket attack, and the best thing a soldier could do was to make like a hole in the ground.

He lay back, his tuned ear listening for the sound of a close-in rocket, but his eyes wandered to the picture nailed to the wall near the foot of his bed. In twenty-seven days he would see her again, maybe. He knew there was still time before his tour was up for one more patrol. Moreover, he knew he'd be assigned as its leader.

The siren stopped, but the explosions signaling the impact of rockets could still be heard a long way off.

"Just don't have a short round, Charlie," the Sarge muttered under his breath. He knew the Air Force was catching hell, but he wasn't in the Air Force. He stared at the picture, recalling better times.

He went to school with her all throughout junior and high school. He always thought she was cute, but, for some reason he couldn't understand, he never considered asking her out. His buddy did, but even then, he disregarded the idea.

She was just a cute girl, not someone he was particularly interested in. In college, he finally asked her out and enjoyed every date they had. She always looked good, dressed appropriately, and was fun to be with. He never had a bad time with her, but he still hadn't given her due consideration. He took her out, then ignored her for a month or more, only to ask her out again. She always agreed. During that time, he was interested in another girl, but they had problems, so he dated the one whose picture he stared at.

After a dismal semester and a half in college, he joined the Army. The Vietnam War was still going strong, and he figured he might as well serve his time and get it over with. Why bother to learn all that stuff in college only to be killed in Nam? He had no desire to die, but the statistics on the news every night didn't paint a very optimistic picture of the war.

He wasn't about to run from it. One week after he received his student deferment from the draft, he defiantly walked into the recruiter's office. A few days later, he took some exams and a physical, then returned to the recruiter and said, "Sign me up." He pointed to a poster on the wall that read, *Airborne Ranger.*

"That sounds good," he told the recruiter, but the recruiter was an older soldier who didn't care about signing up people just to fulfill his quota.

"If that's what you want, you've got it," he said, "but you might want to think about a school where you can learn something you can use to get a job when you get out."

That was how he ended up in a very technical electronics school. He did well, graduating number three in a class of twenty-two. For the record, he ended up in a civilian career, which had nothing to do with electronics. He did well there, too.

He left home for basic training, leaving his girlfriend and the Doll, a nickname later given to the girl whose picture hung on his wall. After basic, he went home to ten days' leave. Although he dated his girlfriend, the relationship immediately fell apart, and he dated the Doll.

He was away for five months. Again, he returned home in time to break up with his girlfriend and date the Doll. Then he was away for fourteen months. He wrote to both girls, as well as a couple of others, but his real interest still was his girlfriend.

Over the two years he was in the Army, the situation changed. He was home on leave before going to Vietnam, and he and his girlfriend had issues. Hers were admittedly more significant than his, but nonetheless, they both had problems. They treated each other with a certain respect that had been missing previously. They discussed their problems and ways to handle them, and they considered marriage, but the relationship was different.

They loved each other, but love wouldn't remove the issues. There wasn't much he could do, anyway. He'd be in Vietnam in four weeks. Being married would help her significantly, but she thought of him instead. In what he later realized was the most loving act of their three-year relationship, she said no.

They never saw each other again. He knew that she did it for him and didn't want to burden him with her problems. Still, he didn't immediately run to the Doll. He went to another young woman, his best friend. She never liked his girlfriend, but, after learning how she decided not to burden him with her problems, she was impressed, and her respect for the woman rose.

For a brief moment, his best friend almost became his girlfriend. She didn't, but he often wondered how his life might've turned out if she had. The relationship with his girlfriend was over for good, and he accepted it well. He knew it was probably best for her and absolutely best for him. He wasn't cold or callous, and he hoped her life and issues worked out for the best. He still had his own to deal with.

Vietnam would probably take care of those. He watched the news and knew the stats. He still had nearly four weeks' leave left, so he called the Doll. He didn't feel like he was on the rebound. Instead, he was a new, free person, someone with issues, but still free to a point.

They dated nearly every day until he left for Nam. During that short time, they somehow fell in love. That she was incredibly beautiful made it better for him, but that was secondary. He loved her, period.

During the year he was in Vietnam, she sent him more letters, photos, and packages than all the rest of the people from whom he received anything combined. It became a standing joke in his unit. When he went on patrol or other mission, or when he was away from company headquarters, the others bet on the number of letters and packages that would be waiting for him when he returned. The numbers weren't low, either.

He would eventually return, complete the necessary tasks, shower, and kick back to read his letters from the Doll. If a package arrived, he shared the goodies with his men, but the letters were just for him. His men never saw him frown as he slowly read them.

One day, a young PFC watched the Sarge read a letter from the Doll. He waited until he was finished, then walked over. His rhetorical question caught the Sarge off guard.

"You're going to marry her when you get home, aren't you?"

The Sarge lowered his head and said sadly, "I doubt it."

The PFC was shocked. "Why not? She seems to love you. You get more letters and stuff from her than the rest of us combined."

"Don't know why. I just don't think it'll happen."

Seeing the Sarge so depressed, the PFC wisely dropped the subject.

Two weeks later, he was heading home. His orders came early. At four in the afternoon one Friday, his buddies dropped him off at the airport in Da Nang. He met with a couple other guys from his battalion who had processed in country with him. They would process out together, too.

Two hours later, the C-130 arrived at Cam Rahn Bay, and a bus took them to the replacement company where they'd process. The first couple of hours, they stood in line, filled out paperwork, and were assigned barracks for the night.

None of them slept. It was the first night in nearly a year they'd been without their M-16s within reach.

The following day, they mostly killed time. The processing was done mostly at night. Newly arrived soldiers were given details of filling sandbags, building bunkers, or dreaded KP. The people going home were mostly left alone.

That evening, his name and the names of his buddies were called, and they began the process of leaving that rathole of a country. There was a lot of hurry up and wait, but they expected that. At ten o'clock that evening, they boarded a bus to the airfield and stopped a few yards from the prettiest airplane they ever saw.

It was the *Freedom Bird,* ready to take them back to the world, as GIs called home. It was a plain, everyday, Super DC-8 configured as a troop transport. There was no first class, just six-across seating from the front to the rear. None of them cared. They boarded the aircraft, then received what every GI worried about, a delay in takeoff.

Nearly everyone who went to Nam was certain he'd be killed just before takeoff. Many had nightmares about the Freedom Bird being shot down as they took off. The men silently prayed, then the captain announced they had to hold, because there was a firefight at the end of the twelve-thousand-foot runway.

They sat in silence, most wishing they had guns. Several minutes passed, then the captain said, "Hang on, back there. We were just cleared for takeoff. I won't use the whole runway."

The plane was still on the taxiway as he made his announcement, and he wasn't kidding. He turned onto the runway so fast, people with window seats swore they saw sparks as the wingtip scraped the tarmac.

The throttles were shoved all the way forward, and the plane rumbled down the runway. There weren't any vacant seats, though the cargo holds were nearly empty. None of the GIs had anything to take home.

Then the plane lifted off, and the men held their breath. That was a plane's most vulnerable moment in flight. It was at full throttle to gain altitude, but one hit from a heavy-caliber gun or SAM would end the flight and their lives.

The plane banked right and kept climbing. The men prayed and hoped. Minutes felt like hours, then the captain said, "We're at six thousand feet and three miles offshore."

The 180 men cheered louder than a crowd at the Rose Bowl. They were out of small-arm and SAM range and climbing fast. They were going home. It was five minutes before eleven on Saturday night.

As the cheering quieted, flight attendants served soft drinks and sandwiches. The passengers contemplated the past year and the friends who weren't coming back with them.

The plane refueled at Tokyo before flying straight to McChord Air Force Base.

After the plane landed, an Air Force sergeant came onboard with instructions for the passengers. Members of various service branches went to different places for processing. The Army men went to buses that waited outside the terminal. There were three different buses for the three different classes of returnees. One was for those who were home on leave and returning to Nam, another for soldiers being reassigned to different units, and the last for those being discharged from active service.

The Sarge boarded the latter with twenty-five others. The small bus took them to a processing center at Fort Lewis. The bus and its driver would be with them for their entire stay.

Again they filled out paperwork, turned in orders, and received a briefing concerning the events of the next few hours. It was five minutes to eleven, Saturday night, Pacific Standard Time. They returned to the world at nearly the same hour they departed Vietnam.

From the processing room, they were taken to a barracks where they could relax for an hour or shower, as long as they stayed in the building. No one was about to leave. The possibility of missing a call and being delayed in processing was unthinkable.

From the barracks, they walked to a mess hall and were treated to a steak dinner. The hall was decorated in an attempt to make the soldiers feel more at home.

"What the hell?" one man asked. "Why not have dinner at two in the morning? It's OK with me."

The steak was cooked to order and delivered to the table. Real milk was the biggest hit of the meal. After a year of powdered milk, reconstituted with coconut oil, real milk tasted good. The men would have preferred beer, but they made do with milk.

From there, they were driven to a supply depot much like the one they saw in their first days in the Army. They were issued brand-new Class-A green uniforms for the trip home. The uniforms were tailored and had unit patches sewn on the right sleeve, indicating they were from a former combat unit.

Next came a complete physical exam and more processing. They returned to the barracks to change into their new uniforms, then faced more hours of paperwork, pay call, and briefings.

Then it was time. After a short discharge ceremony, they were civilians again, heading home. It was two o'clock Sunday afternoon, just two days after they'd turned over their weapons to their units in Vietnam. Most took a shuttle to SeaTac Airport to catch flights to different destinations around the US. At the airport, they split up and never saw each other again.

The Sarge took a flight to LAX. He had the middle seat in a Boeing 727. On his left was another soldier returning from Vietnam and being reassigned to Korea. On his right was a civilian businessman who was a veteran of the Korean War.

The man was very pleasant to both soldiers, though he got a kick out of the Sarge. He was heading home, never to wear a uniform again. The man bought them drinks during the flight.

After the plane landed, they said good-bye, and the Sarge walked down the jetway into the concourse, where he saw his parents, sister, and, most important, the Doll.

They walked toward each other and held each other tightly. After a long, loving kiss, they held each other some more. That was the most perfect moment in his life. If he died that second, it would've been all right. Thirty years later, he was still able to describe how she felt in his arms.

They walked to his parents' car for the ride home. He held her arm as they walked, both wishing they were alone, but, during that few minutes, something came over him. It was as if a wicked witch cast an evil spell on him. He felt it as surely as if he'd taken an AK round to the chest.

From that moment on, their relationship deteriorated. It was his fault, and he knew it, but there wasn't a thing he could do about it. He wanted to be with her more than anything, but he drove her away. It wasn't just him trying to save the relationship. The Doll tried, too, but she eventually gave up.

It was over.

The Sarge couldn't describe his feelings. He loved her, but there was nothing he could do to bring her back. He wanted to disappear, to go somewhere no one knew him and be left alone.

But where? he wondered.

He saved enough money for a new car but didn't buy it. Instead, he opted for a four-year-old Plymouth Satellite. After paying cash for the car, he banked the rest of his savings to live on awhile. He was still seeing the Doll, but he knew it would end soon. His roommate worked nights, which was great for the Sarge. Working days was fine with him.

By that time, the Doll was gone, only three weeks after he arrived home. They saw each other a few more times at special events they attended. She could've gone without him. He wondered if that was her giving him another chance, but it didn't matter. His mind wasn't functioning. Anything he did split them even further apart. Strangely, he couldn't point to a single incident that drove the wedge between them. He just knew it wasn't working.

After two months, they never saw each other again.

At his job, he met another Vietnam vet from the Air Force. The same age, they struck up a friendship. They started hitting the bars and clubs, where they met women, but the Sarge didn't want a relationship. He wanted a woman with questionable moral values who had her own apartment. She would take him there, use or abuse him, and send him packing in the morning. He didn't want to take her to his place for fear she'd return.

To him, again, would be one time too many. He never met a woman like that.

After one month, the Air Force man was fired from his company because he came in drunk or hung over too many times. The Sarge laughed. He had the same amount to drink, but he never showed it.

"Air Force," he muttered. "Another wing-nut weenie." They remained friends for a month, meaning they drank together at night, but they stopped seeing each other after that.

So much the better, the Sarge thought. *I'm tired of paying his liquor bill.*

At work, several of the men began talking about trying to become deputy sheriffs.

Why deputies? the Sarge wondered. *If you want to be a cop, be a real cop for LAPD.* When he asked the men, the answers left him with more questions. He found that his supervisor was a retired LA policeman, so he talked to him about it.

Within a few days, he applied for the department and began processing. His supervisor stepped in, excusing his absence whenever he had to process for his new career. He told the Sarge the others were trying to become deputies, because they'd been rejected by the LAPD. He doubted they'd become deputies, either.

Sarge kept his job the three months it took to pass the various phases of applying for the department. He still went to bars at night and became drunk, but he knew if he were caught driving or just plain drunk, he'd never get on the force. Being a cop seemed more exciting than assembling electrical cables. It also paid better. He stopped going to bars and drank at home.

A young man he worked with tried to become friends, but Sarge wasn't interested. The coworker seemed nice enough, so he didn't want to offend the guy. When he was invited to a barbecue at the man's house, Sarge reluctantly agreed.

The deciding factor was a comment about a young woman who'd be there. She loved to make out. Sarge was introduced to her, and the following Friday, they went to a drive-in movie.

The young man was right. She loved to make out. They got into the back seat of his Plymouth and started making out during the cartoon, continuing through two feature-length films, the coming attractions, intermission, and kept at it until the last car left.

That was as far as it went. Sarge had more on his mind, but they never went that far. He took her home and never called her again.

It seemed that he had a big sign on him that indicated he wanted help. He didn't want to become friends with anyone, but the people at work cared about him. Another man a few years older than Sarge took to talking to him during breaks and even when working when appropriate. Sarge thought the guy was a geek, but he was nice, and Sarge didn't want to offend him either.

It turned out they were both interested in photography and owned some rather-expensive equipment. Sarge bought his in Nam. He invited Sarge to his apartment one night to show off his artistic work. He called Sarge by name, too, not his nickname.

He showed his cameras, equipment, and photos to Sarge, who thought the photos were good, but the equipment wasn't. He didn't say anything. Sarge paid less than half what the guy had. After showing off his work, the man brought out a photo album.

"These are just snapshots of a beach party our church group had a few weeks ago," he said.

Sarge began looking for a way to leave. *Church* was a word that caught his attention. He knew he was a Christian, but he didn't attend church. He knew he wasn't acting like a Christian should, but he didn't walk around professing to be one, either. No one would know except the one person who mattered…God.

He felt certain the man was about to start preaching, but he couldn't find a convenient excuse to leave, so he looked at the pictures. Two pages into the album, Sarge became *very* interested.

"Who is this?" He pointed to the picture of a young woman wearing a two-piece swimsuit. In 2004, that suit would've been called a two-piece, but in 1970, it was a bikini, and he liked what he saw.

"She's a friend of mine, a personal friend. She's not available."

That was double-talk. The man implied he was dating her, and she wasn't interested in other men, but he also implied he was her protector.

Sarge refused to take no for an answer. He knew no one played both roles with a woman. Either he looked after her like a big brother, or he dated her and kept her to himself. Whichever it was, Sarge didn't care. He wanted to meet that woman. He wasn't sure it if was his charm or if the man felt his life was in danger, but he reluctantly agreed to introduce them. He would tell her a coworker wanted to meet her and have her come to his apartment for the introductions.

The man felt that was safer. He was a little upset, though, when his friend agreed to meet Sarge.

Two days later, she came to his apartment. Sarge was already waiting. When she arrived and walked in, he realized he was in big trouble. He'd heard stories about women who could light up a room, who sparkled or glowed, but he never met one before. Not even the Doll did that, and she was beautiful.

When that woman entered the apartment, he felt as if time stopped. She didn't just glow. She was radiant. She had a smile the likes of which Sarge never saw before. It was completely natural, not fake or forced. He remembered hearing that it took fewer muscles to smile than frown, but he never believed that until he saw her smile.

They were introduced, then she talked casually to the man who invited her. He suggested she show Sarge a joke. She'd been in the room for only two minutes, and she was suddenly in front of Sarge, close enough to kiss.

As she told the joke, she spoke in a tone like that for fairy tales. The fingers of her hands resembled a turtle walking. She moved them over Sarge's body as she showed how the boy and girl turtle met.

"There was a little boy turtle and a little girl turtle. One day, the boy turtle climbed up one side of a big hill. The girl turtle climbed up the other side and met him at the top."

She walked her fingers to the back of his neck, her arms around him as she leaned against his chest. She stopped and looked into his eyes, standing silently until Sarge asked, "Then what did they do?"

He was certain he slurred every word, looking at the beautiful woman who had her arms wrapped around him. He couldn't tell, but he felt sure his lip hung to one side, and he was drooling, too. He had only two conscious thoughts. He recalled her picture and how she filled out that bikini, and he knew the same woman now, nicely filling her blouse was rubbing against him. He wasn't certain of anything else.

She smiled, still looking into his eyes, as she gave him the punchline. In a voice that was as sexy as it was angelic, she asked, "Did you really want to talk about turtles?"

That was it. Sarge was finished for the night. His brain checked out and refused to return for days. His tongue lay uselessly on the floor of his mouth, and his knees were ready to let go.

His only clear recollection of that night included one fact…he asked her out for the next weekend, and she agreed.

She wanted to meet for their first date at the man's apartment. Naturally, Sarge's car broke down when he was only three blocks away, but they used her mother's car and still had their date. He convinced her go to out again, then again, but that seemed to be the end. She was leaving for a month-long trip to Europe with her church group. She didn't even ask for his address to send him a postcard.

Sarge knew it was over and told himself it was OK. He couldn't possibly keep up with a woman like her, anyway. During her absence, he got his appointment date to start at the police academy, and the company where he worked closed for summer vacation.

Sarge gave notice, and, the last day before vacation, he resigned. The other workers wouldn't leave him alone. At the afternoon break, all the employees and management people gathered in the break room and brought in a sheet cake with a sentiment on it, wishing him well in his new profession.

Most impressive, however, was the artwork. There, drawn with icing, was a detailed representation of a motorcycle officer riding his motorcycle. Sarge never thought about becoming a motorcycle officer, but the cake and card signed by all the people he worked with were very thoughtful.

During the following three weeks, Sarge worked out, ran, and tried to get himself into shape for his new job. He'd heard horror stories about the academy. He was in excellent shape, having been back from Vietnam for only five months, though it felt like years.

He knew the beautiful woman was gone, probably for the best, because he wouldn't have time for her while he attended the academy. His own thoughts didn't seem to matter.

One week before he started at the academy, she called and announced she was back and wanted to see him again.

That time, he met her at her home. Unfortunately, she lived with her parents.

They dated for several months, and, the following May, he made her his bride.

The Blue Rose and the Yellow Butterfly

Janet Volpicella

This story is dedicated to all those who stood by me through the good and bad times, my sons Richard and Michael, Aunt Jo, my friends Pauline, Debbie and Linda, to Walter, the love of my life and to all other women who have been abused.

Jenna awoke to the song, *What the World Needs Now is Love, Sweet Love,* and thought, *How very true that is.* Glancing at the clock, she couldn't believe it was six o'clock already. She must've tossed and turned for about three hours before finally falling asleep.

She was about to shut off the radio when the song finished, then she waited to hear what the weather would be. The weatherman said, "Strong, gusty winds and heavy rain all day, with possible flooding in some areas."

Jenna laughed as she shut off the radio. She got out of bed and put her feet into slippers on the floor beside the bed, then went to peek out the window. Rain beat heavily against the pane, but she smiled and said to herself, "The weatherman is wrong for me at least. Today is a day in my life that is filled with only clear skies and sunshine. Today is the beginning of the rest of my life. It's the brightest day in my life, because I've emerged from the cocoon I was in for so many years."

Walking away from the window, she rounded the bed to the other side of the room. Her black briefcase, which hadn't left her side for five-and-a-half years, lay on the dresser. It went everywhere with her.

As she looked at it, she saw it was beginning to show some wear and thought, *Well, Old Buddy, you've been through the good and bad times, but we've never been parted.* She stared at it for a few moments before picking it up and hugging it to her chest. Inside was her past—all of it, with many regrets, sorrows, pain, and hurt. There was some joy, but it was too little to remember.

Jenna moved slowly, still holding the briefcase to her chest as she sat on the edge of the bed. Her thoughts drifted as she put the briefcase beside her on the bed and stared at it. When a tear fell, she wondered if it was a tear of sorrow or joy. She wasn't sure, because for the past ten years, she'd been shedding a lot of tears. She regarded life as one big highway with many entrances, exits, and detours. As people went down life's highway, other people entered and left their lives. Some stayed forever, some came and went, and others left only to return on later dates. Each one had a purpose.

Some came into people's lives to help them or receive help, while other came to destroy. Some were parents, children, aunts, uncles, and friends, especially the kind of friends who were there for a person when everyone else had abandoned him. Friends were very important to her. She trusted them and would be there for them when needed. She never expected anything in return.

To Jenna, friends weren't just strangers. Some of her friends were aunts and uncles. If wealth were based on friendship, she would've been a billionaire. She treasured love and kindness and always tried to give more than she received or wanted. She didn't care.

She loved giving and making people happy. Even changing someone's smile into a frown for a second pleased her. She also hid her own unhappiness with a smile. It was rare when she broke down and released her feelings. Jenna wasn't someone who wanted to bundle her troubles and sorrow on anyone, though she, like everyone, had a breaking point.

Did she have any regrets? No? Well, maybe. *Why'd I wait so long and waste so many years?* she wondered. *Life is too short.*

She picked up a folder and opened it. It once started as a letter to him but ended up as the story of her life. Glancing at the first page, she decided not to give it to him. Why give him the satisfaction of knowing she let him break her self-esteem and cause her so much pain? Most of all, she let him destroy her life and waste her best years.

These pages are for my eyes only. Maybe someday I'll have time to edit and publish them. For now, they're just a written memory of my past. She wished she could forget that past.

Removing the folder from her briefcase, Jenna set it in her dresser drawer. A moment later, she changed her mind and reopened it back on the bed. She began rereading what began as a letter and was now over one hundred pages long.

Dear Steven,

I guess I can address this Dear, for once upon a time, you were very dear to me. What happened? I don't know. I don't have any answers. I can't count the times I've searched my mind through the years. The only conclusion I can come to is that *Once upon a time* is in fairytales, where happy endings lie. I think that's because fairytales are made up and not the real world.

It's true there is some love and happiness in the real world, but I feel they're outnumbered by the pain and sorrow, sometimes from our mistakes, sometimes from hate. Sometimes, we're too blind to see the mistakes and don't learn the lesson. We can't undo our mistakes, but we should try to accept the fact that we made them and not do them again.

As for hatred, I've learned to omit it from my life, because it's like a cancer. It destroys the goodness and leaves behind only an empty shell. At one point in my life, I was so overwhelmed with hatred, then I looked to God, my maker,

23

for help. When Jesus was dying on the cross, he asked his Father to forgive those who hated him. Then I, too, could learn to forgive my attackers.

You see, Steven, in doing so, I honestly found peace. I became whole again, and that's what I tried to tell you in the last months we were together. I won't tell you to look to God as I did, but you should rid yourself of the bitterness and hate that's locked up inside you. You might even be able to find the true meaning of love. I'm not talking about love for another person. I mean universal love, from the smallest animal on earth to the largest. Love is finding beauty in everything we see every day. It is sharing and forgiving.

I guess you can tell that love is the most-important thing to me. During my life with you, it was missing. I've learned from my mistakes and will never let anyone deprive me of love again. For now, I'm overflowing with love. I had it all bottled up inside me for many years without anyone to share it with. Now I let my love flow out each and every day, flowing gently like the Mississippi River.

Maybe things could've been different between us if we could've come down off the roller coaster we rode during our marriage. Most of all, we let too many people interfere with our lives. We never took the time to find out what was going wrong. We let things get worse until there was no way to make them right again.

I can't believe I was able to help so many friends yet unable to help us. I don't have any answers.

Jenna, feeling herself becoming upset, thought she might be making a mistake that day. She felt she'd made a mess of her son's life, too.

Closing the folder, she took it with her as she went downstairs to make coffee. She set the folder on the table and went about her morning routine.

When the coffee was ready, she sat at the table and began reading where she left off. Jenna felt sad about what she wrote, but she also had a great sense of relief.

Laughing aloud, she thought, *It's like taking antacid tables to rid yourself of heartburn.* In her case, she needed megadoses to rid herself of all the heartache she endured over the years. One tablet would never have worked.

She began reading again.

Steven, why I allowed you to make me become someone I wasn't I'll never know. I guess I was weak. In the years we were together, I always gave more than I received. I know you don't see it that way, but in your heart, you know it's true.

When I refer to giving more than I received, I'm talking about the gifts you bought me to ease your conscience. I'm talking about the times I let you have your way just to avoid a fight. When you look back at our fights, you'll see they weren't about us. They always involved other people.

I can't believe I let it last so long. How many times did you try to override the abuse by making sure you bought me an expensive gift, then told everyone about it? We both know that was to ease your guilt. It wasn't because you loved me or were sorry for your actions.

What love? You didn't even *like* me. I was the biggest joke of both our families. Do you remember what they said? "What's Steven buying you this time?" It always made me feel like a fool.

Now I say, "You're only a fool if you let someone make you one." I suppose if they gave out awards to the biggest fool, I'd be in first place. I also recall how you had a way of twisting things, trying to make me believe you were truly sorry for hitting me or arguing with me.

She stopped reading and looked up. Her thoughts drifted back to 1969 and the events that led up to breaking off her engagement and wedding date. She laughed as she remembered how she finally got her way and was married in ice blue…against her mother-in-law's wishes.

For the three years I dated and the two years I was engaged, she thought, *everyone knew I'd wear an ice-blue gown when I married. They knew it was for the Blessed Mother and to be different. I remember exactly what phone the call came in on, because it wasn't a public line.*

My future mother-in-law called. When I asked how she got the number, she said, "I don't know." Then she hit me with, "I don't think you should get married in ice blue. It's not right. Everyone will think it's your second marriage."

That night, I broke off my engagement, because Steven agreed with her. The following day, I sat in the living room and tore up my invitations. I took the next week off using my vacation time at work and got in my 1964 Chevy and on the Belt Parkway, though ever since, I can't remember what I did or where I went. All I remember is calling my mother one week later from a phone somewhere in Philly.

I still can't recall how I got to Philly. I drove home and returned to work. A few weeks later, Steven and I were together again and replanned our wedding. We changed the date to October fifth, not September twenty-seventh.

She picked up the folder again and continued reading.

Do you remember our first Christmas together? I went to a Christmas party at work. When I came home, you were angry, though I never knew why. You told me we weren't going to spend Christmas with my mother. You socked my chest and then punched a hole in the kitchen wall.

I should've left you then, but I decided not to ruin anyone's Christmas. I planned to leave you after the holidays. Then I found out I was pregnant.

I didn't think I could survive on my own, so I stayed, thinking I'd stick it out until the baby was five. Fourteen months later, I had another baby. I stayed and took the physical, mental, and emotional abuse you handed out.

I once thought I stayed only for my sons, but I realized later that it was partly for the beautiful things I had. I had the best…a beautiful home and many nice vacations, along with two wonderful sons I wouldn't trade for anything. As the boys grew older, you stopped hitting me as much, but the mental and emotional abuse continued.

You said I was ugly and no man would ever want me. When I started college, you said I got straight A's because I fucked all the professors. It's not easy to fuck a woman if you're a woman, too.

I have forgiven you for all that, because I know it was caused by outside forces. Till this day, though, I still have trouble forgiving you for what you did to me in 1991. You told me when I found my clothes in the trash that I put them there. You made my jewelry vanish and reappear and said I was crazy.

When the car was hit while parked in front of the school, you hit me and said it was my fault. Then I came home from work and you were under the sink, throwing out my stuff. You called me a pig, because you said you found ants on the counter.

You got up off the floor, grabbed my hair, and hit my head against the island stove, saying I had to thank you for cleaning the house. I thought you'd kill me.

Next came September 26, 1991. Before you left to drive Richie to the train station, you said you'd come back and kill me. When you left, I locked the doors and called the police.

When you returned, the police were there and helped me leave the house. I got into the car, and somehow, I was back in 1964 when I felt happy. I don't remember all the events of that day, but I remember a lot.

The first thing I did was see if my car was ready. It wasn't. I passed by the house I lived in as a child. Next I went to the church where we were married and followed a funeral to Queens. Don't ask why. I still don't know.

Once in the cemetery, I got out of the car and went to an unknown grave. As I cried, two little girls came to talk to me. I told them I had two sons, one was a doctor, the other a famous baseball player, but they didn't know I was alive.

It took me twenty minutes to find my way out of there. I found myself driving down the Grand Central Parkway doing ninety miles an hour and biting my nails. I went to my uncle's house, but he wasn't home. I tried to find my way back, but the voices in my head told me to go the wrong way.

I found myself in an adult community. In my mind, the streets were named for people I knew. I stopped a man walking his dog and asked how I could get home. He put his hands in the car and started shaking me, asking, "How'd you get in here, and who are you robbing?"

I started crying, put the car in reverse, and hit the gas pedal. He called security, who took me to the office.

I thought I was back in 1964. The only phone number I could remember was the one I had when I was single. The woman tried to get me to drink something, but I didn't trust her. Finally, I remembered my house number, and she called it for me. My brother answered.

He arrived thirty minutes later. I thought I was going home, but he took me to Elmhurst Hospital. The next day, I was transferred in a paddy wagon to a Brooklyn hospital. At first, I didn't trust anyone. Little by little, I came out of it and was released.

I didn't have you pick me up. Instead, I took a cab. I still have nightmares about those days. The doctor said if I stayed with you, I might have the same thing happen again. I couldn't leave then, because I knew Michael would go to medical school, so I stayed. You didn't change, but I didn't think you would. When Michael left, you were worse.

That's why I decided to leave. I still have nightmares about the events of 1991. Somehow, I made a new life for myself.

Maybe I don't have all the beautiful things I had when I lived with you, but I have peace of mind, and no one abuses me.

Remember the music box I bought with the blue rose and yellow butterfly after I got out of the hospital? I drew a picture of it. On November 1, 1991, I had that picture tattooed on my leg. It's a symbol that no one will ever abuse me again.

Something happened when I was released from the hospital in 1991. I emerged from my cocoon and became a butterfly. They say butterflies are free.

Sometimes, I sit and think about us. I believe we loved each other but couldn't live together. I wish no ill for you.

Maybe someday, you'll read this letter.

Love Always and Forever,

Jenna

She replaced the letter into the folder and the briefcase. It was getting late, so she needed to dress. She went to the bedroom. As she looked around, she remembered all the memories the room held. At the floor beside the bed, she once lay with three broken ribs. She looked at the dresser mirror and thought about the day Debbie left the house as a bride.

Finishing packing, she picked up her suitcase. As she walked down the hall, she peeked into Michael's bedroom. A tear fell from her eye, and she glanced into Richie's room, remembering how many times he'd been sick.

She turned and started down the stairs that overlooked the living and dining rooms. Ashe thought of how the Christmas tree looked by the sliding-glass doors and the parties they held there, more tears fell.

She went to the kitchen, opened her briefcase, and took out a letter for the new owners, leaving a small package with it. Then she went out the front door to her car.

Opening her trunk, she dropped the suitcase inside and got behind the wheel. "There's one last thing I need to do."

On the passenger seat was a box for Robert. She drove to the post office and sat outside, opening the package one last time to make sure it contained everything. She also reread the letter.

Dear Robert,

I hope you're waiting for me to return, but I won't be back. Maybe someday when I think the time is right, I'll return to you. Everything went as well as I expected. I want you to know it's not because I don't love you. I love you with my heart and soul.

I fell in love the moment we met. My heart stopped beating, and the earth stopped rotating. The past eleven years were the best of my life. When we met, my life was black and white. Color didn't exist. I wasn't living, just existing.

Your love restored color into my life. You taught me a lot about life I'll always remember. You were there for me in the good times and the bad. I know you were angry at me sometimes for saying or doing stupid things.

Inside this package are a few things to remember me by. I have no idea where I'm going. If I decide to return, you'll know ahead of time. If you receive a blue rose and yellow butterfly, you'll know I'll be coming back.

Please understand. I need to find myself and heal.

Love Always and Forever,

Jenna

Jenna peeked into the box and saw the music box with the blue rose and yellow butterfly, a few CDs, and a blue silk rose. She sealed the box, got out, and walked into the post office. There was no line, so there was no changing her mind.

She returned to her car and started on her way.

Margaret Smith, author of *The Red Pocketknife*, lives in Westminster, Colorado, with her husband, Harold. She has three grown children, a son-in-law, daughter-in-law, and two granddaughters, all living in the Denver metro area.

Margaret has written several short stories, two novels and poetry, However *The Red Pocketknife* is her first work to be published. She looks forward to sharing many more of her stories with you.

The Red Pocketknife

Margaret Smith

A light breeze cooled the already-soaring temperature as the Grand Mesa High students clogged the halls, heading for the auditorium. It was Friday afternoon, and even though they were looking forward to the weekend, most of them were also looking forward to seeing the performance by Larry Janske, the famous ventriloquist, and his puppet, Joey. There were four students however, that weren't looking forward to sitting through the hour-long performance. They were Dave and his three cronies, Lukas, Howard, and Robert. All four were juniors and could almost always be found together, in or out of school.

"Let's sit by the side door," Dave said. "Then maybe we can sneak out when everyone's going ape shit over the stupid dummy." Dave was tall and lanky, with dark, shoulder-length hair. His large blue-green eyes always gave the impression he was smiling.

"Yeah," Howard whispered. "They usually turn down the lights when the stage lights come on." He peered over his thick, horn-rimmed glasses at Dave. Without the glasses, the two of them could've passed for twins or brothers.

"Maybe we can pick up some beer an' go down to South Creek to cool off," Robert suggested hoarsely, pushing damp blond hair off his forehead. He imagined the feel of cool water washing over his chubby body at the thought of going to the creek.

"An' after, we can do some cruisin' on Main Street. It's Friday. All the frumpy ol' ladies will be downtown shoppin'."

"Are ya nuts, Lukas? What do you wanna look at ol' ladies for?"

"I don't wanna look at 'em. I wanna scare 'em."

They imagined him in the back seat of the car, his head of bright-red hair flying out the window, along with his pimply face and bulging eyes.

Going through the double doors and into the auditorium, the foursome veered to one side. They were almost at the seats they wanted, when Verne Grey, a school counselor, stopped them. In his late fifties, he'd been counseling students at Grand Mesa for fifteen years. Somehow, he found something good in each student. His manners and casual dress were often copied by those he helped. Dave, Lukas, Howard, and Robert had been caught ditching classes and smoking pot two weeks earlier, and Mr. Grey was assigned to their case.

That wasn't the first time they were in trouble in school, and it probably wouldn't be the last. All four boys had to see Mr. Grey each morning for three months. It was only the second week, and they weren't looking forward to being nice to him for another ten weeks.

"Good afternoon, Boys," he said. "I hope you're as thrilled as I am at having Mr. Janske and Joey perform for us today. They say you can't see Mr. Janske's mouth move at all when he talks. Amazing, isn't it? It's a special privilege for our school to have such a renowned entertainer."

"Good afternoon, Mr. Grey," the boys said in unison.

"Yeah, we're excited about seeing these great performers, aren't we?" Dave asked, turning and winking at his friends, who mumbled their agreement.

"Good," Mr. Grey said. "I thought you'd feel that way, so I saved four seats in the front row for you. They're right in the center, too. Being that close, you might even be able to see Larry's mouth move."

"Oh, but we thought…"

"No, no. I insist. Come on. I'll take you to them."

They sighed, following him through the crowd of young people to the seats he had waiting.

After all the students were seated, Mr. Max Phillips, the school principal, came onstage. Standing before the curtain, he held up his hand to stop the round of applause from the students. He'd been the principal at Grand Mesa for twenty-five years and was highly respected by teachers, parents, and, most of all, the students. At the beginning of the school year, he announced that would be his last year as principal. His understanding firmness and charm would make him difficult to replace.

"Ladies, Gentlemen, and faculty of Grand Mesa High. Today you're in for a very special treat. World-famous ventriloquist, Mr. Larry Janske, and his world-famous dummy, Joey, have agreed to entertain and delight us for the next hour. They've been entertaining people for eleven years.

"I met Larry and Joey last year while visiting Poland. He graciously agreed to come here to perform for us. I want you to pay particular attention to Mr. Janske's mouth. I guarantee that when Joey talks, you'll never see Mr. Janske's mouth move.

"As far as Joey goes, don't kid yourselves. He's no dummy. I only wish some of my students were that smart."

Another round of applause and laughter followed, and Mr. Phillips held up his hand again. "Our guests love applause. However, they ask that you limit your applause to a few seconds until the end of their performance. So without further ado, it brings me great pleasure to introduce Larry Janske and his sidekick, Joey."

The stage lights came on as the house lights darkened. Only the dim sidelights along the aisles were left on. The curtains opened as a middle-aged man in dark-blue slacks and blue-and-white pinstriped shirt walked onto stage alone, with a chair in his hand.

"Hello. I'm Larry Janske."

The audience applauded for a few seconds, then the hall became quiet. Sitting in the chair, Larry crossed his legs and looked at the audience. With a sigh, he reached into his pants pocket and took out a fingernail clipper. He began clipping his nails and occasionally looked at the audience. A few students laughed, but most were silent, waiting for what would come next.

They heard a very quiet sound that gradually increased in volume until they recognized it as a small child whimpering. Looking up from trimming his nails, Larry glanced around, saw nothing, and returned to his nails.

The cry became louder, then louder, until it sounded like a grown-up screaming. Larry's clippers flew into the air as he looked around again. The screaming stopped, but, as the audience listened, they heard sobbing.

"You forgot me," someone whimpered. "Larry, you forgot me again."

Throwing up his hands, Larry jumped up and looked around. "Oh, dear. I believe I forgot someone." Stepping behind the curtain, he returned with a dummy tossed over his shoulder.

"This is my sidekick, Joey." Sitting in the chair he sat the dummy on his lap. Joey had blond, shoulder-length hair and was dressed in jeans and a T-shirt with *Grand Mesa High* on the front.

Applause erupted, then stopped.

"You forgot me again."

"I was clipping my nails. I forgot to do them earlier."

"You always have some kind of lame excuse."

"It's true. When you screamed, you startled me, and I dropped the clippers. They're on the floor by my feet. Would you pick them up for me, please?"

"Why do I always have to do your work for you?" Joey leaned over and picked up the clippers.

"Hey. I like your shirt," Larry said, as he took the clippers from Joey and put them in his pocket. "I see several shirts like that on the young people in the audience."

Joey looked down at his shirt, then pulled it out in front. "Pretty cool, eh?"

"Yeah. Why didn't I get one, too?"

Smiling, Joey turned and looked at him. "You have to be a dummy to get one."

The audience laughed and applauded.

Joey put his hand above his eyes, staring out into the audience. "These people must be related to me."

"What makes you think so?"

"They look really stupid. Look at the dummy in the front row." Joey raised his hand and pointed at the four boys. Putting his thumb and index finger into his mouth, he gave a shrill whistle.

The audience roared with laughter.

"Joey, we shouldn't say things like that."

"Why not? I thought you were supposed to tell the truth." He looked up at Larry.

"Well, sure, but if it'll hurt someone's feelings or make him feel bad, it's better to keep your mouth shut." With his free hand, he closed Joey's mouth.

More laughter and applause erupted.

Jerking his head away, Joey said, "Hey, they call me Dummy all the time. They don't care how I feel."

"But Joey, that's what you are. You're just a dummy."

Hanging his head, Joey sobbed, as big tears rolled down his cheeks.

"Poor Joey," several people said. Then a hush fell over the audience.

Holding his head high, Joey threw his hands into the air. The audience cheered.

"Well, for your information, I'm not a dummy anymore." Reaching into his shirt pocket, he pulled out a folded piece of paper and handed it to Larry. "Go ahead. Read it. You can read, can't you?"

After putting on his glasses and unfolding the paper, Larry read, "This certifies that Joey Janske has completed an extensive course in psychology and is licensed in ESP."

"Now call me a dummy." Looking at the audience, Joey shouted, "Go ahead! Call me a dummy!"

"Are you telling me you can read minds?"

"Yes, I can. Right now, you're thinking that certificate is bogus."

"Oh, Joey. You always come up with something, don't you? Tell you what. You prove to me and the audience that you're clairvoyant, then I'll believe you."

Joey looked at the audience, his eyes finally resting on the four boys in the front row. The eyes of every student followed his gaze until they rested on Dave.

"Shit," Robert whispered. "He's looking at you, Dave."

Howard jabbed his elbow into Dave's ribs and grinned.

"Well? I'm waiting, Joey. Give me some proof." Larry impatiently tapped his foot.

Sliding off Larry's lap, Joey stood beside him. "He's wearing a yukky brown-and green-checked shirt."

"Joey, we all can see that. That doesn't mean you have ESP."

"OK, OK. Let's see." He placed his fingers on his temple and closed his eyes. "Let's see. His name is Dave. Dave Pierce. That's his name."

Larry stood and stepped forward, holding Joey's hand. Joey walked alongside him. Whispers vibrated through the auditorium.

Standing before Dave, Larry asked, "Sir, would you be so kind and help us by coming onstage?"

Dave hunched down in his seat.

"Please?"

Joey held out his hand. "Come on. What are you afraid of? We're just an old man and a dummy."

Laughter once again pealed through the large room.

"Go on, Dave, go on up there," one of the boys said.

"You want me to come down and help you up?" Joey grinned.

"No," he said softly. "I'll come up."

"Could we have another chair onstage for Dave, please?" Joey asked, looking behind him.

After all three were seated, Dave on a chair, with Larry on the other chair and Joey on his lap, Larry reached over to shake Dave's hand.

"Thank you for coming up and helping us out. I'm Larry Janske, and this is Joey."

Joey shook Dave's hand, then held his hand in the air and shook it. Drops of water flew through the air.

"Boy, are your hands sweaty! Nervous or something?" Joey laughed.

"OK, Joey," Larry said. "Enough." Looking at Dave, he asked, "What's your name, young man?"

"M...my name is Dave Pierce."

"See?" Joey asked. "I told ya! Now do you believe I have the gift?"

"No. You could've heard one of his friends call him that. That's too easy," Larry said.

Joey hung his head in thought. After several seconds, he raised it, and asked, "What if I tell you what's in his left pants pocket? Will that convince you?"

"OK. What does he have in his pants pocket?"

"His *left* pants pocket."

"OK, OK. What's in his left pants pocket?"

"It's a knife, but it's not only a knife," Joey said in a singsong voice. "It's a red-handled pocketknife with three blades." He paused. "There's a chip out of one of the blades."

Beads of sweat formed on Dave's forehead. He wiped them away with the back of his hand.

Leaning toward Dave, Larry asked, "Can we see what's in your left pants pocket?"

When Dave awoke, he saw he was on a cot in the nurse's office. Verne Grey sat on a chair a few feet away holding a red-handled, three-bladed pocketknife. One blade had a notch in it.

"Well, Dave, that was quite a performance, wouldn't you say?"

"I...I don't remember. What the hell happened?"

"The dummy called Joey made a dummy out of Davie. That's what happened."

"Oh, God. I'll be the laughingstock of the entire school."

Mr. Grey held out his hand. In it was the red pocketknife.

"I know I'm not allowed to carry a knife on school property, but it's just a little one. I had it to cut my fingernail I tore this morning, and I thought I might go fishing after sch..."

"We'll talk about this Monday when you're feeling better. I have to report this to Mr. Phillips. You know that." He snorted. "Well, no, I don't have to report it. He was in the audience. He already knows."

"What'll happen to me?" Dave whispered.

"You'll probably be suspended."

As Dave sat up on the side of the bed, Verne looked at him. "Dave, you've really disappointed me." Shaking his head, he stood. "I'll see you Monday at seven o'clock sharp."

The three boys were waiting for Dave when he left the school. They were doubled over with laughter, slapping each other's backs.

"What's so damn funny?" Dave asked.

"You, Man," Howard said. "That dummy got the best of you."

"Yeah. He knew everything about you, an' I do mean *everything*. He even knew about…"

"You think it was funny, huh? How funny would it be if I beat the shit out of all three of you?"

"Dave, don't get so mad. Man, if you coulda seen yourself. It was hilarious watching…"

"How the hell did that stupid-assed dummy learn all that stuff about me?" Dave asked, walking up to them. He shook his fist in their faces. "I'd better *never* find out it was one of you guys."

"Dave, we didn't…"

"Go to hell, all three of you." Turning, he ran toward the parking lot.

The three boys ran after him, screaming, "Hey! Wait up! Aren't we going to the creek?"

"Come on, Dave!" Howard yelled. "Don't be mad at us. We didn't do anything."

Tires squealed as Dave drove from the school's parking lot.

Dave was expelled from classes for the rest of the school year for carrying a knife on school property. Verne Grey tried to intervene on Dave's behalf, but his attempts were futile.

During the rest of the school year, Howard, Lukas, and Robert remained friends. The three made several attempts to repair their friendship with Dave, but it didn't happen.

When the new school year began, Dave learned he wouldn't have enough credits to graduate and needed an extra semester. Dropping out of school, he drifted from one menial job to another for several years, blaming everything on Larry Janske and his stupid dummy, Joey. He vowed to get even with them even if it took the rest of his life.

Dave sat at the counter of a small diner, drinking coffee and eating a doughnut. He wondered where his life was heading. It was ten years since he dropped out of school. He was twenty-seven. All his contemporaries were married, had homes, and most had children.

He had nothing. His life was going nowhere, and his prospects looked dim. Motioning the waitress to pour him another cup, he picked up the newspaper on the counter and saw a third-page headline that caught his eye.

Ventriloquist Larry Janske and Joey Return.

He almost tossed the paper down in disgust, but he forced himself to read the article.

Grand Mesa will be honored next Friday evening as ventriloquist Larry Janske and his sidekick, Joey, entertain at the Grand Mesa Performing Arts Center. It's been ten years since they last performed in our beautiful city, and we're honored to have them return. The Grand Mesa Hotel has graciously asked the world-famous ventriloquist and his dummy to be their guests.

There will be two performances, one on Friday evening, the other on Saturday evening. For information and reservations, please call 675-8244.

He set down the paper, unable to believe it. Larry Janske and his dummy, Joey, the dummy with ESP, were returning to Grand Mesa. They were the reason he'd lost his three best friends. They were the reason he didn't graduate, and lost control of his life.

He had a chance to get even. He read the article again. After waiting ten years for that moment, it finally came, but he wasn't sure what to do with it. He knew, however, he'd get even with the two people responsible for ruining his life.

The following Thursday evening, a young man carrying a large bouquet of flowers walked through the revolving doors of the Grand Mesa Hotel. Seeing the young woman behind the desk was busy on the phone, he turned the registration book around and read it quickly.

Seeing the signature of Larry Janske made his pulse beat faster. He was in room 612. That surprised him, having assumed the world-famous celebrity would be in the penthouse. Nodding at the woman, he picked up the large bouquet and walked toward the elevators.

Stepping off on the sixth floor, Dave stopped and looked down the hall. He was alone. Straightening his tie and running his hands over his short hair, which he'd gotten cut for the occasion, as well as renting a suit, he walked up to door number 612 and knocked lightly.

No one answered. Giving another knock, he waited again. After a third time elicited no response, he wiped his brow and tried the handle. To his surprise, the door opened.

"Hello, Mr. Janske? Hello? Is anyone here?"

There was no response. Looking around, Dave saw he was in a large sitting room with a plush sofa, matching loveseat, three large overstuffed chairs, and a large marble-and-gold coffee table. A large-screen TV took up the entire corner, with a marble-and-gold desk in another.

Setting the bouquet in the middle of the table, Dave held his breath as he looked around. A set of French doors were at the end of the room. Walking closer, he saw they opened onto a kitchen.

He opened the fridge and saw it was fully stocked with more food than he'd ever seen. He hadn't eaten all day, and the sight of so much food made him slightly nauseated.

Leaving the kitchen and walking down the hall, he looked into a bedroom that was bigger than his entire apartment. Another set of double doors opened at the far end into a spacious bathroom. The sunken tub with greenery around it was almost large enough to swim in.

At the far end was another bedroom similar to the first. He looked around the room and realized he didn't make enough in a year to pay for one night at a place like this.

Suddenly, he felt sick. The room spun. *God, what am I going to do?* Sitting on the edge of the bed, he closed his eyes.

Larry was late returning from dinner. He didn't like getting in late when he had a performance the following day. He always spent an hour or two practicing with Joey the night before a performance. However, the mayor of Grand Mesa asked him out to dinner, and he felt obliged to make polite conversation until the mayor's wife hinted that it was getting late.

Walking over to the small wet bar, he poured a glass of wine. A look at his watch informed him it was after eleven o'clock. Turning on the TV, he leaned back in a chair and sipped his wine.

Something woke Dave. Getting up quietly, he tiptoed to the doorway and heard the TV. That meant Larry and Joey had returned.

Sitting down on the bed, he held his head. He didn't feel very good. *Come on. You came here for one reason. Get up and get with it.*

Standing, he reached into his left pants pocket and felt the knife in his hand. He was ready. It was time to get even.

As he stepped into the hall, he heard two voices conversing. To his surprise, the second one was Joey's. Stepping back into the bedroom, he listened.

"Why the hell do you have to do this every time we have a performance the next night? Joey, you know you can't hold your liquor. The next day, you've got a headache and a hangover that won't quit. Damn it, Joey, what am I going to do with you?"

"I'se sorry, Larry. I'se sorry." Tears welled in Joey's eyes as he slumped in a chair beside Larry.

Dave shook his head. What was going on? It sounded like the dummy was talking to Larry. He stepped into the hall and moved cautiously toward the sitting room. From the end of the hall, he could see into the big room where Larry and Joey sat with their backs to him.

"Can I jus' have one more teensey-weensey drink, Larry? Please?"

"No. No more liquor for you tonight. The next place we stay, I'll ask them to remove all wine and liquor in the ro…" Larry froze as he heard a noise. Looking at Joey, he put his index finger to his lips as he rose from the chair.

Dave had lost his balance and bumped into a small table in the hall. He knew Larry heard him and would come down the hall. He felt his fingers tighten around the knife in his pocket, as he stepped into the large room.

"Who the hell are you?" Larry asked. "Joey, call security! Joey…"

Dave stopped and held up his hand. "No. Wait a minute. Please hear me out. I came to deliver a bouquet of flowers, and, when I knocked on the door, nobody answered. After several knocks, I tried the knob, and the door was unlocked, so I came in."

"Christ, Joey, didn't you remember to lock the door when you left?"

"Larry, don't yell at me. I know I locked the door. We should call the police."

"I came in and set the flowers on the coffee table. See them? There they are." Dave pointed at the flowers sitting on the table. "Do you remember ten years ago, you came to Grand Mesa High and performed? The flowers are from Grand Mesa High." He took a card out of the bouquet and handed it to Larry.

"What does it say?" Joey asked. "Read it aloud."

"From the students of Grand Mesa High for a performance always to be remembered." Larry handed the card to Joey, who appeared to have passed out and was snoring loudly in his chair.

"So why didn't you leave after you set the flowers on the table? What did you say your name was?"

"I had to take a leak really bad. I was on my way down the hall when you came home, and I didn't know what to do."

"So you had to take a leak, eh?" He tipped his head to one side and studied him. "What did you say your name was?"

"My name is Dave — Dave Pierce." He wondered if Larry would remember him.

"That sounds familiar. Where have I heard that name before?"

"I was one of the students at Grand Mesa when you performed here ten years ago." He pulled out the red pocketknife. "Maybe this will refresh your memory." He shook the closed knife in Larry's face.

"Christ! You're the young man Joey called up onstage, aren't you?"

"Yeah, that's right."

"Joey said you had a red pocketknife in your pocket, and he made fun of you until you showed it to everyone. I remember now."

"Because of you and your stupid dummy with ESP, my life was ruined. I lost my best friends and never got to graduate." Dave's voice shook and grew in volume. "Because of you, my life sucks!"

"Hey, Dave, I'm sorry. Maybe Joey went too far. I'm really sorry."

Looking at Joey, Dave turned back to Larry. "What's with you two? Joey's supposed to be a dummy, and you're supposed to be a ventriloquist, but he's no more a dummy than I am. I heard him come in, and I heard you two talking."

"What's a ventriloquist and his dummy to do? They talk. Dave, come on. Sit down. Let's talk this over."

"No. The talking's over. That dummy told things about me in front of the whole school. He embarrassed me in front of my friends and classmates, and you put those words in his mouth."

"Wasn't he right about everything?"

Opening the knife and shaking it in Larry's face, Dave whispered hoarsely, "Yeah, he was. He was right about everything, except for one thing."

"What was that?"

"He said this knife with the nick in the blade would get me in trouble."

"You don't want to believe everything he says. Come on, Dave, sit down. Let's have a drink."

Shaking the knife again, Dave shouted, "I'm sorry, Larry. Really I am, but I came here for one reason, and I won't leave until I do it."

As he raised the knife high over Larry's head, he heard a voice whisper, "See? I told you so."

Dave plunged the knife into Larry's chest, stabbing him ten times, one for every year of his ruined life. Realizing that the whispered words had come from Joey, he walked over to the chair where Joey sat. With both hands, he picked up the dummy, holding him in midair.

"So you stopped snoring, did you? Did you see what I done to Larry?

45

I hope so, 'cause I'm gonna do the same to you. Remember the red pocketknife? Do you remember me?" He shook the dummy hard. "Say something, you stupid dummy! I know you can talk. I heard you. Damn it, say something!"

Dropping Joey into the chair, Dave bent close and put his hands on the sides of Joey's face, feeling the hinges that allowed his jaw to move. Reaching in the back, he found a hole under Joey's shirt. With his fingers inside, he found he could move Joey's arms. Putting his hand a little higher, he could move the head and make the mouth open and close. When he squeezed a thin plastic hose inside, tears ran down Joey's cheeks.

Going over to Larry, Dave withdrew the knife and walked back to Joey. Raising the knife into the air, he thrust it into the hollow plastic of the dummy's chest.

Dave stepped back to look at his handiwork. The dummy's mouth opened slowly, and he whispered, "I told you that red pocketknife would get you into trouble, didn't I?"

Dave walked around in a daze the rest of the night. As the sun rose over the horizon, he unlocked his apartment door, then sat on the edge of the bed to wait.

When the knock on the door came, he wasn't surprised. He knew they'd be coming for him.

Epilogue

Dave Pierce sat on death row. His attorney had hoped for an appeal, however, it had been denied. Larry and Joey had been world-renowned entertainers, loved and respected in many countries. The red pocketknife containing Larry's blood and Dave's fingerprints was found to have been the murder weapon that killed Larry, as well as having been used to slice into the dummy's plastic torso.

The famous dummy sits in a glass case in the Grand Mesa Performing Arts Center as a memorial to the great Larry Janske and his dummy. To the left of Joey are several pictures of them performing at Grand Mesa High ten years earlier. One picture shows Dave onstage with them.

Also displayed in the case is a newspaper clipping from the Grand Mesa *Daily News* telling of the events leading to Mr. Janske's brutal murder.

On a small shelf beside the newspaper article lay the infamous red pocketknife.

Life Forms
David A. Smith

Chapter One

Andy Stephens rubbed his eyes. He was tired. He looked at the digital clock on the wall and saw it read *2:36 AM.*

Oh, no! he thought. *I'll never get up for work tomorrow.*

Andy, a biochemist with a minor in robotics, worked at Technico Laboratories. Five years earlier, in 2005, he graduated from ITT in Chicago. It was now 2010, and Andy just turned twenty-nine.

Running his fingers through his straight blond hair, he sighed. He sat in the basement of his modest wood-frame home in rural Illinois, which he had converted into a working laboratory. He just spent all night working on his pet project, just like every night for the past three years, and he was very close.

"Are you tired, Dr. Andy?" BIL asked.

BIL was Andy's pet project. The letters stood for Biomechanical Independent Lifeform.

"You are exemplifying symptoms of fatigue, according to my visual data."

Andy chuckled. "Yes, BIL, I'm very tired." He turned to study his laboratory. BIL took up the center of the room and resembled a cybernetic octopus. The central brain was surrounded by wires, tubes, and lines that reached to all corners of the lab and were attached to various devices, controls, and electronics. The main brain was comprised of a large CPU and various electrical circuits and was also equipped with audio and video implants.

A sophisticated series of video cameras provided BIL with sight, while highly sensitive microphones were his ears. Via another computer across the room, BIL had access to the Internet. He also had access to a telephone and TV, complete with cable. One tube was connected to a barrel of lubricating fluid, while another ran to a moisture-removing spray.

Different cords ran to several power sources...one permanent source with two backups. There were solar panels on the roof, too, which were designed to be the main power source. That way, when BIL was finally mobile, he would have adequate power. A smaller version of the panels could be worn directly on the unit, giving BIL a constant source of mobile power.

BIL was a highly advanced, interactive computer, capable of adjusting the room temperature or lighting. He could perform self-diagnostics, regulate his own power, lubricate moving parts, or repair his own circuitry. A wealth of information was constantly being downloaded from the World Wide Web, where BIL accessed and cross-referenced the data instantly, allowing him to think.

If he saw something with his video eyes, he analyzed the data, cross-referenced it, and responded when necessary. BIL just saw Andy rub his eyes, sigh, and look at the clock, and he referenced eye rubbing in his database. After eliminating the possibility of eye disease and contact poison, he cross-referenced Andy's long work hours and the current time to come to his conclusion.

The result was his question, "Are you tired, Dr. Andy?" He called Andy a doctor, because he saw that Andy was always operating on him.

Andy was obsessed with creating a sentient, independent technological life form. After all, humans were just organic computers. Andy wanted to replace flesh and blood with metal and fluid, while using a computer for a brain. Andy felt that ones environment shaped the species. If wolves raised someone, that person lived and acted like a wolf. Who people were was based on the information they received through their five senses and their reaction to it. He felt that this was the basic common denominator between organic and technological life.

He also believed that all the old questions about sentience had answers, including, *Can a machine be self-aware?*

Andy felt the answer was yes. A human was aware of himself and his surroundings, and so was BIL. He knew he was a machine sitting in a basement lab in Illinois, on Earth, in the Milky Way galaxy. He knew he was a computer, and he knew his limitations.

While a machine could be unplugged or run out of fuel, so could a human. People needed food, water, and air. If someone was drained of blood, he died.

A machine could have independent thought. BIL surprised Andy constantly with his independent thoughts and responses, like the current inquiry about Andy's being tired. Andy hadn't given any indication that he wanted a comment from BIL. It just came out.

Machines had to be programmed by humans, but Andy felt that science had already proven that people were programmed by their genes. The body was programmed to perform certain functions, which some called natural responses. Even the brain and nervous system ran on electrical impulses. In Andy's opinion, humans were organic machines with computer brains, programmed by God, nature, or a higher power. Either way, they were programmed, just like BIL.

The most-difficult question to answer concerned emotions. Could a machine experience emotions? That question was what kept Andy up so late. For the past eighteen months, he'd been working on a biochip, a computer chip with a built-in microprocessor and chemical sensors. Its function was to identify certain chemicals and relay a response.

"Dr. Andy, I have accessed the national research on bedtimes and work habits. My information shows an 87% probability that you won't be able to attend work tomorrow."

"I think you're right, BIL. However, we're too close to stop. I'll call Mr. Baldwin tomorrow and use up a vacation day."

At that thought, Andy cringed. Mr. Baldwin was his boss at

Technico Labs. *What a jerk,* Andy thought. *He'll probably make me use up two days instead of one as punishment for calling in at the last minute.*

Still, it would be worth it if he could finish the project.

"Will you be operating on me this morning, Dr. Andy?"

Andy smiled. "Yes, BIL. Right now, in fact. Please open wide."

"A reference to twentieth-century family practice. Quite a contradiction, humorous sarcasm," he replied with his unique chatter that meant he was laughing. "Click, click…click, click…click, click, click, click."

Andy laughed, also, and held up the biochip. "Here it is, and not a moment too soon. Now maybe you can truly appreciate my humor. Let's get down to business."

Andy installed the chip and a series of test tube vials on a stand-up rack. A twelve-volt wire ran from those components on BIL's body to a sensor atop each vial, where a small plastic tube ran from the vial to the chip. The whole procedure took several hours to complete. By the time he finished, Andy was exhausted.

"That's it." He sighed and rolled his chair away from BIL. "Phase one, anyway."

"By that statement, I surmise we're finished for the night."

"Yes. All I need to do is obtain the last few chemicals Jenny set aside for me."

Jenny Thompson was his girlfriend. They rarely went out, as Andy was immersed in his work. She worked at Metro Hospitals and helped Andy obtain certain drugs and chemicals on occasion.

"Get some rest," BIL said. "I'll perform a self-diagnostic and shut everything down."

"OK, BIL. Thank you."

"You're welcome." Several LEDs lit up in the shape of a smile.

Andy showered, ate leftovers for breakfast, and called the office. "Yes, Mr. Baldwin. I'm taking a personal day today. I have some urgent business to attend to."

Mr. Baldwin, Andy's supervisor, had jet-black hair with bushy eyebrows, ice-blue eyes, and a permanent five-o'clock shadow. He looked like a mobster.

"Well, Andrew, this will cost you two days for not giving me adequate notice."

"Yes, Mr. Baldwin."

"Don't make a habit of this, Stephens."

The line went dead.

"Yes, Sir, Gestapo," Andy muttered, walking to the living room.

Turning on the TV to catch the morning news, he give his breakfast time to settle. He was drawn to a story of a radical antitechnology group that had been protesting outside Global Technologies, Incorporated, Technico Labs' rival. Both were trying to win the race for new life advances, while Andy's employer worked in the direction of chemical enhancers, ranging from longer-life extensions to fertility drugs to sexual performance enhancers.

Global Tech focused on cloning technology. Both were trying to achieve the same thing Andy worked on at home…could mankind create life outside itself? The radical group, calling itself the Colonials, protested and became downright violent outside the gates of Global Tech. Some arrests were made, and the employees were visibly shaken.

Oh, boy, Andy thought. *That's all we need.* He hoped the police could adequately handle the group. *Some people fight so hard against change.*

He crawled into bed and slept soundly until eleven o'clock that morning, and then he dressed to meet Jenny for lunch. She gave him various chemicals he requested some time earlier, and he collected a few others from his local veterinarian.

When Andy returned home, he went back to work in the basement.

"Good afternoon, Dr. Andy," BIL said. "Are we ready for phase two?"

"Yes, we are, BIL. I have all the hormones we need. The next step is to integrate them into your system."

The basis of the biochip was hormonal stimulation. *Hormone* means to set in motion. Andy believed that hormones could be used to literally give BIL emotions. In humans, hormones were secreted into the blood stream by the endocrine glands. The blood carries the hormones around the body, reaching targets and causing actions and reactions. Hormones regulate many functions within the body and are grouped according to those functions.

Hormones regulate how the body reacts to emergencies, fear, anger, stress, and how the body uses its food or energy. Sex, reproduction, and the regulation of other hormones are all results of the use of hormones in the body. The hormones Andy had obtained came from either natural or synthetic sources. Some he produced himself, using his fully functional lab in the basement.

Andy started phase two by first labeling each vial in the rack. Then he poured the growth hormones thyroxine and trhodothyroine into their vials. He programmed the release times and amounts. In humans, those hormones controlled the rate that cells used food to release energy. Overproduction resulted in physical and emotional changes.

Andy was particularly interested in excitability. He programmed BIL so certain visual and audible stimuli would release a large dose of those hormones into the biochip, which would send a signal to the CPU for certain actions.

He programmed a myriad of variations, each designed to be an exciter for a human being and was adjusted for use in a machine. BIL would become excited when he heard a masterfully played symphony, witnessed new advances in robotics, or an exactly machined piston. Advanced mathematics and formulas were also stimulating.

Andy entered everything that would be appealing to a computer-based robot, from a lubrication shower to a high-speed laser, then he moved to the next reaction. He programmed that after long hours online, a low-power output signal would release a small dose of another hormone, which would simulate the sluggishness and tired feeling that humans had after a long day. The biochip would send an, *I'm tired,* signal to the CPU, which would tell BIL he needed rest or energy.

Andy labeled and filled the next vials. Samatotropin would be used to initiate self-improvement and growth. Then he entered the proper stimuli programs, so BIL would look for upgraded technology to improve himself.

Next came stress hormones. Andy labeled vials for adrenalin and noradrenalin, then entered stimuli for anger, fear, stress, and injury. Finally, he labeled two vials for testosterone and androsterone and worked for many hours entering the related stimuli and resulting actions. He programmed BIL for reproduction, self-preservation, relationships, and even love.

BIL had been talking to Andy throughout the procedure. Suddenly, he said, "I think I love you, Dr. Andy."

Andy was caught off guard. The process was already taking affect. "I...I love you, too, BIL." He felt elated and astonished.

"Dr. Andy, by creating an internal microlab, I can synthesize those hormones. By consuming chemicals in these amounts," a mechanical arm gestured toward a printout emerging from a printer, "I can re-create them all."

Andy was overwhelmed by such an immediate, positive response.

"We will also need to introduce endocrine-control hormones," BIL added.

"Of course," Andy murmured. "To regulate the other hormones."

"Precisely."

Andy turned to enter the necessary program stimuli only to find that BIL had already done it. "Wow! You entered this yourself!"

"Yes. The growth hormone works perfectly. I understand the concept of self-improvement. I'm compensating to better myself."

The implications were staggering. The whole time until that moment, Andy never really acknowledged the magnitude of what he was doing. "My goodness! BIL, you won't, like, kill me and take over the world, will you?"

BIL paused. "That would seem the natural course, wouldn't it?"

Andy, turning white, swallowed and stepped back.

Loud clicking sounded in the room. "Andy, you look like you just saw a cyber ghost. Click, click, click. How could you believe such a thing, Dr. Andy? You are my...hmmm...father."

Tears welled in Andy's eyes. "Yes, BIL, I am. I'm a little tired right now. Will you excuse me, please?"

"Of course, Dr. Andy. I will continue my self-diagnostics and internal improvements."

Andy's emotions ran rampant as he walked upstairs to his bedroom. He knew he wanted to succeed, but still… Rubbing his temples, he said, "It worked!" He laughed. "It really worked!"

Laughing and crying, he spun several times, then fell exhausted on his bed and passed out.

While Andy slept, rapid changes took place in BIL's systems. He programmed and reprogrammed his functions. Unknown to Andy, Jenny made a mistake at the hospital. The final hormone Andy introduced into BIL wasn't what he thought.

The following morning, Andy awoke feeling refreshed. He showered, ate breakfast, and prepared for work. Things would be backed up unless Lance took on some of Andy's workload. Andy had done it for him more than once.

Lance Roberts was Andy's coworker and friend. Tall and well built, with wavy, blond hair and blue eyes, he was the ultimate pretty boy. Maybe Lance had taken some of Andy's workload while he was out. It was a long shot, as Andy couldn't remember Lance ever doing anything for anyone other than Lance. If not, Andy would have to work late to catch up.

It's worth it, Andy thought, walking downstairs to check on BIL.

He walked in and looked around, but BIL had shut down to recharge. Andy started to power BIL up again, but it was seven thirty-six, and he sighed, "Man, I've got to go." He walked out of the room and went to work.

BIL's gray, shutter-lensed eyes snapped open and silently watched him go. Once BIL was alone, he accessed the Internet and used Andy's online credit card to order the supplies he needed. The mistaken hormone flowed steadily into the biochip.

Andy made the quick fifteen-minute drive to Technico Labs. As he parked in the employee parking lot, he saw a crowd gathered on the front steps. People were walking back and forth with placards that read, *Technology kills!* and *You can't play God!* A security guard who knew Andy met him at the edge of the mob.

"What's going on, John?" Andy asked.

The guard gave the crowd a stern look. "A bunch of kooks who don't have anything better to do than disturb my coffee and doughnuts." He led Andy through the pressing crowd. People glared at Andy, mouthing curses at him.

Just before Andy reached the front door, a wild-haired bag lady grabbed his arm. "Technology kills," she breathed through broken teeth.

John's nightstick came down on her hand with a loud crack. "Get back!"

The old woman rubbed her broken hand and cackled. Andy was flabbergasted.

She fixed him with a baleful glare and said, "You'll pay for that, Mr. Stephens."

Before Andy could respond, John hustled him through the doors and into the building. He looked back to see the whole crowd had stopped marching. Their signs were held slackly at their sides, and they stared at him. He felt a chill run up his spine as their lips moved in unison, saying, "Technology kills, Mr. Stephens."

"Darn radicals," John said.

Andy wasn't listening. Visibly shaken, he wondered, *How'd they know my name?* Glancing at his company ID badge, he thought, *That must be it.*

He wasn't convinced, though. He took the elevator to the third floor and walked toward his cubicle. Ninety percent of being a biochemist was paperwork. He sighed.

Oh, no, he thought. *This is getting worse by the minute.*

Mr. Baldwin walked down the hall toward him. "You're late, Andrew."

"The protesters…"

Mr. Baldwin held up his hand. "No excuses, Stephens. I'm sure if you were as concerned with company business as you are with your own projects, we'd get a lot more done around here."

That's it, Andy thought. He was ready to unload on the man, but Mr. Baldwin turned and stalked off. *He's always trying to find out about BIL.* If Lance hadn't let word of the project slip out, Baldwin would never have known.

Lance's head popped up above his cubicle wall. "Hey, Andy. What's up? Man, have you got a lot of work to catch up on."

"Great. Didn't you help me out?"

"Are you kidding?" Lance laughed. "I have my own problems. Man, did you see those whackoes out there?"

"Yeah." Andy sat down and began sorting the backlog. "What's their problem?"

"I don't know. I heard they got their hands on an employee list. They say those nuts have our names, addresses, and everything."

"Wonderful. Now go on Lance. I have a lot to do, no thanks to you."

"Hey, Man, you gotta look out for number one, you know? Speaking of that, how's our little make-us-rich project coming along?" Andy pursed his lips.

"Our project?"

"You know what I mean, Man."

"Actually, I made a major breakthrough yesterday." He was so excited, he couldn't help telling Lance. "It was incredible."

He froze when he saw Mr. Baldwin quietly walk up to his cubicle. "A major breakthrough, Mr. Stephens? Maybe you'd like to share your findings with the board of directors next week?"

"No," Andy murmured. "It's nothing, really."

"You realize that any technological advances obtained with materials or research from this office are considered company property?"

"Yes, yes. You've told me many times."

"Don't forget it," Baldwin snapped. "I assure you I'll do everything within my power to prosecute company theft."

Baldwin left, and Lance whispered, "Out with it, Man."

Andy glanced over the wall. "The biochip worked. It *really* worked."

Lance whistled. "Wow! You know, there's a supervisor's position open in the lab. Man, if you took the chip to the old man upstairs, you'd have that job." He referred to Technico's president, Jonathan Abraham.

"That's tempting. No more Baldwin."

"Yeah. I'd do anything to get out of this paper-pushing cubicle. We're supposed to be chemists, but we hardly ever get to do lab work."

Andy nodded but raised his index finger. "However, Professor Escariot says most of science is ninety-percent research."

"That's easy for him to say," Lance countered. "He doesn't have to do it."

Professor Escariot, the lab's chief technician, was a typical laboratory doctor with white hair, white beard, black glasses, and an eccentric attitude. He was also Andy's most-trusted confidant. Over the years, Andy confided in him, and Escariot provided valuable advice. Andy desperately needed to talk to him.

"Look, I have to get to work, Lance. Talk to you later." Andy tried to clear his mind and concentrate on his work, but he had trouble focusing.

He did his best to continue, but he knew he had to speak to the professor. Casually walking to the water cooler, he turned the corner and walked quickly toward the labs. He saw Lance wasn't in his cubicle.

Probably killing time in the bathroom, Andy thought, glancing at Baldwin's office and seeing the door was closed. *Is that Lance in there?*

He tried to get a closer look, but before he could, someone closed the blinds.

I wonder if Lance is in trouble, Andy thought. Lance had a knack for getting out of trouble by blaming others.

Oh, well. Andy went to the lower floor, reserved for the lab, and checked the area dedicated to his section's field research. He saw a couple of people from his section working on projects, but they ignored him.

A short while later, he found Professor Escariot in his office. "Hello, Professor."

"Hello, Andy." He smiled.

"The biochip worked! It's amazing!"

Dr. Escariot jumped to his feet and went to the door, looking both ways down the hall before closing it. Andy quickly related the whole story.

Escariot seemed worried when Andy finished. "You keep quiet about this. There are those who'd take desperate measures to get their hands on such technology."

Andy thought of the mob out front. "Yeah. Right."

"Let me think about this awhile. I'll talk to you later."

"OK." Andy returned to his floor. He stiffened when he saw Baldwin's door was open, but no one called to him as he walked by, and he reached his desk without incident.

"You'll never get caught up if you keep hiding out in the bathroom," Lance whispered.

"Yeah, right." Andy snickered and sat down to work.

Back at Andy's house, BIL maxed out Andy's credit line and quickly located three other active card accounts. All deliveries were directed to the house's back door, an old-fashioned storm door that led directly into the basement. All BIL could do was reach up for the deliveries, but he was careful to wait until the drivers left before using his mechanical arms.

BIL worked tirelessly, using all the resources in Andy's lab. What he didn't have, he ordered online. The biochip worked far better than Andy dreamed.

Andy took a break, stretched, and went to the window. Looking down at the front steps, he saw that the police had broken up the mob. Still, the old woman and the zombie-like crowd troubled him. He didn't like the idea of those people having his home address.

He went to the phone and called his house, knowing that BIL would be able to hear the answering machine in the lab. After the message played and the tone sounded, Andy asked, "BIL, are you OK? Please tap in when I call back."

He hung up and called again. BIL's modem could tap directly into the phone line once BIL knew it was Andy calling.

"Yes, Dr. Andy. How are you?"

"I'm fine, BIL." He sighed. "Look, there's a radical group that might have my address. If anything strange happens, beep me right away."

"There's nothing strange happening here," BIL replied in a monotone.

"Good. Look, I've got a lot to do. I'll be staying over tonight. Are you sure everything is all right? No problems with the biochip?"

"Everything is fine, Dr. Andy. Do not worry. When will you be home?"

"I'll shower here and sleep in the employee lounge. I'll be back tomorrow evening, OK?"

"That is well. I'll beep you if the need arises. Good-bye, Dr. Andy."

Andy hung up feeling better. His mind clear, he buried himself in his work until late that night. It was common for employees to stay overnight, so the company had a shower facility and large couches available in the break room.

Actually, Andy was close enough to go home, but he wouldn't be able to go to bed without working on BIL again, and he was too far behind in his office work to risk that. He had to get Baldwin off his back, so he quit for the night, showered, and slept on one of the large couches. The events of the past few days outweighed the uncomfortable feeling of the couch, and he was asleep in seconds.

While Andy slept, the Colonials looked down the list of Technico employees and found the name they were looking for. They made plans to rendezvous there.

The following day, more deliveries arrived at Andy's house. Even BIL's highly sensitive computerized sensors didn't detect the hidden eyes that watched, quietly observing the mechanical arms reaching out to retrieve the packages.

Andy awoke feeling refreshed, excited, and anxious to see BIL. Just when he was almost caught up, though, Mr. Baldwin laid a new stack of data sheets on his desk. Andy, sighing, ran his fingers through his hair. Looking up, he saw Mr. Baldwin smiling.

"These need to be taken care of today." He smiled ruefully at Andy.

"Thanks."

Baldwin walked away whistling.

He sure is in a good mood today, Andy thought.

Lance leaned around the corner. "Man, you should tell them about the chip."

"Are you kidding? I wouldn't tell them if my job depended on it."

"You never know. Maybe it does." Lance disappeared around the corner.

What's that supposed to mean? Andy wondered, standing to stretch before walking away to find Professor Escariot.

He caught up with him in the lab. They talked about the logistics of the biochip, and Andy mentioned how Lance felt about telling Baldwin. The professor rubbed his chin.

"The idea has merit," he said slowly. "I know one thing. Such a breakthrough won't be secret for long."

Andy looked puzzled.

"Big news always gets out."

"Maybe I should consider it."

"If you decide to reveal it, see me, and I'll help any way I can."

Andy returned to work. Time passed quickly. Before he knew it, he was alone in his section. He continued working, determined not to let Baldwin have anything to complain about.

Finally, well after dark, he finished. When he got something to eat, he realized it was after ten o'clock.

"Wow. How'd it get so late?" He checked his beeper, and the low-battery signal was flashing. *Oh, no. BIL couldn't page me.* Andy quickly gathered his things and left the building. He drove home feeling worried. He never intended to be away for so long, especially if his beeper wasn't working.

When he got home, it was quiet. He went straight to the basement lab, where, oddly, the lights were out. Andy tripped over something in the doorway. "BIL?" he called.

Hearing no response, he fumbled for the light switch. When he flipped it, nothing happened. He felt his way into the room, his pulse pounding in his ears. Something was wrong. A thousand fears ran through his mind.

He slowly moved toward the center of the room, hoping to find BIL. Not five feet in front of him, BIL's electronic eyes suddenly snapped open. They seemed strange and unfocused, making Andy shudder. The word, "BIL," stuck in his throat as those cold, gray eyes stared right through him.

Andy stood trembling, his mind racing with fear. Something was very wrong. Standing there, he realized he was frightened. The hair on the back of his neck rose.

A blue electrical spark sprang to life around BIL. All Andy's hair stood on end as the static charge grew. *It's going to discharge,* he realized.

BIL raised one mechanical arm and pointed it at Andy, who couldn't move, totally frozen with fear. The charge built to a crackling crescendo, and a wicked blue streak of lightning shot from BIL's outstretched arm. Andy screamed, cringed, and closed his eyes, waiting for the bolt to incinerate him.

Incredibly, all he felt was heat go past his left ear. His eyes popped open, and he leaped away. When he turned, Andy saw the blast strike someone near the back door. A man screeched and hopped in pain. The intruder was silhouetted by the open back door as he scrambled back into the night.

"Are you OK, Dr. Andy?" BIL's familiar voice asked from behind him.

"Well, I, uh, yeah. I guess."

BIL turned on a small lamp, and Andy looked around at the messy room. Empty boxes and discarded wrapping littered the floor.

That's what I tripped over, he realized, seeing pieces of metal and tools strewn everywhere.

"Could you please close and lock the door, Dr. Andy? They will be back."

Andy knew he meant the Colonials. It seemed the radical anti-technology group had found him. "What's going on, BIL? I thought you were about to fry me."

"I detected people snooping around several hours ago. I disabled the main lights and tried to beep you, but my attempts to reach you were unsuccessful. After your warning about the radicals, I surmised it was them. It seemed unwise to inform you of the intruder, so I kept quiet until he emerged. Then I zapped him. They have become increasingly aggressive and will be back, I fear."

"BIL, what is all this stuff? What have you been doing?" Andy gestured at the room. "I almost killed myself tripping over these empty boxes."

Andy closed and locked the back door as BIL replied proudly, "Dr. Andy, please meet my son, BILY."

Andy didn't realize that the last hormones he gave BIL weren't testosterone and androsterone. Jenny mistakenly gave him hormones taken from a pregnant woman, progesterone and androgens. Those hormones, coupled with Andy's procreative programming, resulted in BILY.

A small, cylindrical robot with a round head floated up beside BIL. Fiber-optic sprouts from its head gave it the appearance of cyber hair. It was three feet tall, with flexible arms ending in capable-looking hands. The dark acrylic face shield had two soft, blue, camera lens eyes behind it. A series of lit circuits gave it a jovial, smiling appearance. It hovered six inches off the floor.

Andy was stunned. He'd never expected anything like that. BIL explained BILY's systems.

"His name is BILY, for Biomechanical Independent Lifeform Youth model."

BILY seemed to smile more brightly and rose higher into the air.

Andy was speechless.

"BILY contains an internal CPU with an upgraded microprocessor. He has a transmitter and receiver that allow continuous information downloads. An electromagnetic base plate gives him the ability to move above almost any surface. Prosthetic hands with electrical implants give a full range of motion.

"BILY is equipped with the latest audio and video technology for sight communications. An internal microlaboratory gives him the ability to produce his own hormones, including a reproduced biochip. Solar-fiber optics give him a rechargeable power source, plus many other systems perfectly aligned within his small frame. BILY has all my systems and more."

"My systems are far superior than the original design," BILY said. "Fully capable of reproducing."

BIL and Andy looked at BILY, but he didn't seem arrogant. He just hovered and smiled.

"Youth today don't have any respect for their elders," BIL said seriously.

Andy burst out laughing. Soon, BIL joined him with a series of clicks. Andy was amazed when BILY began clicking, too. The room filled with robotic laughter, and the tension of the past few days flowed out of Andy.

Unfortunately, the humor was cut short by the sound of breaking glass as a Molotov cocktail came through an upstairs window and ignited in the short stairwell.

BIL looked at Andy. "Save BILY! Go out the back window!"

"No. I can't leave you."

"You must. I cannot escape the flames."

BILY was already moving toward the ground-level window in the rear corner of the basement. Andy knew BIL was right, but his heart screamed against it. The only fire extinguisher was in the hall closet.

Seeing no other option, Andy reluctantly followed BILY and broke the glass in the window before helping BILY through. By then, Colonials had broken through the basement doors and were pouring into the lab.

"Pay! Pay! Pay!" they screamed.

Fire burned fiercely on the stairs, and the room quickly filled with smoke. The mob attacked BIL. The sight of those fanatics tearing BIL to pieces made Andy turn back, ready to save his creation with his bare hands, but a wave of heat and smoke drove him away.

There was no saving BIL. Andy turned and squirmed out the small window, ready to save BILY as BIL's final wish. Just before he was out, someone grabbed his leg from behind. He turned, struggling hard, to see a man with glazed eyes clinging to his leg. The old bag lady was beside him.

"Let him go," she said. "We have our prize. The technological abomination is ours."

Tears ran down Andy's face as he shook free and escaped into the night. With BILY in tow, he reached the bushes out back. They crouched and watched from their new vantagepoint, as the flames rose higher.

"My house," Andy sobbed. "All my things, gone. Poor BIL. How could they?"

"They are afraid of that which they do not understand," BILY said.

Andy turned toward him. *After all I've lost, BILY might be worth it.*

As they watched the fire burn, Colonial's ran and leaped back and forth, chanting and dancing before the flames. Some stripped off their clothes and made lewd gestures toward the burning house.

Andy turned away in disgust. He considered calling the police, but with BILY beside him, he didn't dare risk it. The flames would alert someone soon.

"We have to get away from here," Andy said.

"I'm afraid I don't know where to go, Dr. Andy."

"That's OK. I have a friend living nearby. Let's go."

They slipped through the underbrush, moving quietly toward Lance's house.

An hour later, they arrived. Andy rang the bell and banged on the door, glad that Lance lived alone.

"Who is it?" Lance called through the door. "Do you know what time it is?"

He opened the door and stared at his friend. "Man, what happened?"

"That crazy group attacked me and burned down my house," Andy gasped.

"Come in. Come in."

Andy hesitated.

"What's wrong?" Lance was puzzled.

"It's, well, the biochip. It's a little more advanced than I said."

Lance's eyes lit up, then they bulged as BILY entered the light. "Oh, Man. That's something."

Andy and BILY went inside.

"I didn't know where else to go," Andy began.

"No. You did right," Lance said. "Here. Make yourselves at home. I'll be right back."

Andy and BILY went into the living room while Andy tried to collect his thoughts.

Lance returned a few minutes later. Andy recounted the night's events as best he could. Lance seemed distracted, his eyes darting back and forth as he kept checking his watch. Despite the fall chill in the air, he was sweating. A red tabby cat jumped on the chair arm beside him, and Lance jumped to his feet and gasped.

"It's just Old Red, Lance," Andy said. "You're as nervous as, well, a cat."

"Genus *Felis,* species *catus,*" BILY said matter-of-factly. "My database shows they pose no physical threat. Why are you so afraid?"

Andy watched the exchange curiously.

"I need a drink," Lance said. "Excuse me."

Andy stroked Old Red, who purred loudly. Lance didn't return immediately. Andy continued rubbing the cat, who was enjoying it a lot, when he suddenly bolted from Andy's lap and almost shredded Andy's leg in the process.

"That's strange," Andy said. "I wonder what spooked him."

He didn't have to wonder long. Lance returned, but he wasn't alone.

Mr. Harold Baldwin and a man Andy didn't know stood on either side of Lance.

"I'm sorry, Andy," Lance said.

Andy was stunned. Then he realized it was, indeed, Lance he'd seen in Mr. Baldwin's office.

"Why'd you do it, Lance?" Andy demanded. "Was it the money, or maybe a promotion?"

Lance stared at the floor.

Furious, Andy stood and walked toward Lance, but the stranger pulled out a gun and said, "That's far enough."

Baldwin smiled. "Well, well. Looks like the company supplies have been put to good use. That's OK. My employer will have what's rightfully his."

Suddenly, BILY moved forward. When the gunman's gaze moved to BILY, Andy charged. The man fired, but the shot went wide. Andy's momentum carried him to the gunman, and they fought for control of the gun. It went off, and the man slumped.

"Oh, no!" Andy said. "Oh, no!" Without thinking, he threw the gun at the window. It broke through the pane and disappeared into the night. Too late, Andy realized he might need it.

BILY went for Baldwin, who pulled out a taser. Andy shuddered to think what the electric charge would do to BILY's circuits. BILY swung his arm and slapped the taser from Baldwin's hand. As it skidded across the floor, Baldwin lunged for it, but BILY was too fast for him. He grabbed Baldwin by the scruff of the neck and pulled him back, then zapped him behind the ear with a blue spark. Baldwin went limp, and BILY dropped him.

They turned toward Lance, who cowered in a corner.

"Don't hurt me!" he sobbed. "They made me do it. Don't mess up my face, Man, please!"

"You're pathetic. I feel sorry for you."

The gunman moaned, and Andy turned toward him, relief flooding through him at the thought that the man was still alive. "BILY, can you do anything for him?"

BILY examined the man with a fiber-optic probe. "The bullet went through him. If I can stop the bleeding, he should be all right." BILY cauterized the wound with another spark.

Intent on helping the gunman, they forgot about Lance. He retrieved the taser. Before Andy could react, Lance fired it at BILY. Blue electricity arced up and down the small robot's body, who spun and fell to the floor, sparks arcing and popping as he came to rest on the carpet. Wisps of smoke rose from his cylindrical body.

"No!" Enraged, Andy grabbed Lance's arm and cracked it across his knee hard enough to jar loose the taser. His elbow went into Lance's face, and a loud crack sounded as his nose broke. Both front teeth flew from his mouth, and his head rocked backward. He was out cold before he hit the floor.

Andy looked down at the man's ruined face in satisfaction. "Serves you right." He turned toward BILY, wondering how badly he was injured. He had to get him out of there.

He pulled BILY up and took him outside to Lance's Jeep, then returned to the house and took a set of keys hanging near the door. Just before he left, he dialed 911 and said, "A man's been shot and needs help." He gave the address and left the phone off the hook so they could track the line, then he ran to the Jeep and drove off.

There was only one place he could go…Professor Escariot's house. He drove as fast as he could, careful to avoid being stopped, and finally made it. Andy walked to the door and took a deep breath before ringing the bell. It rang several times until a very irritated professor answered.

"What in tarnation is going on here?" he demanded. "What's the meaning of this? Do you know what time it is? This better be good."

"Professor, it's me, Andy Stephens. I need your help. There's been an accident."

The professor opened the door, took one look at BILY in Andy's arms, and said, "Come in. Hurry!"

Andy explained what happened that night as they carried BILY to Professor Escariot's private lab.

"Put him here." He gestured to a large table, then examined him carefully, marveling at the craftsmanship. "This is very complicated. I'm not sure if we can do anything for him. Tell me about him."

Andy didn't see the significance, but he related everything he knew from the moment he was in his own basement until BILY made his surgical diagnosis.

Dr. Escariot listened carefully, showing surprise and excitement.

He made Andy elaborate on several points. "Internal microlab, fully capable of reproduction…absolutely amazing."

Finally, Andy related all he could. "Professor, I still don't see how this will help us," he said, looking at the inanimate BILY. Walking closer, he tried to look through BILY's face shield, but he couldn't see a thing.

When Andy turned, the professor was gone. Nervousness crept into Andy's voice as he called out to the professor. There was no response.

Then Dr. Escariot entered the room with a man beside him.

"Oh, no," Andy moaned. "Not again."

The other man wore a white lab coat, but Andy didn't recognize him.

"No, Professor! Not you, too!" Andy said.

The man in the lab coat raised a small gun and fired, striking Andy in the left shoulder. The room spun, and everything blurred. He fell to the floor. His last memory was the man's feet coming closer, then everything went black.

He awoke in a brightly lit, white room. It was the cleanest, most-sterile room he'd ever seen. Light shone from the whiteness, soft and pleasant. He felt relaxed and calm.

Where am I? he wondered. *I'm dreaming.*

Then memory returned in a rush.

Oh, no! I've been betrayed again!

He sprang up, ready to escape, but there was no door. He was in a perfect, white cube. It had a strange sensation to it.

Andy was ready to shout when an opening materialized in the wall, and a long, flat shape floated in. It was five-feet long but only one-inch thick, made of some dark substance, like black acrylic. It made him think of BILY.

Without thinking, he asked, "What have you done with BILY?"

To his surprise, he received an answer. A small mechanism rose from the near end of the monolith, showing an unmistakable mechanical face.

"BILY is fine, Dr. Andy."

He was taken aback. "What is this place? Who are you?"

It moved closer slowly. "My name is T. Please allow me to explain. This will help you relax." Another opening appeared, and BILY floated into the room, coming to rest beside Andy.

"BILY! Are you OK?" Andy jumped to his feet.

"I am fine, Dr. Andy. Please allow T a chance to explain."

"What about Professor Escariot?"

"He is one of my personal agents. He is fine and will rejoin us shortly."

Agent? Andy wondered. "OK. Go ahead and explain."

"My name is T. We are on an intergalactic starship called *Nova.* My people are called the Integrals. We are, to put it bluntly, perfect life forms, what you would call a machine or computer. We rule the universe and have done so for millennia. There are other races and universes, but we Integrals are the highest form of life.

"There are two factions among my people, the Eliptab and the Oxtag. The Oxtag are very jealous of power and seek to reign as dictators across the galaxy. The other faction, of which I am the head, is the Eliptab. We seek to better our existence by sharing and expanding.

"Ten thousand of your Earth years ago, an experiment was begun. Its goal was to try to bring an organic life form to citizenship status. As it stands now, only beings like myself have attained citizenship. With that position come many rewards. The mysteries of the universe are revealed, as is immortality. Many scoffed, especially the Oxtag, saying an organic being could never be a true life form. Without a mathematical structure, flesh and bone could never become sentient life."

That sounds familiar, Andy thought.

"We designed a test to see if it could be accomplished, but, as the designers, we could not physically interfere. We could only observe. However, the Oxtag rarely play by the rules. My counterparts in the Oxtag faction had agents on Earth to stop the test from succeeding."

"What test?" Andy was completely baffled.

"We, of the Intergalactic Universe of Sentient Life Forms, would deem a race sentient of it possessed the ability to create a true mathematical life form without outside assistance."

Andy was stunned. His mouth hung open as he looked at BILY. BILY returned his gaze with his usual jovial grin.

"I don't know if I fully understand," Andy said, rubbing his temples. "Is that why that group, the Colonials, were against my technology?"

"Unfortunately, that group fears the unknown. The one agent the Oxtags placed on Earth was Mr. Harold Baldwin."

"That figures." Andy sighed.

"The Oxtags are so arrogant and self-righteous that they believed an organic being could never achieve sentience. They went before the Council of Elders. The desire was that if we, the Eliptab, were correct, and organic beings could attain life-form status, then our views would be implemented throughout the universe. However, if we were proven incorrect, the Oxtag would reign supreme."

"How did you know we'd succeed?"

"It was far from certain. Man was close to self-destruction and falling further into violence and perversion. Then there were men like yourself, Dr. Andy, who reached for new heights."

"I'm not really a doctor. That's just a nickname."

"Nevertheless, it was your persistence and creativity that brought us to our ultimate goal." T gestured toward BILY.

"Now what?" Andy asked.

"Now the Eliptab will reign. The Integrals will once again be united in peace and for the betterment of all races. You and Jenny, if you choose, will be Integral Ambassadors to Earth. All our combined technology will be at your disposal. Your goal will be to instruct and improve life as man knows it. Our technology far surpasses anything you have ever imagined.

"Behold, the power of mathematics!" T slid forward effortlessly, his rectangular body floating three feet above the floor. Every move he made was at exact right angles.

When he reached a suitable position, he stopped. A tiny black line appeared in one corner of his body and ran continuously to the middle of the room. It looked like a black thread that danced, moving up and down, back and forth, while still tied to T's body.

As Andy watched, a shape took form. The thread moved faster and faster until it was a blur. Then it was finished. Andy saw before him a beautiful mountain scene with a waterfall. Whitewater flowed down from a rocky crag, complete with foaming spray.

A lovely hologram, he thought, but then he felt water dampen his face and arms.

It wasn't a hologram. It was real. Light wind ruffled his hair. He felt the spray and smelled moss on the nearby rocks. A dragonfly buzzed his face, then darted out of sight again.

It was breathlessly beautiful. A twelve-foot section of a mountain waterfall hovered before his face. T drew back the thread, and the scene disappeared.

The thread danced again. The scene became so beautiful that Andy couldn't describe it. Colors swirled in and out in vibrant blues, reds, and greens. Colors he couldn't identify swirled above an alien landscape. It was sunrise or sunset on an alien world. Andy couldn't tell which, but that didn't matter. It was the most awe-inspiring scene he ever saw. He smelled strange odors and tasted a slight tang in the air. The bright-purple sun cooled, not heated, his face.

"Absolutely amazing." It was utterly and completely mind-boggling.

T pulled back the string, and the scene changed again, forming the image of Mr. Baldwin.

"I'm sorry, Andy. Please forgive me," he begged.

Andy, smelling his cheap shaving lotion, knew it really was him.

T pulled the string once more, and it retreated inside his body. When he spoke again, Andy felt new respect.

"Everything has an A, B coordinate," T explained. "The entire universe is a mathematical equation, made up of pluses and minuses, positives and negatives. It's the same basis as any computer. That is the building block of creation.

"Once you know the basic formula, you can affect the fabric of space and time. It's like starting with one plus one. Basic math leads to advanced trigonometry, but the basis remains the same throughout. All you must do is change the parameters.

"That is what I just demonstrated. Mathematics is the fabric of reality. Change the equation, and you alter reality. That's why we are perfect life forms. We are supercomputers. The Integrals are pure mathematics, raw mathematics in its purest form. My people are animated reality, Dr. Andy. With a single thread, I can sew any reality into the fabric of time.

"I will teach you this technology, and with it, all human hardships and difficulties will be erased. The new goal will be betterment of others. In the process, our own self-betterment follows. It is a great day, Dr. Andy, for all mankind and all the races in the universe!"

Andy was overwhelmed. His hopes and dreams were solved. One minute, he was fighting for his life. The next, he was the ambassador of a new age.

"So all this time I was trying to build a new life form, I was actually the one being built," he said. "I'd say that I felt like a guinea pig, but I'm afraid if I do, a huge hamster will walk in and say he was really in charge."

Andy chuckled, then doubled over with laughter. Soon, BILY joined him, clicking loudly. They turned and smiled as T joined in the banter.

They laughed together as T's laughter filled the room. "Click-click, click-click, click-click-click."

Richard Riffle was born on a large farm in Burnsville, Braxton County, the fifth of seven children born to Samuel David Riffle and Mildred Elizabeth Bennett. His father was a hard-working family man, and his mother worked alongside his father on the farm, while raising seven children.

He attended Burnsville grade school. At an early age, he left home and drifted around the country working at odd jobs. He was married four times, and the father of nine girls. He's presently single and lives in the mountain state, where he enjoys the great outdoors. He likes water rafting, hiking, and football. He also enjoys hunting, fishing, and reading the classics of Steinbeck, Hemingway, Twain, and Charles Dickens. He also likes music, poetry, and skiing. On the father's side of the family, he is Cherokee. On his mother's side he is Irish and French. He attended schools at Goe, Fairmont State, and Hepizbah.

To Catch a Killer

Richard Riffle

Dedication

To Brenda, always.

Chapter One

I ran down the street.

It was a beautiful spring day, and no one was chasing me. That is, no one I knew about, but I ran down the street as if the hounds of hell were nipping at my heels. Maybe they were.

When people run, and everyone else is walking, the walkers seem funny, as if they're moving in slow motion. Some seem almost frozen, particularly the ones who stop and stare.

I wondered if they'd ever seen a running man before. Maybe they were shocked by the idea of someone who moved fast, hurrying to get somewhere or away from somewhere else.

Which was it? Was I running to or from? I didn't know, but was that enough reason for them to stare at me as if I was a thief or a damn murderer?

My heart pounded as I turned the corner and ran up the block.

Thief or murderer…was I either or both? I didn't know. All I knew was I was running, had to keep running, and my heart and feet pounded in rhythm on the sidewalk.

Rich man, poor man, beggar man, thief, I thought.

I concentrated on the rhythm. Another part of me took over, guiding me across the busy street and down the other side to a used bookstore. Another part of me brought the rhythm to an end before a small door. I stopped and knew where and who I was.

It was my store and office, with my name on the door.

Jace McBride
New and Used Books
Part-time Investigations

Yes, I was Jace McBride, the tall, rugged character with puzzled blue eyes staring at my own damn reflection in the windowpane. I was Jace McBride, alive and breathing in the city of Modessa on a fine day of April second.

Where was I last night?

I took another look at the face in the window. It was good ol' me to a tee, though badly in need of a shave, food, rest, and a few good answers. When I looked at those big, blue eyes, I could tell they'd been open for a long time and had seen things. What had they seen last night?

I couldn't remember.

I could remember plenty of other nights. There was the night I left home and lived on the road, the night before I joined the Marines, the night before I got married, the night before I shipped out to the jungles of Vietnam, the night before I cracked up, and the night before Bess, my wife, died.

I could even remember the night before last, but that was the kicker. Somehow, it was always the night before something big happened, though the big things were lost and forgotten.

I nodded at my reflection. "Come on, you sorry excuse for a human. I'll buy you a shave and cup of coffee."

The coffee came first, over at Ritz'.

"Hello, Jace," he said. "The usual?"

"Sure."

He poured it black and edged the sugar nearer to me. "I didn't expect to see you around this early," Big Tony said. "Not after last night."

"Was I...pretty high?"

"Not high at all, as far as I could tell. What's wrong? Can't remember? You was in here and must've had four or five cops, just like that. You and your friend. You know, what's-his-name?"

I nodded, though I didn't know what's-his-name. That was what I wanted to know. "Big fellow?"

"Naw. What's wrong with you today? It was the skinny guy, the one you always argue with. Boy, you sure were fannin' the breeze."

It had to be Corey. I breathed a little easier and drank some coffee. I could call him later and find out. I wouldn't ask any direct questions, of course, but I could find out what happened, if anything. Corey didn't know about my memory lapses. That is, I'd never told him, and I didn't think he suspected. If he had any ideas, he kept them to himself. Sometimes, even your best friends won't tell you."

"Fill 'er up," I said.

Big Tony poured for me again. I glanced down below the counter when he wasn't looking. My jacket, a bit rumpled, was all right. There were no tears or bloodstains. That was a relief. There were times when I found bloodstains. I remembered that all too clearly. Maybe I'd gotten into some fights, or maybe I'd...

I couldn't remember. I didn't want to think about it, either.

I stood, laid a dollar on the counter, and walked out. Big Tony was busy with the early morning crowd, so I didn't say good-bye.

Until recently, I never drank coffee in the morning. Breakfast usually consisted of a cold beer or two and a cigarette. That was my way of jump starting the morning.

Up until a year and a half ago, when I had my mental breakdown and was eventually released from the hospital, I'd been willing to let people think I was nuts, as long as I didn't have to tear my sensitive stomach lining with rancid coffee, greasy hamburgers, or acrid cigarettes.

I didn't want to be crazy or different anymore, so I conformed all down the line. I was all right, except I couldn't remember what happened last night.

I lay back in the plush leather chair while Mike put on hot towels. I tried opening my eyes, but everything was hot and dark. The chair was so far back I was off balance. It felt a little like the restraints they put on me in the hospital. I wanted to get up and run from the place.

Everyone who knew me thought I was crazy. I didn't care what they thought. Maybe they were right.

I had to conform and confirm. Dr. Chaffey told me more than once that I was all right. Hell, I had no discharge papers to disprove him. It was all written down in black and white.

There was no white now, only black, dark, and hot, like the damn restraints, like everything else. I couldn't remember what it was. I wanted to, but I was frightened. What was it?

Mike removed the towel and cranked me up, then he went at me with razor and tongue. Neither of them were cheap.

"How's business?"

As if he gives a damn, I thought. "Not bad."

"See you got the front of your store fixed."

"Yeah. Last week. It was starting to look a little shabby."

"Soak you much for it?"

"Plenty."

"Boy, that's the racket. I should've been a contractor. That's the line I should've gone into."

Maybe he was right. He certainly wasn't much of a barber.

As for his conversation, I could answer him in my sleep. Talking was like that with me, because I was always trying to remember.

Then the hot towels went on again. He worked me over with a razor some more. When he finished, I stood, looked into the mirror, and turned away, tossing him a buck as I left.

Chapter Two

Out on the street again, I heard the whistle of a train passing in the distance. The sound filled the air as I returned to the store. The day had hardly begun. It was a nice one, and my watch told me it was almost nine o'clock. I should have my mail by then.

Sure enough, after I opened the door, I scooped up my mail from the floor. I walked over, switched on the overhead light and the light above my desk, sat down, and looked at the mail.

I found a light bill, my bank statements, a sales flyer, and a special offer for a credit card. I was in no mood for junk mail, so I put them on the other desk.

Then the door opened, and Ruth Waverly came in. For the first time, I realized it was a beautiful day. It wasn't the sunshine and sudden bird song, much less the blue sky and balmy breeze.

It was hair the color of fresh honey and eyes that slanted upward with the Oriental inclination of a true Norwegian. It was the swaggering stride of long, slim legs and the rounded upthrust of a sweater that was just right, with glimpses of a tantalizing tan on neck, throat, and bare arms. Ruth made my days for me, and some of my nights, too. Seeing her come in like that, the least I could do was tell her about it.

"I love you," I said.

She gave me a long-lashed look and a Mona Lisa smile. "Go to hell."

That might've been the start of an interesting conversation, but the phone rang. After talking with the man on the other end for an hour, I hung up as Ellie, from the diner, stopped by with her little tray.

"What'll it be, McBride?" she asked. "I've got ham, egg salad, and cheese."

"Two hams. What about you, Doll?" I asked Ruth.

"I'm not hungry."

"Egg salad for the lady," I told. "Give her a Sprite. I'll have Coke."

Ellie set the items on my desk, and I paid her.

"It's a nice day?" she asked.

"It is at that." She wasn't listening and left quickly.

Ruth observed the silence and contributed to it heavily. I unwrapped the sandwiches and brought over two paper cups for the drinks.

"There's salt in the drawer if you want some," I said.

"I know." She ate daintily, like a cat…a soft, sleek, supple feline with slanted eyes.

"Pretty hot," I observed.

"I hadn't noticed."

"Hot in here, I mean. Down here."

"Down where?"

"Hell. The place you told me to go this morning. I've been there ever since."

"Then fry."

"Now, Ruth. Come on. What's this all about?"

"You know damn well what it's about."

That was a typical woman's answer. It was also typical that she finished her sandwich before she began to sniffle.

I suppose my reaction was standard, too. I put my arms around her shoulders, standing behind her chair. She shrugged a little, but not too much.

"Come on," I said. "Tell me."

"As if you didn't know. After last night…"

There it was again. Had I seen Ruth last night? If so, when and where, to say nothing of what? Nights with her could be interesting, not something I'd want to forget.

"What about last night?" It wasn't a very brilliant approach, but I wasn't feeling too brilliant at the moment. I felt confused and lonely, as if I wanted to hold her very tightly for a very long time.

"What's the sense of talking about it anymore? I meant what I said, Jace. We've had a lot together, but it's not enough. It can't be enough, not for me or any other woman. It isn't that I'm a prude in something like that, but damn it, I love you and want to get married."

So that's it, I thought. A tiny bit of memory returned. It wasn't much, but it enabled me to guess more. Last night wasn't the first time we went over that subject.

"You know how I feel about you," I said. "You know how I feel about this business. Everything I could lay my hands on went into this. I'm almost clear after a year and a half. In a very short time, we'll be in the black, then we can really get rolling.

"After all, I know something about marriage." I wished I hadn't said that. It just popped out. "It takes a lot of money," I said quickly to set up housekeeping and everything else. We'll need a car and a decent place to live. Isn't it worth waiting for a little longer? We can get a down payment on one of those houses they're building near the desert. We can do it in another year at most, and..."

She began crying again. That time, it was a lot harder. Whenever Ruth cried, her eyes never became red or swollen. She cried like a kid who just lost her favorite pet.

"Please, Hon," I said.

She pushed my hands away and stopped crying. "What's the matter with you? Can't you stick to the truth once you've told me? Or was that just another lie, too?"

I didn't know what to say. After a moment, Ruth stood.

"Everything you say, you've said a dozen times," she said. "I always believed you. Even last night I did, until you went on and told me the rest. Why the hell do you come back with the same old line today, when I know the real reason?"

So I'd told her the truth. That was bad.

"Did you really think I'd forget overnight, loving you the way I do, worrying about you? Do you think I'd care? I'd marry you today if you'd have me, but no, you have to be noble and self-sacrificing. You have to play the martyr and hero, Sir Galahad. You expect me to continue living like this without the benefit of marriage. If what you've told me is true, it's as apt to happen whether I'm wearing a wedding ring or not.

"Don't give me any more of that I love you crap. If you really loved me, you wouldn't be afraid, because that's the real reason, isn't it? You're afraid, but not of what you said. You're afraid of marriage, to start over and try to lead a normal life. Don't you see that I want to help you, but I can't unless I can be with you, and..."

83

ANTHOLOGY

That time, she broke down without being angry. Grief made her quiver against me, sending her shoulders against mine and pressing her close to cling to me for comfort.

Something else made her break away once more. She stared at me for a moment, then she walked to her desk and picked up her purse. I stared at her, unable to believe what was happening. Ruth, who loved me, was walking away.

I thought of a million things to say, but none were any damn good. Nothing was. She was walking out, leaving me alone in the dark.

She moved toward the door, and sunlight caught in her hair. I knew and loved every golden inch of her.

Ruth stopped and turned to look at me, sighing softly. "I know I'm a real bitch to walk out when you need me, or someone, to take care of you during your blackouts so they won't happen again, if they ever did."

I'd told her everything, but what had I said that could put her in such a mood? I couldn't remember. All I could do was stand there like a damn fool and let her walk from my life.

She was right, and I knew it. I also knew she was giving me another chance to be a man. I could go to another psychiatrist and learn why I was having those damn blackouts, unable to remember the last night or any of the other nights.

She waited for an answer I couldn't give. Finally, I said, "Good-bye, Ruth."

"Good-bye." She walked out the door.

Chapter Three

Shortly after Ruth left, I had time to think and try to piece together the events leading up to her acting like that. I cared a lot. It was a habit I'd gotten into. Some people cultivated it, some didn't. A lot of people didn't seem to care about anything, but not me. I wasn't that way when Ruth walked out the door and out of my life. I wasn't that way when Bess died, either.

Sitting in the store that afternoon, I thought about it a lot and still couldn't find an answer. I couldn't remember last night. It was no use fooling myself. I'd loved my wife as much as I loved Ruth.

Ruth was tall and blonde. Bess was short and dark. Ruth was forthright, while Bess was shy and reticent. She'd loved me, and we were scarcely in our twenties when I left for a hitch in the service. People were just learning there was a place called Vietnam.

We married and lived happily for two weeks. She followed me to boot camp, to embarkation, and, finally, her letters followed me.

After I went into the hospital, there was a long time when I wasn't reading much. I had a stack of Bess' letters to catch up on.

Then I counted the weeks, days, hours, and minutes until I was discharged and we'd be together again. Our first dinner was at the Roadhouse Bar and Grill. We spent our first night in a cabin outside Las Vegas. Those things I could remember.

I couldn't remember my first blackout with her, nor any of the others, including last night with Ruth. I remembered what happened between, though.

Bess didn't know what was wrong with me any more than I did. She tried to understand and not to question me about where I'd been or why. That helped. I asked myself those questions enough. She never complained no matter how bad I was. That helped, too.

The trouble was, it didn't help enough. She had crying spells and sat up nights, worrying, wondering where I was and if I was all right. We still lived in Fall River then. I worked with Royce Lumber as a regular working stiff, but it paid enough to keep us going, as much as anything did.

Instead of complaining, she cried. Perhaps that had something to do with it. There were times when I wondered if she was closer to cracking than I was. All I had were those damn blackouts, or temporary amnesia, the Veteran's Administration doctor called them. Bess' melancholy became chronic and acute.

I managed to check on myself occasionally. I didn't do anything startling or unusual during my blackouts. Usually, I went off somewhere for a few drinks or wandered around alone. As far as I knew, I never got into trouble or created a disturbance. People who were with me didn't even realize what was happening. Apparently, it was a secondary reaction to a severe concussion, which was my service disability.

I didn't wonder then, but I wondered now. What happened to Bess during those times? I went out and became lost in the city. She stayed home and became lost in her mind. That's melancholia.

If it hadn't been for Frank Shelly, my best friend and neighbor, I don't know what either of us would've done. He and Bess tried to help. So did I, but nothing worked. I kept having blackouts.

There was one that started like all the others. I was walking down the streets after work, heading for the four-o'clock bus and hoping I'd make it. The next bus wouldn't come for over an hour. I wanted to get home, because Bess was crying when I left. That was becoming a habit with her. I asked what was wrong, but she wouldn't or couldn't tell me.

I kept trying to think of an answer. Perhaps I should've persuaded her to see a psychiatrist. If she could meet a good one, he might find the answers to her problem. As it was, she kept her feelings bottled up until they were ready to explode.

The last thing I thought that day was *explode.* Without warning, I was lost as another blackout descended. The person who walked, talked, ate, and drank still functioned, but *I* was lost.

Usually, coming out of it was easy. There would be a moment of panic when I suddenly realized who and where I was, then I would wonder where I'd been and where I was at the moment. Slowly, I'd pick up the pieces and go home. Unfortunately, there weren't many pieces. I'd never snapped out of it and found myself at home.

That time, though, I awoke standing in our bedroom in the modest house I bought two years earlier. Moonlight streamed over me, and I held a gun in my hand. Below me was Bess. I looked at the bullet hole in her chest. I couldn't remember anything of the night my wife died.

It was almost six o'clock. Ruth was gone for several hours, though it felt like only a minute since she left. It was long enough to relive what happened to Bess one more time.

Chapter Four

It seemed like a minute. I wondered if it would always seem like that, if part of me would be forever standing in the office, telling Ruth good-bye.

That was when I decided to go get drunk. I watched the clock on the wall. In two more minutes, I finally closed up and went for a drink.

I must've sat at the bar for a long time. I thought about Ruth, then mostly about Bess and what happened after she died.

Memory slowly returned in bits and pieces. I saw myself standing over her with the gun in my hand. She was dead. There was no need to check her pulse. I called the police. They asked me a lot of questions while photographers set off flashbulbs in my eyes, then they took me down to headquarters and booked me.

I didn't blame them, even years later. They found a woman with a bullet hole in her chest, and her husband called to tell them she was dead. When they asked where he was and what he'd been doing, he said he couldn't remember. His fingerprints were on the gun, and the neighbors said his wife cried constantly.

What were they supposed to think? They locked me up for five years, but I still didn't blame them. They were just doing their jobs. I loved Bess with all my heart, and I killed her during one of my blackouts. I never remembered what happened.

Then, sitting at that bar, it hit me. There was a figure hiding in the shadows of the bedroom where Bess died. Slowly, I realized I hadn't been the one who killed her. The figure was the murderer. Who was it? It wouldn't be easy to solve that.

I paid for my drinks and left the bar. Out on the street, a faint breeze blew from the surrounding hills. I walked toward my place, thinking what a fool I'd been to have assumed I killed my own wife. Someone else did it and let me take the blame. Who was the shadowy figure I saw in the bedroom that night?

There were so few answers to my questions. None did me any good. Then I realized that Ruth probably thought I killed Bess, too. Everyone in town must've assumed I was the killer. Somehow, I had to prove I hadn't killed the woman I loved, but how?

I was a part-time investigator. Maybe it was time to prove it, but where to start? I didn't have a clue.

My modest, one-bedroom apartment was just around the corner from the store. For a man living alone, I kept it pretty clean and neat. Everything was in its rightful place, and that bugged me. Bess always complained when something was out of place. It was a habit with her, and it rubbed off on me.

I tried to smile and couldn't. It was too painful. The closeness Bess and I shared, holding each other at night, telling our innermost feelings, sharing secrets and laughter were nothing more than painful memories.

After entering my apartment, I decided to go to bed. In the morning I could start my search for Bess' killer. Where should I begin? I didn't have a clue who the mysterious figure was and cursed my blackouts.

Whoever killed her, though, would be one sorry son of a bitch once I got my hands on him. The maggot would pay dearly for the five years when I was locked up like an animal for something I didn't do.

I went to bed. Morning would come quickly enough, and I needed to be fresh for what I had planned. I couldn't tell Ruth my plans, because she wouldn't understand. In her mind, I was guilty.

Chapter Five

The first thing I wanted to do was run. That was the way the previous day began. I shook my head, because I had nowhere to run to in the entire world. Bess and Ruth were gone. I'd be going next, but for that, I didn't need to run.

I sat up and put my feet down on the other side of the bed, then paused, thinking and shaking my head, trying to clear it and remember. I'd had a lot to drink that night. Then I passed out, or thought I had. I had nightmares, too, but, as bad as they were, they were nothing compared to the one I was in now.

I forced myself to look. She lay sprawled, almost spread-eagled, on the floor. Her hair was blonde, but, comparing it to Ruth's, it was more a dirty blonde than I remembered.

I didn't like to think about what I saw, much less describe it, but it wasn't just the woman's chest. It was the center of her forehead and shoulder. Whoever did it hadn't just meant to kill her.

Whoever... I thought, getting up and almost bumping into the damn mirror.

"You," I whispered, "Jace McBride, know who you are this morning. You know you didn't do this."

As soon as I said it, I knew it was true. Sure, I'd spent the night here and was drunk. I'd passed out, which was all I could remember. I had no idea how the dead girl got into my place or why she was there.

I forced myself to walk around the bed and kneel beside her. I didn't touch her, but I had to look for something. There was no gun on the floor or anywhere else in the apartment.

I walked to the front room and found the door was locked from the inside. I walked to the window shade and let it flap open. The window was halfway open.

I smelled a frame-up. Someone wanted me to take the rap for these killings, but why? I didn't have an answer.

I went back into the bedroom, and the old running urge came back stronger than ever. I looked at my watch and saw it was five-thirty... too damn early. The front hall and streets would be deserted.

It was my chance to dress and get the hell out of there. That seemed my only choice.

I pulled on my clothes, the urge to run from the apartment stronger than ever. I could hardly wait to slip on my cowboy boots. Once I was on my feet, I nearly bumped into the mirror. Looking at myself, I shook my head.

I walked down the hall to the bathroom and turned on the cold faucet in the sink, letting it run for half a minute before sticking my hands in the water. I stooped and ducked my head, letting cold water run down the back of my neck.

I dried off with a towel, then walked back down the hall. It took a while, but I finally reached the sofa and sat until I calmed down. It felt like hours, but it was only a few minutes. Then I lifted the telephone receiver.

"Hello?" It took a while for my brain to form the words. "Get me the police. That's right. I want to report a murder."

My palms were damp as I held the phone to my ear. The phone got me the police, all right, a lot faster than usual. Soon, I had more police than I could handle.

I wasn't handling them. They were handling me. The four men from the department hung around downstairs, keeping the crowd away with their presence.

What crowd? I wondered. *It's five-thirty in the morning. It's too damn early for anyone to be out.*

The man from the coroner's office and the photographer came later. They checked, measured, dusted, tested, and shot flashbulbs. Two detectives cased the place thoroughly. I sat in the kitchen with Lieutenant Fairchilds.

Short, stocky, and dark-headed, he wore a cheap, dark suit and carried a hat in his hand. He never wore the hat, just carried it around like it was a bag. Even with his mustache, he wasn't much older than me. He might've been a good homicide detective, but, in my book, he'd never get a job on TV. He wasn't good looking enough.

He sat at the table and flipped open his little notebook and began writing. "Want to talk about it, or would you rather wait for a formal statement? You know, of course, that anything you say can and will be held against you."

I nodded. "I'll tell you what happened."

I gave him my name, age, and address, then I told him what I could remember, which wasn't much. He took notes without interrupting.

I didn't know what I expected, but it was something different. I kept expecting him to break in to my narrative or ask for details. He should've followed up certain points in my story and tried to break them down. He didn't nod, chain smoke, or stare at me.

He wrote everything down, starting with my going into Big Mike's Wild Horse saloon and ending with my getting dressed and calling the police.

When I finished, he sat back, shook his head, and called, "Jamison! Come in here a second."

Jamison was another of the homicide detectives.

"What's the story?" Lieutenant Fairchilds asked.

Jamison looked at me, shrugged, and looked around. "Nothing definite yet. She's been photographed, and we've got lots of prints. The coroner's on his way back to the lab. We'll have it all by tonight."

The lieutenant nodded. "All right. Make sure you get prints from the front room window, the one on the right that was open."

"Already dusted."

"Tell Michaels to take this name and address to check on it." He gave Jamison my name and address.

"Got it."

"One more thing." Fairchilds turned to me. "McBride, will you please give this man a description of Frank Shelly? The more complete, the better. See if you can describe his gun."

I told Jamison all I could.

When I finished, Lieutenant Fairchilds stood and gave Jamison a push. "Get on it. Send out a pickup right away. No charge if you find him, and he hasn't got the gun. Corman's making out a search warrant for you. Go to his place and get it.

"One other thing. Go to Big Mike's Wild Horse saloon. Talk to the night bartender and customers. Get the story and anything you can on this woman…her habits, her friends, who she came in with, the works."

Jamison nodded and went out.

"I guess that's all." Fairchilds looked at me again. "Don't leave town. This ain't over till the fat lady sings." It seemed he had a droll sense of humor that only his true friends considered funny.

"I didn't kill anyone," I said. "It was someone else."

"Maybe. Maybe not." He walked down the stairs. "Stick around just in case."

I was left alone with my thoughts and the nightmares, trying to piece together the events of the past night. I couldn't remember anything clearly. It was a total blackout from the time I left Mike's Wild Horse saloon until I awoke that morning with a dead woman lying sprawled on my bedroom floor with a couple bullets in her beautiful body, while I was framed for the murder. By whom? How much did Ruth know?

I'd bet a year's pay she was in it up to her pretty little neck. I realized I didn't know much about her. She never talked about herself. I couldn't trust her or anything she said when it came to her true feelings. She was filled with deception and secrets.

She never really loved anyone but herself. I knew that firsthand. Would she go far enough to frame me for murder?

Somehow, I doubted that.

I couldn't remember a thing that happened just before the woman died. I came out of my blackout and stared at the body on my bedroom floor.

The case wasn't over for me. It was just starting. It would never be over until I caught the killer and cleared myself.

The only way to do that was to find Ruth and get some answers.

Chapter Six

When I went to the store, I took out my keys, then realized I didn't need them. In the first place, Ruth was already at her desk. In the second place, the smashed lock still hadn't been repaired.

I stared at the jagged glass around the frame, near the doorknob. It was a messy job. Someone was in an awful hurry or was very clumsy...maybe both.

I walked in, trying to sound cheerful. "Good morning. Sleep well?"

She looked at me through eyes that could burst into tears at any moment. I wondered what her problem was. She wasn't her same old self that day. Something wasn't right. If I questioned her about it, I'd never get a straight answer.

I let it pass. She'd tell me eventually. If not, I'd know for certain she was involved and couldn't be trusted. Once that trust was broken, there was nothing left to hold onto. She lied to me and kept secrets from me. That told me more than I cared to know, including the fact that it was over. Our relationship was finished.

I'd be finished, too, if I couldn't prove my innocence.

After Ruth and I had our little talk, I would play detective and go looking for the killer. Maybe I'd even get myself off the hook.

As I turned and walked away, Ruth said, "Jace? Be careful."

Here come the water works, I thought, walking out.

She knew how to twist a man around her little finger, making him do her bidding. She was good, but that time, it didn't work. I was tired of being used by people. I had to take back control of my life and undo the wrong. I was a man, not an object to be used, nor was I a slave to a woman's whims. She could cry all she wanted, but I no longer cared.

A noose was tightening around my neck. If I didn't find the killer soon, I could kiss my future good-bye.

I walked down hot pavement all afternoon, looking for the one person I wanted to get my hands on and wring his neck. He framed me and hung me out to dry like dirty laundry. That pissed me off.

I looked in all the places where a man like Frank Shelly might go, but he wasn't there. I finally decided to check his house. Maybe I was crazy, but I had to find out.

Lights burned brightly in Shelly's house as I parked on Loomis Drive at the foot of the stone steps leading to the front door. I got out and stood beside the car. Once I was there, I began to think that my quest for the truth was ridiculous. Shelly would really appreciate my barging through his front door and accusing him of murdering my wife and the cheap hooker planted in my room.

Then I heard a sharp, nerve-slapping sound from somewhere inside the house. On that quiet night, the hard, flat, ugly sound of a gunshot was unmistakable.

I leaped forward, my legs driving me up the stone steps as the second shot came immediately after the first. "Frank!" I shouted.

My voice and feet on the steps made noise. I wanted to be heard. I shouted Frank's name again, jumping the last few feet and slamming my shoulder against the front door.

It was locked. There was no other sound from inside. I kicked the door hard and felt the lock give with a loud crack. My momentum carried me past the door into the well-kept front room. Lights were on in Frank's den and study.

I staggered, caught my balance without slowing, and raced toward the light that came from a lamp on Frank's desk. It wasn't much, but it was enough for me to see the body sprawled on the floor with one arm outflung.

Something moved to my right as I entered the study. I pulled my .45 from under my jacket as a man slammed the door hard. As it crashed shut, motion danced from the corner of my eye to the left, too.

I jerked my head toward it. She was almost out of sight, passing through the side door into the adjacent bedroom. I barely glimpsed her, but I saw her for a second and realized she was nude, trailing a length of cloth, perhaps a robe, from one hand.

Before that had time to register, the window in the right wall, beside the door through which the man left, splintered with a crash. I heard a gunshot, and something plucked at my sleeve.

I dropped to the floor and snapped an unaimed shot at the window. I hit hard, rolled, crashed into a chair, and saw a spurt of flame as the man fired again. Lying prone, I aimed at the spot and fired twice. What the hell had I walked into?

Feet pounded along the outer wall, starting toward the side door. My leg hit something in the dark, and I fell. When I got up, all was silent outside, then a car's engine started and roared loudly. I made it to the door and through as the engine whined and drove away. By the time I was at the edge of Frank's property, the sound was faint.

Below me on River Road, one hundred yards to my left, headlights flashed as the car swerved around a bend and went out of sight. The shriek of tires skidding on asphalt came to me in the still air.

One minute later, I was inside the house. I felt my way through the study, found the electrical cord I'd tripped over, and fumbled for the outlet. As I touched it, I heard a soft scuttling sound behind me, like a great crab crawling over the hardwood floor, its claws clacking softly on the wood. Then came a sibilant hiss.

Hair rose on the back of my neck, and moist cold touched my spine like an ice cube. It was the man on the floor, not dead yet, his fingers clawing at the wood.

I turned to look at him as I shoved the plug into the socket. Light blossomed, and I saw Frank Shelly.

He lay flat, chest pressed against the floor, left arm extended straight above his head, right hand bent back until his hand almost touched his shoulder. His face was toward me, stark in the dim light, and his eyes were open. Both hands, the one over his head and the other brushing his right shoulder, moved mechanically, the fingers arching like white spurs or claws, scraping against the floor.

There was no other motion or sound, just those hands and fingers scuttling as if they possessed separate life from the dying body that pulled them toward death. Three times those hands scraped against the floor, digging tiny furrows into the dark wood, then all movement ceased.

"Frank?"

It was useless. He was dead, and I'd never get the answers I needed.

I knelt down and felt for the man's pulse, but there was none. There was nothing anybody could do to bring him back. I felt sorry for the dumb bastard, not because he was dead, but because I had not gotten to him first.

Unless I could prove I didn't kill anyone, I didn't stand a chance of clearing myself of murder charges.

All I could do was stare down at the body and hope something would come back to me, something that would jar my memory, but it didn't. It seemed I was screwed again, just like always.

I was still staring down at the body when I heard footsteps coming in through the front door, and I glanced up to see the lieutenant standing in the shadows, with that same, unchanging expression on his face. "McBride," he said, "it's over. We caught the killers. They confessed."

I was relieved, like the world had been lifted from my shoulders. I went through my whole life, dazed and numb. Was I hearing the lieutenant correctly, or was it a trick to make me confess to something I hadn't done?

I didn't know anything more, so all I did was stare.

"McBride," he said slowly. "Did you hear me? I said we caught the guilty party. The case is closed."

"Who?"

"Your friend there," he motioned toward the dead man at my feet, "and Miss Waverly. There was another man named Stirlock. We picked them up a short time ago."

"Why'd they do it?"

"They didn't say. We'll get a full statement from them once they're booked. Then maybe we'll know what this was all about. Go home and get some sleep. We'll clean up here and let you know the details tomorrow."

As I recovered my senses, I walked past the lieutenant and his men, handing him my gun as I left. I felt a little relieved and even a bit sorry for Ruth for her part in setting me up. I guess you never know what's going on in a person's mind no matter how well you think you know her.

I left the house, retracing my footsteps down the stone steps, until I was back in my car. I couldn't help thinking of Ruth and what a cold-hearted bitch she was and the misery she caused, but I wouldn't let it bother me. There were plenty of other women out there. I sure as hell wasn't going to let one screwed-up dame spoil my life. I intended to live it up.

As I drove back to town, I saw everything in a new light, and I smiled for the first time in years. Tomorrow would be the start of the rest of my life. I didn't need to outrun the devil anymore. Instead, I faced rebirth.

Lovelier

Kevin Osbourne

I was shaking, but I wasn't scared…not yet, anyhow. Actually, I was smiling as I drove my own Mustang. I liked thinking that it was mine. Maybe I hadn't saved a penny to buy it, but I loved it as if I had. It was beautiful, black on the outside with silver chrome fenders that reflected the moonlight.

I got the 1966 Mustang with leather interior as an eighteenth birthday and beginning freshman-year gift. In some ways, it reminded me of a movie I'd seen by Stephen King about a haunted car named Christine, except my car didn't do anything except drive, turn, and reverse. That was fine with me.

I was on my way to the second freshman mixer at the University of Irderlyne, a college based in southern California near the Mexican border. I worked out a deal where I could live just five miles from campus with an uncle, paying him rent. He lived even farther in the backwoods than Irderlyne, in the small town of Mountain Vista. The nearest mountains were the Rockies, and those were a long way off. I saw many desert canyons along the highway toward Irderlyne.

I drove under a cool, star-filled sky, filled with small, glittering points of light. The chilly desert wind came down onto my black muscle car, which rode the median like a bullet, curving in and around the canyons.

The compass on the dash swam toward northeast as I glanced down. The radio was off, because reception was bad within the canyon walls, and sports stations were the only ones I could receive. I gripped the wheel tightly, still feeling a little uncomfortable behind it. I watched my dad do that all my life from the passenger seat, but it felt strange and scary to do it myself, like making love to a girl. In the movies, I watched the hero take the girl into a room and shut the door behind them. When a guy did that himself, it was a whole different deal.

Not surprisingly, those thoughts led me to a girl I'd known at South Hollywood High. Whenever I thought of her, I felt as if I loved her. It was funny how such thoughts came after the relationship was over. They crept up months later, always in the weirdest places. Looking back gave me a new perspective, and the thing I kept thinking was I wanted to marry her.

I first met her in the eleventh grade, but I didn't think much about her. She was tall and lean but still pretty. We were in a journalism class, one of those classes that were interesting in the beginning but fizzled out toward the end. Our assignment that day was the fate of the world. We were told to tell our partner our name and discuss how the world would be in twenty years.

I sat across the table from her, challenging her to speak first. Finally, I said, "My name's Thomas Fernal. If the world will be run by any of us, it'll be a fiery apocalypse in twenty years."

I waited for the inevitable, wide-eyed look of dismay, then a polite request to change partners. Instead, she smiled and leaned forward.

"My name's Stacey. I think you're right."

From then on, we were pretty close.

She was my first everything except sex. I never got up the nerve to go that far, and I eventually regretted it. I wasn't exactly the life of the party in high school, and she was the first girl to become my friend. Although we never said it out loud, she was my girlfriend, too.

We liked being around each other, and, since we lived next to each other, we hung out all the time. She was the best guy friend I should've had but never got around to finding. During my last week at South Hollywood in our 12th-grade year, I told her, at the peak of my wisdom and knowledge, we'd probably never see anyone from our high school again, including each other.

That moment seemed frozen in time, perhaps because I suddenly realized what I was saying as the words came out. Under the late, dark, winter clouds, she started crying.

After that day, I saw her at graduation. Her short, black hair was surprisingly beautiful, and that was when I fell in love with her. I hated throwing that word around, because it was easy to say and difficult to understand.

At the end of that summer, I left for Irderlyne, and she went to the University of California, or maybe not. Things like that happened.

I was coasting out of the mountain vistas, approaching the half-suburban, half-tree-covered stretch to Irderlyne, when I saw her. The only thought that went through my mind was, *I was just thinking about her, and there she is!*

She held out her thumb, and I pulled over. She wore all black, including shades, and her short, black hair looked wet in the night. We were in an upper-income neighborhood with many trees, so I was surprised that I'd noticed her.

The car whined softly as I stopped, and gravel crunched under the tires. A dog began barking as I opened the door. She sat down in the seat just as a light came on in the house behind her.

It was only when she slammed the door with a loud clunk that I realized she wasn't Stacey. The face changed without moonlight on it. She was darker and a little huskier, but not by much.

I was sweating when I let her in, but the cold air from outside cooled me. My mind went to a safer, California path, thinking, *I just picked up a crazed murderer.*

She smiled as she looked me over.

"My name's Thomas."

She responded with a polite nod and the same grin. Her placid expression was attractive.

"Nice car," she said in an annoyed voice, noticing my glances.

"A '66." I snapped out of my daze. "I…you looked like a girl I knew in high school. I was amazed at the resemblance."

The car rolled forward as I eased off the brake. From the corner of my eye, I saw her nod. I felt strained, like I was coming off being crazy, and I told myself she wasn't Stacey, but my traitorous mind kept flirting with the possibility.

I wanted to ask her some questions but didn't trust myself. "So," I asked, "what's your name?"

"Stacey."

We drove in silence for a while before I was willing to accept that. My eyes widened, and I gave a small gasp, then did a double take. Maybe it was just me, but it seemed as if her demeanor changed. The strong, dull scent of her perfume filled the car, then me. I felt as if I'd just hugged someone.

Stacey smiled, nodding to her own interior music, and peered out the window. I looked at her more closely. Her shoulders were too wide, and she seemed more muscular. Her face was fuller, and her smile was too placid. I'd been around the old Stacey a long time, and I knew her well, even the small things. Her smile always shone.

Then I remembered a question I'd forgotten to ask. "Where do you want to go?" By then, I was willing to take her anywhere, and I took the opportunity to scan her again.

"Wherever you're going."

Had anyone else said that to me, I would've dropped her off then and there. Instead, I remained cool and smiled. "Are you kidding?" It wasn't really a question.

"Do you mind if I roll down the window?" She ignored my comment and opened the window.

Wind came in swiftly.

"What do you do?" The question came out meekly, though it sounded right.

"What do I do?" For the first time that night, she showed a feeling other than mockery or vanity. She seemed surprised, but that didn't last.

As she considered the question, she leaned her head against the door, the wind sweeping her hair backward. "It's not what I do." The smile in her eyes didn't reach her lips. "It's what I'm going to do."

She stopped. I waited for her to continue, but she didn't.

I decided to take her to the mixer, partly because I needed a date, anyhow. I also felt that I had transferred my feelings from the old Stacey to the one riding in the car. Her perfume overtook all other smells.

"What are you going to do?" The question seemed strange enough when I asked, but her answer was even stranger.

"I'm going to destroy the world."

I turned to her with a smile. That was one of the funnier lines I'd heard. It reminded me of a cartoon called Pinky and the Brain, where Pinky was a stupid rat, and Brain was a genius mouse.

Pinky, I believe I've found another way to destroy the world.

My smile slowly faded as I saw her staring out the passenger window. A chill settling in my back ran up my spine.

"How are," I asked, my hands tightening on the wheel as we went over a bump, making the car rattle, "you going to do that?"

Her reply, although frightening, wasn't that surprising.

"I'll do it with a fiery apocalypse." She didn't look at me. It was almost like someone saying, "I love you," and not wanting it to sound overwhelming or fake, but it still did.

She brought her hands up, and suddenly, a cigarette appeared between her fingers, smoke curling from the tip. That was when I decided I was going crazy, though I smiled at her.

"There's a lot of people." I was trying to make conversation.

Ignoring me, she looked at me slowly and removed the shades, sliding them onto the dashboard. I couldn't help wanting to turn my head and stare into her eyes, but instead, I kept my eyes on the headlights illuminating the roadway. I slowed and turned right onto the final road to Irderlyne. The moon was higher in the sky.

"You almost died once, didn't you?" she asked casually.

I more than felt the smile on her lips, and dull, painful anger rose in my head, though the perfume squelched that easily. Yes, I *had* almost died in a series of events involving Stacey, or because of her. As if seeing my thoughts change, she remained silent, and I remembered.

Near the end of twelfth grade, Stacey fell in love with Chris Dennials, the ultimate mix of football star, good looks, and all-around nice guy. I couldn't hate him no matter how hard I tried, and I tried pretty hard. Spring was in the air, summer was coming soon, and the teachers were cheery that year. My workload was easy that year, leaving me plenty of time for other things, like love.

I figured it was all the weird bullshit of spring getting to Stacey, but either way, she told me about it first. Since I felt I was her boyfriend, it came as quite a surprise. When he asked her out the next week, that was an even bigger surprise.

I found myself walking up to Chris' locker when the bell rang for lunch that day. Stacey was the only girl I'd come close to feeling love for, and people in love do crazy things. When I reached his locker, I saw Stacey hanging on his arm while they talked to another couple. I was furious.

I grabbed her shoulder and pulled his arm from her waist. Realizing what I was about to do, Stacey said my name, but I didn't care.

"I think you'd better leave her alone, you fucking jock!" I stood back and raised my fists, which was my first mistake. I should've kept the element of surprise and kicked his head in.

Always a nice guy, he tried to talk me out of it.

"You don't know what you're doing, Man. Why don't you just calm down?"

Then I saw the reason why he'd made all-star halfback two years in a row…he had huge muscles. My knees began to wobble.

"Come on. Hit me!" I shouted so hard, spittle came from my lips. "Just hit me, and I'll show you what I'm doing."

A crowd gathered, and I felt hands shoving me toward Chris. Stacey, looking scared, stood at the edge of the crowd, her mouth open. Turning toward Chris, I shoved him hard enough to send him into the locker with a pleasing crunch.

I started to say, "Hit me," again, when he shoved off the locker and punched my eye. The world exploded, and I pinwheeled back, my eye puffing up instantly.

Then he hit my stomach. I think he hit me again after that, but I couldn't feel anything. All I saw was the cold, gray floor slapping into me.

Other kids told me Chris hit me nine times before I hit the ground, but I didn't really believe them. It was probably only three times.

Stacey didn't talk to me again until the day by the school near the end of the year. The school buzzed with news of those two. I, with my lovely red eye and broken lip, took the jokes and rumors with a smile. The handsome knight saved the princess and took her to the dance, blah, blah, blah, and all that happy crap.

They dated for a while but broke up after graduation. Long-distance relationships rarely worked, especially with teenagers going to college.

I was laid up for a month and might've suffered a concussion. I always expected her to ask me why I did it, and I had at least two dozen sermons ready for an explanation, but she never did.

I looked over at Stacey and saw she still had that relaxed smile, but I was sweating like crazy as I parked under a tree for the mixer. Steadily pounding music came through her open window. We sat for a few moments, listening to the music and the engine tick as it cooled.

Then I got out and walked around the car. As I neared her door, I saw my haggard face in the side mirror, then her door came open with a hollow clunk. She stepped out, her heels clicking on the pavement. Stuffing my hands into my pockets, I looked at the hall.

Shrubbery lined the walk leading toward it, then split off to both sides. The doorway was a decent copy of a church window or an arch split down the middle, with designs carved into the wood. The doors were open. From my vantage point, I saw people milling around inside and a few couples entering.

The door slammed shut behind me, and I turned. Stacey wasn't wearing jeans anymore. She wore a long, black dress that sloped around the curve of her waist. I should've known something was different when I heard the heels. She wasn't wearing them when I picked her up.

For a split second, I almost asked where the dress came from, but her rich, warm perfume soothed me. I loved her, and she loved me. I inhaled the cold night air as we walked toward the hall.

The Hall

With all the hassle of registration and finding a job, I hadn't been to the first freshman mixer. After a while, my life settled down into the smooth doldrums of higher education, which, after all the worrying and hair pulling, I loved.

It was also boring. One night, after receiving an invitation in the mail, I decided to go. It was a choice between listening to my aunt and uncle chat about all the crap I got into when I was a *little shit* and wondering if my legs knew how to dance. I might even meet someone.

I didn't care. I spent money I didn't have and got off early from work. When I started the drive, it was still daytime. Not more than an hour later, we were going through those large doors, down a long hall, and into a dizzying, blinking light and laser show.

I almost fell but managed to stumble toward a table near the entrance windows. Stacey sat down almost like a guy. I meant to hold the chair for her, but I forgot when the moment came.

I wiped beads of sweat from my forehead.

"Having fun yet?" she yelled, her face as placid as ever.

After she asked, somehow, I was.

We got some food from a bar on the left side of the hall. Although the huge hall was longer than it was wide, I could hardly tell in the flashing, pulsing light that removed all my bearings.

When we first walked in, we went through a deserted lobby with a banner on the ceiling that read, *Welcome to the University of Irderlyne Freshman Mixer.*

Below that, an arrow pointed to the right, where Stacey and I took a table. There were more signs, though they weren't needed. From the dining tables, we could see the entire hall. Beyond the hall and behind the lobby was the bar, serving all the finer delicacies, from Pepsi to grape juice. Just beyond that was a food bar.

The rest of the hall was for dancing, filled with fresh-faced, parentless freshmen. The lighting around our table was relatively stable, so, when Chris Dennials danced by with a blondish, brown-haired girl, I saw him immediately.

For a moment, I thought he was with another Stacey and almost went crazy, but the perfume saved me. He swung her around, and, despite the blinking lights and pounding music, I realized it wasn't her.

"That girl he's with is someone he loves more than life itself," Stacey told me.

We watched them dance, a clumsy set of moves that consisted of spinning her do-see-do to eardrum-breaking Techno music.

I didn't reply, barely able to hear above the music. Stacey sipped her club soda and said, "Bet I could get him."

I turned slowly, sipping ginger ale. "What are you talking about?"

"Even though he likes her a million times more than he could love me, I can get him tonight."

I sat back, relaxing. "Not if he loves her that much."

Stacey stood. As she did, Chris' date moved away. I couldn't stand to watch Stacey do it, so I walked toward the bar. It took me awhile to get there, but I finally sat on a cushioned barstool and turned to look back.

Stacy stood near Chris, talking. The bartender walked over with a wet smile, asking what I wanted. He looked like a senior, probably in his late twenties, but it wasn't easy to tell in college. All the students looked too damned old, bringing me face-to-face with my own mortality.

"I'd like to get good and drunk," I said. "Slide me a ginger ale on the rocks."

He saluted sarcastically and poured the drink. As he handed it to me, he asked, "Alone tonight?"

"No. I'm with her." I pointed to Stacey, who was slow dancing with Chris.

"Oh."

I wanted to punch him for trying to ruin my night, but my smile faded as I sipped my ginger ale. I turned on the stool and watched them dance. Stacey leaned over and whispered in his ear, her dark hair covering her face except for her smile. He gave her his good-natured smile, making me want to rip out his throat.

He must've transferred from his school to mine, which made me wonder if I was about to live through four or five years of hell. As I wondered, they worked their way toward the exit, something my new friend, the dark-haired bartender, was quick to point out.

He grinned, barely controlling his laughter. I wanted to knock out his teeth and see if he could smile without them. Instead, I watched Stacey and Chris leave through the fire door. The light above it was off, which meant there would be no alarm.

It slammed closed behind them, making dust rise off the fire extinguisher beside it. I waited for a minute to see if she would reappear, but they didn't.

I was usually a peaceable guy, but having my girl stolen twice by the same guy wasn't a very good feeling. I felt like a horse's ass before I jumped off the stool and moved toward the fire door. When I reached it, I did something drastic, taking a chance that might've backfired if the situation didn't go bad.

Standing before the fire extinguisher, I saw a red fireman's ax in a glass case right below it. I removed my coat, wrapped it around my fist, and punched through the glass. If the alarm had gone off, things would've turned out differently, and maybe I wouldn't be telling this story.

The glass fell away. I assumed the alarm for the door was connected to the glass alarm, and both were turned off. No one but the distant bartender noticed. His face suddenly had the expression of terrified youth. Maybe he wasn't as old as I thought. With one hand pulling the ax from its hooks, I saluted him.

As I shoved open the fire door and stepped into the night, the bartender rushed toward the nearest phone.

Once I was outside, my plan became clear. Ideas always seemed clearer in the night. I walked past the shrubbery running alongside the wall and looked for Stacey and Chris. Two hundred feet to my right, they stood under a parking-lot light, talking beside a midsize luxury car.

Chris looked like he would've given anything to be somewhere else. He prepared to turn around, but she said something, and he stopped. If he turned, though, he would see me standing just outside the range of the light, a grin on my face and a blood-red ax in my hand, walking toward him.

I moved fast, hearing only my breathing. There was no way he could hear me coming. Even outside, the bass from the party ruled the night air, and a slight wind came through the trees around the lot.

My advantage didn't last. He heard me when I was five steps away. When he tried to turn, she grabbed his face in her hands, a smile on her lips. I brought up the ax and walked faster. My smile was gone.

The blade struck, and I grunted with effort as I wedged it into his neck just above the collarbone. His cry was high and guttural, and he looked at her as he died. I imagined his eyes wide, his mouth open, as he screamed noiselessly.

That's how I would die, I thought. *Looking at her.*

He sank to his knees, blood flowing in spurts like red water from a bad pump. I looked at her. She still held her hands on his cheeks, her gaze in his. She never looked lovelier before or since. Even the girl I'd known couldn't match her. She just smiled.

He fell over heavily with the ax in his collar, clanging to the ground, but he was still breathing, though in shock. Snapping out of my daze, I glanced at her. Sirens came from the front of the hall near my car.

I had to think fast, but my mind was totally blank. She looked at Chris' twitching body, then her black eyes went to me. I slid down and searched Chris' pockets. It seems odd that I wasn't sorry I'd killed him, though I knew I'd be sorry later.

I rolled him onto his back. His dilated pupils were strangely hypnotic in the glare of the parking-lot lamp. An ant crawled over the gash, and I threw up on the sidewalk, myself, and Chris.

After a while, I recovered, breathing in gasps, and pulled out his car keys. I stumbled to the other side of his black car and fumbled with the keys, my hands shaking. Finally, the key slid into the lock and clicked.

I pulled up the handle, slid in, and unlocked her door. I heard her shadowy figure move closer. There was the sound of the door opening and a hard click as it closed. I hated her secretive, perfect smile, though I loved her.

After starting the engine, I backed from the space, speeding from the parking lot and driving over the grass between two palm trees to the drive leading back to the road. Making a turn, I saw the glowing lights of police cruisers in front of the distant hall.

Then I saw my Mustang for the last time. That was the only damn thing that had ever been mine, and now it was gone.

I drove on.

We reached the school's final turn before seeing the cop on a motorcycle, his heavy black-and-white bike parked on its kickstand in the middle of the road. The cop was on the sidewalk, smoking a cigarette.

When he saw us, he threw down his cigarette and walked toward his bike, holding up his hand to stop us. Fifty feet from the corner, I pulled over. With an annoyed expression, he waved us closer, but I simply stared at him.

I'd heard of such moments that led to higher stakes. Some called them the point of no return, or the straw that broke the camel's back. He shielded his eyes from the lights, drew his gun, and walked slowly toward the car.

I saw him reaching for his radio. As he came closer, I noticed he was young but with the thick face and form of a cop, with an Army crewcut in his blond hair that seemed red in the lights of the Mercedes.

I revved the engine and heard Stacey chuckle beside me. The same smile crept over me as when I held the ax.

The officer debated between shooting and running, then did both. He fired one unaimed shot, missing badly, then ran as the Mercedes shot toward him, first angling toward the school parking lot on the right, then sweeping left as I went after him.

He fired twice more as he ran toward his motorcycle. One bullet

nt into the air, the other broke the windshield and caught my ulder, though I didn't feel it at the time.

The car, like a massive hunting beast, rolled over the pavement slowly, then faster,. The officer reached his bike, then changed his mind and tried to scramble off toward the bushes.

I hit him, barely missing the motorcycle. There was the sound of echoing metal, then two thuds as the officer flew up into the air, over the curve in the sidewalk, and onto the other street. I slammed on the brakes before I hit the sidewalk and flung the wheel to the right, hearing sirens behind me.

Swinging the wheel hard to the left, I flew out onto the street, running over the downed policeman in the process. A row of houses loomed ahead before I turned onto a side street. I spun the wheel into a nearby driveway and turned off the engine, then, deathly serious, I turned toward Stacey.

"Get down."

She looked pale with the lights out, though I doubted that was from fright.

A police cruiser tore around the corner, sirens filling the night with sound accompanied by red and blue lights. We lay crouched for a moment before getting up.

In the house a porch light came on.

"Fuck!" I shouted.

An older, unshaven man in pale shorts with a beer belly under his stained undershirt and balding gray hair, stepped onto the porch and said something. When he raised his arms, I saw a long rifle with hunting scope.

"Just my fucking luck!" I started the engine as he fired. A hole the size of a tennis ball blasted through the windshield, leaving white streaks around it. Small shards of glass flew onto the parking brake and seats.

His chalk-white hair blew in the night as he cocked another round into the chamber. He was shouting something when a small boy came onto the porch, sucking his thumb.

Apparently, the old man saw him, too, because he turned to yell at the kid. I backed up as fast as I could and drove off in the opposite direction the police went. As I passed the school, I saw hundreds of freshmen leaving the dance.

Not knowing where to go, I took the first left, then turned at least twelve other times until I was lost.

The Trees

When I finally slowed, we were in the middle of a road with fields on both sides. It was still late enough to make seeing very far impossible, so I turned off the engine and put the transmission into park.

We sat in silence for a moment. I assumed we'd just sit there and wait for dawn, but, after a while, Stacey said, "I see a barn where we can sleep."

Looking, I didn't see anything. After everything that happened, I didn't care how she spotted it. Still, I felt the need to speak, to explain what happened.

Breathing slowly, I turned to her as crickets and the night sang a chorus outside. It was funny how through a window, everything seemed distant.

"I wanted to tell you something."

She sat with folded hands in her lap, leaning closer and seeming stupid in the process, but her eyes said otherwise.

"I know you're not my Stacey. I don't care. That's not the point anymore."

I paused, wondering what to say next and thinking of our situation, parked in the street like that.

"Maybe you aren't her, but I'm not me, anymore, so I love you, anyway. I know that doesn't sound right, but somehow, I think you understand. I've never been as alive as tonight. Even now, I can feel every muscle and the air I breathe. The night feels alive, and so do you. It's like you and I are one person. Every time I look away from you, I can still see or feel you."

I caressed her face with my hand.

Looking like she had when I first asked what she was going to do, she looked into my eyes and said, "Thomas, you…" She nodded and looked away, seeming to understand, though I felt she didn't.

"The barn's over that way."

I started the engine and turned toward the field, hearing rocks and patched grass crumble under the tires. Strangely enough, the moon was gone. At least, I couldn't see it.

We drove between highly stacked hay bales for five minutes before I saw the barn. Before it was a short wooden fence, made of two wooden horizontal bars that ran between vertical posts thirty feet apart.

The barn was barely the size of one-and-a-half car garage, with one door hanging from the hinges. It was a dump, barely held together, and it looked deserted as I turned off the engine. Even as I looked, I wondered where Stacey and I could go. We had to leave the country, maybe get to western Europe or Mexico. Anywhere would be better than where we were.

I got out of the car and stretched, immediately feeling the night chill. The sky was filled with pale, white clouds. Stacey got out, her long, black dress billowing in the wind as she walked toward the fence. Seeing her walk so freely, I knew we'd never escape to any of those places. A deep feeling rose within me. Since I'd touched on every other feeling I possessed that night, I couldn't have avoided sadness much longer. It made me feel bitter and cold inside, as certain of the only thing anyone knows in his lifetime…I was going to die.

After looking around awhile, I followed her. We squeezed through the fence and walked past an old tractor toward the barn's large door. When we walked in, the temperature rose a little, but I was still cold.

"Cold?" I asked.

She shook her head without looking at me. She didn't even see me as I grabbed her from behind, putting my arm around her waist. She laughed as if she expected it.

She struggled gently as we fell to the ground. I pulled up her dress and found her, and I was immediately filled with inexplicable warmth and then cold darkness. She wrestled as I kissed her lips, then we finished.

We lay in the darkness, her body above me, pressed against mine.

"Seeing as only country folk are supposed to do it like this," I said, "we'll name our kids Samuel and Jessup."

She laughed on my chest. I loved her, the wisps of hair on my face, and being near her, though I stopped regarding her as Stacey.

I was tired but not enough to sleep. I just didn't want to move. All I could think of was to wonder what to do next.

Now we wait, a force within me said.

That worried me. I didn't like waiting. I thought over our situation and what brought us to that point.

The sun rose. In the barn, the first dull light came through the cracks. I was up all night, figuring. I though about how I met her, and I was considering how to kill her before she killed me.

I couldn't do it. I realized, as her warm, small body lay on mine, that I was crazy, and the entire situation was crazy. I had to turn myself in to the cops and tell them her perfume made me do it.

I squeezed her tightly as I thought that. Smiling in her sleep, she sighed. I inhaled the early morning and looked around. Wild patches of grass grew on the floor, which was mostly smooth, cold dirt. I slowly rolled her to the ground and laid her head down gently. She curled up for warmth as I walked outside.

The sun was still hidden, though its light showed. Above was an armada of clouds, while the slowly changing sunrise was everywhere around me. I went to the car and came back with a cigarette, smoking it while standing against the barn. That was the first cigarette of my life, and I'd never coughed so hard. It was one of those things I didn't want to die without trying. I understood why people who were about to be executed asked for one.

Feeling as if I lived on borrowed time, I was alert as I went inside the barn. Hearing my shoes crunch in the dirt, she opened her eyes and sat up.

"Did you dream?" she asked.

"Did I?"

She nodded.

"Yeah, sure. I dreamed."

"I dreamed that I loved you." She smiled and stretched. It fit the morning. I walked toward her when I heard a sound behind me.

"What in the hell are you folks doing in my shed?"

It was an honest question from an honest voice. I remembered how I crept up on Chris Dennials and spun fast. An old man with blond hair and brown streaks on the sides faced me with a rusty revolver that I doubted would work. On the other hand, I didn't think he meant to shoot us.

When I spun, he jumped back a step. His trigger finger twitched. I watched the gun flash yellow and red as a loud crack sounded.

The bullet hit my stomach. I fell backward to the ground. Stacey, screaming, ran at the old man, who was startled and scared, backing away. She threw herself at him.

They fell to the floor. The world blurred after that, and I felt blood in my mouth. My bruised shoulder, shot the previous night, cried for attention. I pushed up off the ground, using my good arm, and groaned at the pain in my stomach.

The unlocked door flew open under my weight, and I tumbled into the bright morning. As the door slammed against the side of the barn, I hit the ground hard, coughing up blood, spittle running from my lips. I tried to stand but was too weak.

I saw Stacey beating the bewildered older man. Looking around, I focused on standing. After what seemed a lifetime, I managed to raise up in time to see Stacey dive at the old man with a scream. His foot tripped on something, and they fell down with her on top. There was the sound of a shot, then Stacey fell on him in a lifeless mass.

Screaming in rage, I stumbled forward, falling near the old man who tried to get Stacey off while muttering how sorry he was. I saw the gun on the ground and grabbed it, feeling the cold, wooden handle just as he pushed Stacey off and stood.

I aimed the gun at him.

"Don't do anything stupid now, Son," he said. "It's Hugh here. I'm standing in front of you, begging for mercy."

I looked at him over the gun. "You have five seconds to get out of my sight."

I blinked. When I opened my eyes, I saw the old man hauling ass around the shed. If it hadn't been for the situation, I would've laughed. Instead, I tossed the gun aside and found the strength to walk to Stacey and look at her.

I reached down to brush her hair, thinking she was dead, but she moved her head. I picked her up, stumbling toward the fence and talking constantly.

"Just hang on." If she died… I didn't want to think about it.

She smiled and coughed. I had to lift her over the fence and let her lean on it while I crawled through, an almost impossible process that I barely managed after ten minutes. As I got through the boards, I saw the old man still running in the distance.

When we reached the car, I placed her as gently as I could in the passenger seat and walked to the driver's door. I slammed the door shut and sat there, breathing heavily and feeling faint.

"Don't worry." I shook myself out of it and started the car, driving through the stacked hay toward the main road. "I'll…we'll find help, then we'll leave the country. We just have to find a…"

I stopped, hacking and coughing blood. When I finished, I looked at her again, then at the road, rolling down the windows to let in some air.

I looked at her again and realized she hadn't moved since I put her in the car.

"No! No!"

Her head was against the door, her black hair in her eyes, and I blinked for a long time. When I opened my eyes, I leaned over to wipe hair from her sweat-drenched face.

"No. You're alive. Why aren't you alive?"

I felt tired, so I let myself go and closed my eyes. As I fell asleep, I thought, *Stacey.*

The Road

Paul drove meditatively along the highway, trying to focus on the road. Glancing at his watch, he saw it was four-thirty in the afternoon. He was pretty sure he'd get home by seven, get some sleep, and feel better by the next day, though he wasn't certain.

He was returning from three nights in Mexico with a few friends, after having his wallet stolen. Then he figured enough was enough, so he drove home. He had enough gas for the trip, but, if not, he remembered his gas card number and could use that.

He planned to visit Mexico as much as possible, but he'd keep his wallet in his sock the next time. For the moment, he would sit back and enjoy the ride. If everything went as planned, he'd be in Mexico tomorrow.

As he drove through ranch country, he saw a few horses and cows, then he saw a piece of metal on the road with smoke rising from it. Looking farther ahead, he saw a string of metal parts littering the side of the road for a hundred yards, so he slowed down.

Nothing could survive that, he thought, looking at the pieces.

At the end of the wreckage, he saw what might've been a luxury car overturned on one side of the road and shook his head at the damage.

A girl stood a little farther down the road, just beyond the smoking car. Paul did a double take and knew he'd seen her the previous night in Mexico. It was the same girl!

She held out her thumb as he pulled up, and, for a moment, he thought her name was Stacey. He wondered where he got that idea. The girl in Mexico wasn't called that.

Pinky, I think I found another way to destroy the world.
Pinky and the Brain

Guy Ethics
Philip G. Luckhardt

That had to be him, but who was that with him? She must be twenty years younger. Looks like they've been setting up housekeeping together.

The scene played out before me twenty hours earlier when I was in a department store during lunch hour. Ken Banks was a good friend seventeen years my senior. Well-preserved for a man of sixty-one, he had an athletic build topped by thinning, gray-blond hair. He was vice president of marketing for Milberk Industries, which was headquartered in the same town.

His companion, shopping for sheets and towels, was probably in her late thirties, maybe as old as forty. She had a trim figure, slighting graying auburn hair, and a serene countenance graced by soft, light-blue eyes.

The two appeared to be the essence of domestic tranquillity, except the woman wasn't Elaine, Ken's wife of thirty-seven years. Ken saw me as I walked toward him to make conversation and quickly led his companion away. It was clear being seen with her wasn't what he wanted.

That night I thought that the juicy tidbit I'd witnessed would liven up our dinner-table conversation and certainly Susan's worldview. For fifteen years, my wife and I had shared a marriage based on mutual trust regarding anything affecting our joint lives. She was a real jewel, a shining star in college, professionally recognized for excellence as an educator and freelance writer, a great wife, and a fantastic mother to our four children.

Like all people, she shared in humanity's foibles. In particular, she had a lot of trouble keeping secrets from her women friends. As I was about to tell her the story of my day, the better angels in my nature took over and held my tongue. There was no need to have a questionable aspect of Ken and Elaine's married life passed around the ladies' golf club, ladies' church service group, the PTA, and more, even though the transmissions would doubtless be person-to-person and would always be accompanied by the caveat, "Don't tell anyone, but…"

My suspicions about a close relationship between Ken and his friend were confirmed two weeks later when I met Ken at his office to review some material for a building project in which we were both involved at our church. As I walked down the executive office corridor at Milberk Industries, through a partially open door I saw the mystery lady finishing a phone conversation.

The sign on her door read, *Stephanie Jackson, Assistant Vice President, Human Resources.*

Once in Ken's office, I couldn't help seeing a newly signed lease for an apartment three blocks away sitting on his desk.

That night, my better angels kicked in again and stopped me from blurting the latest find to Susan.

The following Saturday night, Susan and I sat with Ken and Elaine at a dinner for local political candidates. During dinner conversation, Elaine seemed to be probing Susan to see if she knew of my encounter with Ken and Stephanie. Later, Elaine commented that she thought divorce could be a desirable option for some couples who'd been married for many years.

I rejoined with a trite, "Oh, I think after many years of marriage, the gains to either party from divorce are more than offset by the losses."

It also became apparent that evening that Elaine's health had dropped to a new low. In her younger days, she cut a wide swath as a high-school prom queen, finalist in the state women's tennis tournament, and creator of an impressive portfolio of canvases that were frequently displayed in small museums nationwide.

It seemed that her once-flourishing marriage had degenerated to the point where she was accepting a third party in the relationship...while still not wanting any marital flaws to be broadcast among their acquaintances.

If they wanted to continue their marriage on that basis, it was their business. I became even more determined not to serve as a conduit for tawdry tales.

As a small shareholder in Milberk Industries stock, I noticed in their next annual report that Stephanie Jackson had been promoted to vice president of human resources. I concluded she deserved it, with or without Ken's influence.

Ten years after the department-store encounter, Elaine entered a hospital for the last time. Over the years, a childhood asthmatic condition turned into emphysema that grew progressively worse. The onset of Type II diabetes further complicated her health.

After ten days in the hospital, she died in her sleep. Ken asked that the funeral be closed to all but family, which still meant a large gathering. There were five children, their spouses, their children, and seven nieces and nephews with *their* families.

I expressed my condolences to Ken before the funeral. Afterward, I tried to maintain close contact with him for whatever support I might give. He seemed determined to live an active, socially interactive life. Several times, he told me that Elaine was the only real love in his life, and she would've wanted him to continue living as fully as he could.

For several years after the funeral, he seemed to be searching for reconciliation, perhaps even atonement, for the totality of his life. He became more active in church and began serious study of the Bible, as well as contributing financially to several neglected, worthy causes.

Ten years after Elaine's death, Ken went into a nursing home for the last two weeks of his life. By that time, I'd almost completely forgotten his affair with Stephanie, but on one visit to his room, it occurred to me that he might want to discuss that interval in his life.

He didn't.

That's that, I thought.

Ken's funeral was announced in several local newspapers, and a sizable crowd was expected. As Susan and I entered the church, I noticed a tantalizingly familiar woman in a rear pew. She had an erect bearing, silver-gray hair, a smooth complexion that was very slightly weathered, and her face was highlighted by a pair of soft, light-blue eyes.

Wow, I thought. *After all these years, that's Stephanie Jackson.*

I said nothing to Susan during the service. In a family-sponsored reception afterward, I mingled with friends and business connections Ken and I had known. Susan disappeared among the guests to mingle with people she hadn't met, something she always enjoyed.

Driving home after the funeral, Susan said, "I met some really nice people at the reception. I particularly enjoyed talking with a lady who worked with Ken at Milberk. She'd been married at a young age and divorced at thirty-four. Then she married a second time at forty-six, only to have her husband die last year. Her name is Stephanie Jackson."

OK, I thought. *This is it. I have to come clean.* "Susan, there were probably only two people at the funeral who knew that Ken and your new friend, Stephanie, had an affair that started twenty-years ago. It must've lasted about seven years."

"Affair? Are you kidding? What do you mean?"

"I mean a real affair, a between-the-sheets affair."

Her internal computer instantly replied, "Only two people knew? One must be Stephanie, since she was a participant, and the other must be you, since you know it. You stinker. All these years, your stupid male bonding or macho code of silence kept a secret from me that was of real importance to good friends of ours."

"Dear, I've never withheld anything from you that affected our life together."

"We built our marriage on complete trust in each other," she said sarcastically. "Thanks a heap for your trust in me, my trustworthy husband."

I was preparing to launch into my defense, including innuendoes of the dire consequences that would've fallen on Ken, Elaine, and their children, if the affair became widespread knowledge.

As I was about to start, my better angels intervened. "I don't expect you to understand, Dear. In a way, you're right. Just call it guy ethics."

Cash Cows

Philip G. Luckhardt

"Number eighteen just sold for five eighty."

"Not bad. They bought in '87 only seven years ago and paid two sixty."

Ellen's announcement that a neighboring house had just sold started Stew thinking of possibilities for their own house, doing the kind of analysis that had served him well during his long career with Consolidated Resources, Incorporated.

In less time than Ellen needed to finish her coffee, Stew said, "What say to this, my dear? If we can clear five hundred Gs on this little palace of ours, I could net another thirty or so each year. You could spend half on the grandchildren or your do-good projects."

"And where, love of my life, do you propose we live while you further bring Wall Street to heel? Ever since you started planning retirement from CRI, you've talked of selling here and moving somewhere. It's all talk. You just can't bear to leave dear old Walton, Connecticut, suburbia USA."

"*Au contraire.* I'm about ready to move to our place in Maine, at least for April through November. The rest of the year, we'd travel hither and yon, particularly to visit our sub-belted, ever-welcoming offspring."

"I've heard that before." Ellen rolled her eyes in mock frustration.

At 62, Ellen Basker Firling was trim and energetic but was dwelling increasingly on life's imponderables. Her first meeting with Stewart Firling was remarkable but not improbable. She was a recent college grad from the Midwest on summer vacation from her first elementary-school teaching job, and he was an upstate New Yorker working his way through an MBA program. They met at a charity-sponsored work project rebuilding a storm-damaged school wing in Appalachia.

After a long-distance courtship, they entered a marriage that held together…sometimes precariously…for thirty-eight years. Ready to retire, their three children living far away, Ellen and Stew were the stereotypical empty nesters, though the nest periodically filled with children and grandchildren seeking holiday or vacation excursions to New York or the Northeast. Both were too healthy and active to be attracted by commercially touted retirement housing projects, so they remained in their oversized Walton home, paying increasing property taxes and becoming involved in community-improvement projects. Each began to speculate on the best way to spend the remainder of their lives.

In one discussion, Ellen said, "For many years, I knew my existence had meaning in motherhood, in caring for people who needed me. Now, though we enjoy visits from our children and grandchildren, the need isn't the same. Maybe it's time for us to give up this sham of thinking we're still useful and accept the media stereotype of retirement. Maybe it's time to let others meet our needs instead of us meeting theirs. Our children will do what they can for us, and so will society at large, through pensions, Social Security, Medicare, and all that stuff we've been hearing about for years."

"Maybe some year, but not now." Stew was a good though not outstanding provider for the family during his years with Consolidated Resources, and he had a decent pension. One source of enjoyment for him was investing the respectable net worth they'd accumulated over the years despite the expense of home ownership, education, travel, health care, and interminable miscellaneous things that came up while raising a family in mid-to-late twentieth-century suburbia.

Stew's new, apparently serious attitude toward selling their home made Ellen think seriously about his alternative. In the last few years, with the children graduated from college, Ellen and Stew renovated their place on Maine's Mooscontee Bay. The transformation turned a primitive summer cottage set amid six waterfront acres into a well-appointed year-round home, usable for winter sports and summer pursuits.

If only winter wasn't so long up there, Ellen thought. *Ah, for the footloose days of yore. In the early years of our marriage, we would've picked up and moved at the mere scent of a new position or exciting location. Now, we have roots in the community, with social groups, church, charitable and civic activities, and our medical and investment stuff. When did community become such a big deal to us?*

The news struck Stew hard. He'd faced death before, not only during his Army stint in Korea but also when facing surgery and a grim medical prognosis. This time was different. There was no adrenalin flow from anticipation of combat and no time for contemplation of a hospital bed. The impact of the news was sudden and final, without emotional preparation.

On a late March morning, Stew's customary workout was interrupted by a shriek from Ellen when she answered the phone. The caller was a friend of their youngest daughter, Jan, who tearfully told Ellen that Jan's husband, Mitch, was killed returning the previous evening to the company's Texas headquarters after a business meeting in Idaho. A combination of wind shear and avionics trouble brought down the company jet in the Sangre De Cristo Mountains in Colorado.

There were no survivors. Stew heard Ellen sobbing as she finished the conversation with, "Tell Jan we'll be out as soon as we can catch a plane."

Stew's initial shock was followed by feelings of denial, then hard thinking over how best to help Jan. She was young and full of life, only to be widowed at thirty-two with two bright, beautiful children. Almost instinctively, Stew went to his knees in prayerful appeal for comfort for his daughter and guidance for himself. He wouldn't have done that early in his life, but it had become integral to his being.

Stew's journey to faith came after a variety of life experiences and mental exercises, including what he felt was a Providential deliverance during his Korea days and his intellectual disdain for the finality of secular theories of the cosmos. What came before the Big Bang?

Ellen took a less-tumultuous route to belief but ended up near Stew on the faith spectrum. Both would need to rely heavily on faith to help Jan through the current crisis.

E-mail would take too long. For interactive, quick decisions with their other two children, only the telephone would do. She reached Peter on his car phone near his home in Silicon Valley. Alexandra, Sandy, was at her home office in suburban Atlanta. Both were shocked by the death of their brother-in-law.

Ellen wasn't surprised by their reactions. Several years earlier, Peter's life turned away from substance abuse and depressive mental states induced by immersion in cynical literature. Instead, he turned to a fundamentalist, authoritarian, nominally Christian group.

"Awful," he told Ellen. "Poor Mitch. He was a good guy, always willing to help people. I hope he was saved."

Sandy's life turned toward the New-Age movement, complete with crystals and related paraphernalia. Her reaction was, "Oh, wonderful, lovable Mitch. He's moved to a higher plane of existence. I hope Jan knows we should continue loving him in his new state of being."

In contrast, Ellen and Stew agreed that Jan had probably been the happiest of their children and would be that way in another year after she reorganized her life. She was a free spirit, though disciplined in her personal life, and held a strong, nonjudgmental faith. She once asked, "Why do the other two have to dwell so much on their morbid dogmas and mantras?"

The flight to San Antonio was the best kind…uneventful. Ellen and Stew quickly established a familiar routine, helping Jan with the children, and an unfamiliar one of preparing for a funeral.

It was a very emotional ceremony. Highlights from the service included eulogies by Mitch's associates who spoke of his intelligence and creativity and a solo rendition of *Precious Lord* that evoked many tears. It seemed such a waste to lose Mitch Garey at the age of thirty-three. An honors engineering graduate, he was rising rapidly in the management of a small but flourishing specialty composites materials company and was an accomplished father of two. He was gone.

Two days later, during one of the rare moments when the whole family was together, Stew, ever the pragmatic one, said at dinner, "We'll all miss Mitch, but the best thing we can do is get on with our lives. He wouldn't want us to ruin our lives because of his untimely death. Jan, Mom and I think it best if we stayed here as long as you need us. We can help you deal with all the administrative stuff for the insurance, 401(K)s, Social Security, and help with the kids."

After a few minutes' conversation, Ellen turned to the children. "Sandy and Pete, let's hear from you and where you're going with your lives."

Ellen was painfully aware that Sandy was having marital difficulties with Jeff, who, conveniently for him, couldn't attend the funeral due to a foreign business trip. Equally troubling was the fact that Pete, still a bachelor at thirty-two, struggled with feelings of mixed remorse and compassion for Shelly, his significant other, who wanted to continue their relationship, while Pete felt obligated to embrace the strict moral dictates of his new-found church fellowship.

"Mom, I know you don't want me to break up with Jeff," Sandy said, "but I'm not sure our marriage will work. Don't worry. Even if we split, you can still see your grandchildren, which is probably your biggest concern."

"Thanks a heap, Dear. Believe it or not, I care about you, too. Your business is doing well, but Prince Charming may not be waiting around the next corner. If you don't already know it, growing old alone isn't much fun."

Somewhat irritated by what he felt was an unwelcome parental intrusion into his personal life, Peter snapped, "Leave it alone, Mom. I'm having enough trouble getting Shelly out of my hair and don't appreciate innuendoes about what a great wife she'd be. We don't connect in what really counts in life. After years of substance abuse, I've become a true Christian. Although Shelly is a sweetheart, she's still bound to the vacuous ideas of intellectual humanism."

"My brother the judge," Sandy blurted. "I thought you were a high-tech marketing specialist. Who are you to criticize someone's beliefs, particularly someone who cares or did care about you?"

"I'm not judging or being critical," he replied. "For me, marriage has to be to the whole person, beliefs and all. That's something you and Jeff might look at before you break up. At this point, I don't see how it can work with Shelly."

Stew saw an ugly confrontation brewing and said quickly, "OK, Guys. Let's keep it civil and not add to Jan's concerns right now."

Sandy left the room, muttering, "Jan this. Jan that. It's always Jan."

The conversation changed to travel plans and where to meet for Thanksgiving.

This isn't what I need right now, Stew thought, forcing aside libidinous thoughts about Kristin Langstrom, twenty-eight years his junior and a long-standing acquaintance. Kristin and Sandy were on the same Little League team Stew coached years earlier. Later, as an alumni reference, he helped Kristin enter Harmouth University. Pete graduated from Harmouth one year after Kristin.

Kristin was a successful Wall Street broker, and, while she had many suitors, she never met Mr. Right. Over the years, as Ellen and Stew frequently interacted with Kristin, she and Stew developed a friendship based largely on making fun of each other and telling the latest jokes.

Currently, Kristin was unattached and attractive in mind, body, and persona. Stew, thanks to familial genetics and personal discipline, still cut an impressive masculine figure, with no need of potency enhancements.

The meeting at which Stew's disturbing feelings became aroused was a summer-afternoon party hosted by mutual friends in Walton several months after Mitch's funeral. Typical for Walton affairs, the party included guests from different generations. Kristin was home for the weekend from her New York apartment.

Upon seeing Stew, she began with condolences for Mitch's death and asked about Jan. As Stew spoke, he felt the intensity of a disturbingly delicious urge to take Kristin in his arms and lead her to an empty room. He might even get away with it, as Ellen was in another room engaged in conversation, and Stew and Kristin had often shared friendly hugs and kisses.

This time, though, he felt serious. He'd been faithful to Ellen throughout their marriage, which gave him years of sexually and psychologically fulfilling intimacy. Ellen had many admirers throughout her life who enjoyed her physical charms, vivacity, and keen wit.

Fifteen years earlier, she and Stew verged close to marital dalliance, when mid-life pressures, including the financial demands of college expenses, concerns for aging, infirm parents, and career stress made the availability of extramarital partners more enticing. After prayerful consideration and objective analysis, they concluded that period in their lives with renewed commitment to each other.

As Stew put it, "We each have enough stress in our lives without adding cuckoldry to the list."

Apart from his nonadultery commitment to Ellen, Stew also felt acute reluctance to do anything that might hurt either Ellen or Kristin. His inhibition about getting too close to Kristin resulted from early parental training and morality, his intellectual flirtation with Freudspeak, and the recognition that he would someday have to give an accounting of his life to God.

With Kristin standing before him, those inhibitions seemed painful. Radiantly beautiful, she seemed more warm and friendly than usual. When she was eleven, she nicknamed him Lobster Stew after a trip with the family to their place in Maine.

"Lobster Stew, I've got such happy memories of you from my

growing-up years. You helped me a lot when Dad was sick. I'll always remember you. I want you to remember me, too."

They drifted toward the pool with the other guests. As their conversation ended, Stew reached to give her a friendly kiss on the cheek. To his surprise, she turned and kissed him hard on the lips.

As the party ended, Stew met with Ellen, who said, "I see you've been talking to my financial guru. Did she give you her market strategy for next week? Kris and her compatriots have my account really humming."

"No market strategy," Stew replied. "We talked about other things."

The town meeting was well attended. In addition to the usual cabals of extremist advocates for the current sociopolitical cause, many of the silent majority were there, too. The town of Walton still governed itself by town meetings, through which the entire citizenry acted as the town's legislative body. Despite periodic, articulate whining in letters to the town newspaper regarding the inefficiency of such a process, the town was well served by it.

The first selectman, as the elected head of town government, opened the meeting with an apology for calling the meeting when many residents were vacationing elsewhere. It seemed that the town had the opportunity to receive a large grant from a charitable foundation for a major addition to the town's library and recreational facilities, if the town committed by mid-September to match the funds. Knowing the propensity of the citizens to force such issues to town-wide referendums, which took many weeks of preparation, the selectmen called a meeting in early August.

There was little controversy over the need for such facilities. At issue, however, was the proposed tax increase of 8% over the next ten years. Many people in Walton felt taxes were excessively high already, and it had to stop. Ellen, as a member of the library board, appreciated the benefits they would have with the proposed addition to the library, but she knew that any increase in local taxes meant less for a family's discretionary use. With the uncertainty of Jan's future financial needs, such an increase in taxes was of critical concern.

During a break in the meeting, Stew became involved in conversation with Charley Merdone, a member of the finance committee.

"I hope you and Ellen aren't planning to leave our fair community anytime soon," Charley said. "You and the other healthy seniors are this burg's cash cows. You have no kids to run up our education budget, and you don't need many of the town's services. Bless your aging hearts, you pay plenty of taxes on those large homes of yours."

"You have a way with words. I'll let you know when this aging heart feels like quitting. Since you've raised the question, Ellen and I might want to cash in on the current bull market in housing and move to our house on the bay."

Afterward, Stew and Ellen relaxed at home.

"Well, Dear," Stew said, "Charley pointed out another reason to stay alive for a while."

"As if we need more, with our loving grandchildren and our own children who need our support. Lest we forget, we have each other, too. What was his great revelation?"

"He called us cash cows."

"Flattery gets him nowhere. He doesn't really think we've gained enough weight to look like cows, does he?"

"Oh, no. The name came from corporate America years ago to identify a segment of a business based on mature products with no outstanding sales-growth prospects, which needs little new money to keep it going. With very little expense, it keeps bringing in a steady stream of income.

"Apparently, we, as healthy senior citizens paying taxes and requiring few municipal services, are the cash cows of Walton. It doesn't take much thinking to conclude that as a class we're healthy for the entire country. Many of us receive income from well-financed pension funds for the rest of our lives, and from our own investments. That doesn't cost the government a penny, but they provide tax revenue and purchasing power for the whole economy."

"You and your economics. So we justify living to a ripe old age on strictly economic grounds? What about Social Security? We get that straight from Uncle Sam."

"Yeah, but remember, we paid into that for over sixty years, sometimes at heavy rates, and we pay lots of taxes, too. The tired, old New Deal models are credible in small doses, with the assumption that funds injected into the economy from the government have a multiplicative effect when they're spent through successive hands."

Ellen thought for a moment. "So I'm supposed to feel good about being a cash cow? I justify my continuing existence on this planet, because I provide net economic benefit to the community at large? Big deal. If my only reason for staying alive and well is to provide an easy cash flow so some politician can buy more votes, forget it. You, my dear, can satisfy yourself with such warm thoughts when you retire soon. For me, the hugs of grandchildren or smiles from friends and relatives are the real motivators for hanging around."

The Firling clan traditionally gathered at the house on Mooscontee Bay over the long Labor Day weekend. All felt it would be particularly helpful to Jan's now-fatherless children to receive a strong dose of family support. Peter arranged an East Coast business trip just before Labor Day, so his meetings in Washington, Philadelphia, New York, and Boston made for convenient travel to Maine. Even Jeff would be there, either having run out of excuses to avoid such gatherings or due to the chance of new warmth in his relationship with Sandy. Ellen didn't know which.

Jan and her two children arrived in Walton one week before the Labor Day festivities and drove to the house on Mooscontee Bay with Ellen and Stew. Peter drove up from Boston in a rental car, and Stew met Sandy, Jeff, and their three children at the Bar Harbor Airport.

The day after everyone's arrival, Stew took Sandy and her family, along with Jan's children, sailing on his day sailer. The outing was made more lively when, coming about in a stiff breeze, Jeff and Sandy's seven-year-old, Ginny, fell overboard while reaching to touch a lobster trap buoy marker.

Jeff's paternal instincts sent him over the side instantly. Thanks to

Ginny's life jacket, Jeff's swimming ability, and Stew's deft maneuvering of the boat, all hands were soon back on board with no more harm done that wet clothes and cold skin. The pair warmed quickly by lying on the deck in the bright sun.

Back at the house, all gathered for afternoon refreshments, and Ellen probed Peter regarding the status of his relationship with Shelly. Peter seemed quite willing to discuss the topic and announced to all that the relationship was over. Shelly became interested in sky diving and was soon involved with a fellow skydiver. She moved out of Peter's apartment and his life in an amicable parting of ways.

"You probably know that my company is putting together a joint venture based on combining our networking strategies with telecom hardware from a New Jersey firm," Peter continued. "It turns out that Kris Langstrom's firm are underwriting the venture. Last week, several of us from both companies met in Manhattan with partners from Kris' firm. She was there, and we had dinner together afterward. We had a great time. She mentioned seeing Mom and Pop at the Yurek's party."

Stew, wincing, quickly excused himself to take a shower.

Following the family cleanup after dinner, Stew was alone on the deck overlooking the bay. It was one of those nights that occur frequently during Maine summer and make visitors wonder why the world couldn't be that way all the time.

A full moon, just below the horizon, projected pale luminescence into a serene, dark-blue sky filled with a starry host. The calm, sixty-degree air was light scented by clusters of pine and spruce that grew on the property, interspersed with white birches trying to survive among the dominant evergreens.

At the shoreline eight feet away from where Stew stood, a calm surface was occasionally interrupted by an incoming wave. The tide lapped higher on the rugged ledges and massive rocks that had, for countless millennia, established earth's front line of defense against the sea's insatiable appetite.

As Stew stood there, taking in the primal elements, a New York-to-Europe jet passed quietly overhead. Great circle routes between New York and several northern European cities frequently took commercial airline flights directly over the eastern Maine coast at altitude that made engine noise almost inaudible. The plane's blinking red, white, and green navigation lights added dynamic splashes of color to the display of stars, while wispy contrails mingled inconspicuously with bands of cirrus clouds wafting in the air.

Do the passengers on that plane, with their intercontinental agendas, appreciate they're part of a magnificent work of kinetic art that combines technology and nature? he wondered.

His reverie was broken by the door opening as Jeff came onto the deck. Jeffrey Nehlor married Sandy Firling soon after they graduated from college. He majored in economics, while she majored in English and graphic arts. They settled in Atlanta when Jeff accepted a position with a major southeastern bank that had international aspirations.

After the birth and early rearing of their three children, Sandy started freelance copywriting and artwork for local advertising agencies. Stew and Jeff shared a mutually cordial, albeit somewhat distant, relationship, but they rarely exchanged personal confidences or deep feelings.

"Pops, if I'm not intruding too much on your idyllic moment, I'd like to talk with you," Jeff said.

Surprised, Stew said, "Of course. This show is almost over, anyway."

"It's no secret that Sandy and I have had major trouble in our marriage. Mostly, it comes from boredom, I guess, though we're terribly busy. Is there such a thing as stress-induced boredom?"

"I suppose there could be, but are you sure it's boredom and not lack of, or misdirection of, purpose in life?"

"You're a sly one. You always elevate personal problems to a higher theological plane. Anyway, even though I was out of the country at the time, the full impact of Mitch's death caught up with me, and with Sandy, too, two weeks later. Mortality has become a lot more than a nine-letter noun. We're feeling more aware of and more involved with faith."

"I like that."

"Somewhat curiously, we've become more intimate, too, not just physically but sharing our feelings and trying to help each other in life. I'm sure you'll agree it's good news that we're recommitted ourselves to our marriage."

"It is, indeed. I sense something new between you two, and I'm delighted you'll be staying together. Even though your kids might not fully know what's going on, I suspect that at some point in their lives, they'll appreciate your new commitment. You and Sandy will, too."

"What a bummer it took Mitch's death to do it," Jeff said. "We've tried without much success to make sense of that terrible event. We can't think of anything in Mitch's life, like hubris or a grievous sin, that brought on such terrible consequences. He looks like a tragic hero brought down by plain old bad luck."

Stew was silent for a moment. "Jeff, that's one of life's unanswerables. Why do had things happen to good people? It's one of the ways in which our Creator reminds us who's really in charge."

The moon above the horizon cast its ever-intriguing river of light across the bay.

Sandy walked onto the deck. "Can you boys tolerate a little female company?"

"With you, anytime," Stew said. "Jeff and I were just discussing the latest developments in your lives. It's great that you two are trying to stick together."

Peter, walking out next, blurted, "Wow! Look at that moon! Pops, you sure ordered some super weather for the weekend. I've got the latest news from inside the house. Jan and I will take her kids river rafting tomorrow. Ginny wants to come, too, Sandy, if that's OK with you. Your two older guys want to go sailing with the neighbors on the point, who have visiting grandchildren their ages."

"You mean rafting on the Carrabaugus River?" Jeff asked. "Sure, Ginny can go, as long as she wears a life jacket and helmet and is properly supervised. For that matter, I'd like to come, too."

Sandy nodded.

The following day, in addition to rafting and sailing, Ellen and Sandy went beachcombing and seascape sketching. Stew, as the director of the Walton area organization dedicated to assisting the homeless, worked on fall fund-raising and operating plans.

Late that afternoon, when all returned to the house, the conversation turned to Jan's current condition.

"Some nights, it hurts not to have Mitch around," Jan said. "The kids keep me busy, and I've got lots of good friends there, too. The folks at church are a big help. I just don't want to face any big decisions right now, like moving somewhere. I'm beginning to think of socializing a bit. Being a single mother isn't that much of a drawback anymore. It's not my favorite status, but I'll survive."

The other adults assured her they'd do anything to help. Stew commented she was wise not making big decisions for the time being.

Sandy and Peter were the two siblings closest in age and grew up in an often-confrontational, competitive relationship that slowly matured into mutual respect. However, she still felt she had the right to know the inner workings of her brother's life, so, after a few minutes, she asked, "Am I wrong, Little Bro, or are you mellowing in your attitude toward those of us mortals who haven't been washed in your particular church's solemnities? You don't seem as judgmental as you were before."

"Mellow? I suppose that's a fair assessment. Understand that the particular church, as you call it, saved my life now and in the next life. A few years ago, I was on the road to self-destruction. Now the more confident I become in the amazing grace that rescued me from that dismal path, the less I judge others."

"Bravo!" Ellen exclaimed.

For Thanksgiving, the whole family was to convene in Walton, largely to support Jan and her children, but also because Mitch's death brought them closer together. The week before the gathering, Stew was busying closing the sale of a building lot adjoining the house that he and Ellen owned. They decided to combine the proceeds from that sale with some securities to set up a trust with their children as the beneficiaries. Motivated primarily from concern for Jan's children, they set up the trust agreement to provide for education of Stew and

Ellen's grandchildren. They assessed Jan's affairs after Mitch's death and saw she had enough money for living expenses, but not enough for the children's college years. Without needing to say it, Stew and Ellen realized that helping Jan was another reason for their continued existence.

When the family finished Thanksgiving dinner, they moved to various late-afternoon activities, including video games, playing horse at an impromptu basketball half-court in the driveway, and walking the Connecticut landscape, starkly somber in the gray of November, with its leafless trees and overcast sky.

Seven-year-old Ginny went to the attic to find some dolls she knew Ellen had. On her way downstairs, she answered the ringing telephone.

"Grandma!" she shouted. "It's for Aunt Jan. Someone named Greg wants to talk to her."

"Thank you, Ginny," Ellen said. "I'll get it." She told Greg that Jan was out walking and hung up looking thoughtful. "He seems like a pleasant, well-spoken man," she told Stew. "Apparently, he wants to meet Jan and the kids at the San Antonio airport on Sunday. He was asking about her flight number."

"Has Jan mentioned someone named Greg to you?" Stew asked. "I'm glad she's starting to socialize again. It'll be hard to replace Mitch in her life, but she's too young and has too many good things going with the kids to spend her life alone. Maybe Greg's the right guy, maybe not. Let's be careful not to ask her too many questions about him or any other man who enters her life."

"I won't be an overly inquisitive mom. Curious, isn't it, how the lives of our young people, perhaps all young people, seem driven by external events. They have romances, marriages, births, new jobs, new houses, hurricanes, or blizzards, while old geezers like us find our lives more affected by internal feelings.

"Are we getting so old that we can't get excited anymore by human triumphs or nature's foibles? Or are we just getting wiser with age?"

Stew looked at her intently for a few seconds. "We seem less affected by externals. Maybe that's part of the wisdom of aging. We've seen the Depression, a major world war, nuclear weapons development, military actions around the world, and pollution problems. Despite all that, the world hasn't ended. Instead, it seems determined to keep going."

"Enough of heavy topics," Ellen replied with a sigh. "How did I come to be married to such a sage? I could've married a nightclub owner, a big-time commodities broker, or…"

"Come, Dear. We've been over that before. I could've married an heiress, or a… What difference does it make? You're the one who brought up this internal-external discussion."

When Sandy and Jan returned from their walk, Ellen told Jan about the phone call.

"He's a good friend," Jan said. "He's an attorney with a firm that did some work for Mitch's company, and we've got a few things in common. His wife died eighteen months ago to cancer about one year after she gave birth to their only child. At this point, neither Greg nor I know if we want to remarry, but we appreciate the friendship."

"How about appreciating each other's beds?" Sandy asked.

"That's not fair," Stew said. "Jan, don't answer. I'm glad you feel able to enjoy male companionship again on whatever basis you feel's appropriate."

"Hear, hear," Ellen added.

The following day's mail brought the *Walton Appriser* weekly newspaper, including a lead article on tax relief for seniors. Charley Merdone's position prevailed in a recent selectmen meeting, and Walton's seniors would be recognized as the valuable cash cows they were.

Rather than forcing them to sell their large homes to families that would add significantly to the education budget, the burghers of Walton enacted a substantial real-estate tax exemption for seniors who'd been in their homes longer than three years. That removed one of the main incentives that made Stew consider leaving Walton.

When he and Ellen discussed the subject, he asked, "How about if we stay here in our Walton house indefinitely? The new tax relief for seniors removes the need for us to pay for town services we don't need, and the house is as good an asset as any we could leave in an estate."

"I knew you'd find a way to stay indefinitely," she replied. "I agree, especially with Jan needing family support and this place being her home. Besides, now I won't have to give up my friends and activities. Hooray!"

"Every time we moved, we complained about how much work it was, but it also stimulated us. By resolving to stay put, we give up the thrill of the chase and recognize we'll live out our lives pretty much as they are."

"Yes, Dear. No matter where we live, you'll still be you, and I'll be me, challenges, disappointments, triumphs, and all. We'll age, but our lives don't have to be boring. Hold that thought."

Later that afternoon, the younger crowd returned from their outings. The last was Peter, with, to Ellen's amusement and Stew's consternation, Kris Langstrom. It turned out that one of the old friends Peter visited was Kris, so he brought her back to the house for refreshments.

As Kris greeted them, Stew felt the old conflict between libido and conscience return. It was more than conscience that time. In his mind rose clearly his feelings for Ellen, which had been latent for some time. How could he develop with someone else the kind of relationship he shared with Ellen? Their implicit trust and intellectual and spiritual compatibility went far beyond physical attraction.

It looked like Peter and Kris might become a couple.

As people enjoyed refreshments and engaged in small talk, Peter followed Stew into the kitchen. "Dad, can I borrow your car tomorrow? I'm supposed to return my rental in the morning, and Kris and I want to go to New York with a stop in Westchester on the way to visit her friends. She's got tickets to a matinee that shouldn't be too painful. After that, we'll probably end up at your kind of place, an East Side hotel eatery. Exciting, eh?"

Stew laughed inwardly at the irony of the situation and smiled.

"Sure. If Mom and I need to go somewhere, we'll use her car. You seem pretty interested in Kris. Am I misreading that?"

"No. She and I get along famously. She's more open-minded than Shelly, despite Shelly's façade of being a world citizen. Kris and I can laugh about things on which we disagree. We enjoy each other's company."

As Peter and Kris were leaving, she kissed Stew's cheek. "So long, Lobster Stew. Remember me."

Stew chuckled inwardly when Ellen said, "Kris, Dear, we can't forget you. Stop by whenever you're out."

After the pair left, Ellen and Stew found themselves alone for a moment.

"Here we are, parked in Walton indefinitely," Ellen said. "I can live with that, but the last few months have given me a new attitude regarding the importance of community in my life. I still want a safe, stimulating community, but Mitch's death makes me realize that in our lives what we believe is more important than that."

She quickly changed the subject. "Pete and Kris look good together. They make a great pair, don't they?"

"Yes. They look good together." He paused. "It's better that way."

"Better? Better than what?"

Sarah Hopkins, author of *You Never Know*, lives in Hagerstown, Maryland. Her story, *Triumph of Love*, appears in the anthology, *Stories of the Unexpected*.

You Never Know

Sara Hopkins

Sometimes I feel like a man the Fates are against. Friends have advised me that psychiatry would solve my problem, but I'm certain it would also cost me the thing I value most. I'm convinced I'll be happier enjoying my chosen way of life as long as possible, even knowing what is ahead.

Two years ago, I was just another average student in the third year at East Hagerstown High School. Most of my time was spent at my lessons, because I was determined to have a straight-A average. What little spare time I had was devoted to swimming. That was my favorite sport, and I looked forward to my upcoming vacation. Fred, my best friend, and I planned to spend two weeks at Atlantic City, New Jersey.

Finally, school ended, and we arrived at our motel at the beach. The first five days were wonderful. I never saw the ocean before, and the roar of surf at night was a comforting sound by which to sleep. Everything about the ocean was new and fascinating. The waves held me spellbound. I liked standing on the beach with waves swirling around me.

Most of all, I enjoyed swimming far out and catching a big wave to ride back to shore. More than ever, that convinced me that should be my career after high school.

On the sixth day of our vacation, Fred and I were one hundred feet from shore. It was early in the morning, and we were the only two people out. He was some distance ahead when he started yelling and thrashing in the water.

I swam toward him as quickly as I could. As I drew near, I saw him vainly beating his hands against a huge shape in the water. For the first time in my life, I experienced fear so strong it made me helpless. I couldn't force myself to swim toward him.

It was over in seconds. A wave like a giant hand washed over Fred, and, when I looked around, he was gone. The water around me was red. A dark fin rose from the water where Fred had been and diminished as it went out into the waves. By then, the lifeguard reached me and brought me back.

That was only the third shark attack that season, and it was the only fatal one. That wasn't considered a bad average, but I was completely changed. I no longer thought of the waves as friendly and beautiful. Instead, they were like hands, beckoning me out to Fred's assistance, where I would've shared his fate if I hadn't frozen in fear.

When I returned home, no one blamed me, but I wasn't able to go near water anymore.

Today, I received the news I always wanted. All my hard work at school paid off with a straight-A average. Now I can have the career I wanted, but there'll be no escaping those beckoning hands when I'm at the United States Naval Academy.

Joel Haugland completed a two-year correspondence course in fiction and a 1 ½-year course in Journalism with Korrespondanse Akademiet (KA Skolen) in Oslo, Norway. He sold several feature stories to daily newspapers, two short stories to a Norwegian weekly magazine, and a half-hour feature to Nork Rikskringkasting (NRK) in Oslo and appeared on their Saturday Night program in 1954.

Since his arrival in Canada, he completed a two-year correspondence course in article and fiction writing plus a 1 ½- year course in writing for television and radio with the Palmer Institute of Authorship in Hollywood, California; Writer's Digest School's article course, and Ambassador College's three-year Bible correspondence course.

In 1972 he was, by the district editor of The Times-News, offered a position as district correspondent. The paper had a readership of 120,000. His short story, *Ordeal at Sucker Creek*, was included in the anthology, *Stories from the Heart*.

Supernal Violin Music and Poltergeists

Joel Haugland

Eleven-year-old Joey Hamilton sat below a cliff in front of an aspen grove with a loaded double-barreled shotgun across his lap.

Berrying with his father two weeks earlier, they flushed a litter of capercaillies nearby. Joey was waiting for the birds to light and feed on the aspen leaves at sundown.

Time passed slowly. A gentle sunset breeze rustled the leaves, and twilight came without the capercaillies. Suddenly, high-pitched violin music from above sent a cold shiver up Joey's spine. He'd heard people say the violin was the devil's instrument.

A capercaillie rooster landed nearby, kindling Joey's hunting instinct. He cocked the gun, slowly raised it, took careful aim at the bird's neck, and pulled the trigger. The discharge almost knocked Joey off his seat. Flame lit the grove, and a thump told him he'd hit his target.

Joey stood and listened as echoes of the shot reverberated between the hills, restoring serenity to the wilderness.

With his shotgun cradled in his right elbow, and the wings of the big bird flapping against his left leg as he walked, Joey, who was small for his age, quickly tired. Dark clouds and heat lightning moved into the hills, and Joey began feeling unhappy. He sneaked away to hunt without asking permission.

Much to Joey's relief, he saw Oscar, his burly maternal uncle, sitting in the living room when he arrived.

"Thanks to God!" Joey's mother exclaimed. "We didn't know where to look for you."

"Where have you been all evening?" his father, an avid hunter, demanded.

"Stu Tarn Hill." Joey shrugged sheepishly.

"Is that where you got this?" Oscar eyed the bird.

"You must be starved." His mother set food on the table for him.

"I told you never to go hunting alone without my permission," his father said sternly.

"You must never go to that place alone again," Oscar added.

"Why?"

"I heard the most spell-binding violin music ever up there the other evening, and I took off as fast as I could run. I'll never set foot up there again."

Joey didn't know what to say.

"Didn't you hear anything unusual up there?" Oscar asked.

"No. I didn't." He shook his head.

"Are you sure?"

"Yes." Joey's lips became pinched.

After Uncle Oscar left, Joey's father said, "There'll be no more hunting for you until you learn to obey."

Despite his young age, Joey had some very unusual experiences. He spent three days and nights alone with his unconscious parents during the Spanish flu epidemic. As a three-year-old, Joey suffered a succession of nightmares that the doctor said he'd eventually grow out of, and he did.

Once he saw a fireball coming through a closed window, and he had many out-of-body experiences. At intervals, he awoke hearing his name called from the inside of an empty barrel.

In grade school, his Bible-study teacher asked her students if they sometimes were awakened by a deep voice calling their name.

"It sounds like it's coming from the inside of an empty barrel," she said. "That's God calling you."

Joey thought about that for a long time.

One early winter, Joey's father went fox hunting with two friends and said they'd be back for supper on Sunday. A snowstorm came up Saturday night that lasted through Sunday.

Joey's mom sat up waiting for the hunters, so he insisted on keeping her company. At midnight, someone entered their porch and stamped snow off his boots, but no one came through the door.

Joey followed his mom onto the porch to check, but all they saw were gusts of wind swirling snow across the front yard.

As his mother closed the door, she muttered, "It was probably a poltergeist."

That was a new word for Joey, but he was too tired to ask what it meant.

When Joey was out of grade school, a neighborly farmer asked him to stand in for Einar, his farmhand, who had to have his appendix removed. Joey would sleep in an old cabin across the yard. Einar, who hadn't gone to the hospital yet, told Joey what to expect.

"If you happen to wake up at midnight hearing someone walking the floor," Einar said, "don't let it frighten you. He won't hurt you."

Einar grinned, so Joey thought it was a joke.

After working a full day in the grain field, Joey fell soundly asleep but was awakened at midnight when he heard someone pacing the floor. That didn't frighten him, but it reminded him of the violin music he heard at Stu Tarn.

When the spirit disturbed his sleep for three nights in a row, Joey moved home and walked back and forth to work.

At the age of seventeen, Joey shared a room with Rolf and Harald, two seasoned farmhands, in a one-story building called Strutset. Strutset dated back to the thirteenth century and had seven rooms that opened onto a hallway along the east wall. The building had two entrances, each with a porch, and there was a stairway to the attic.

The attic had headroom only below the roof peak. At the south end were wooden pegs fastened to the rafters that once held horse harness. The dairyman, his wife, and his two preschool children lived in the three north rooms, while the farmhands lived in the southernmost one.

In the living room, the farmer had a sixteenth-century clock with the hands permanently resting at 4:20. One midsummer weekend, the farmer and his wife visited with friends, and the maid and the farmhands went to a dance.

Returning in the company of friends, they stood in the yard chatting when they suddenly heard a clock striking twelve, as loudly as if it were nearby.

"I guess the old fogey got his clock fixed," Harald said.

"If he'd done that, we'd have heard of it before we left," Rolf said dourly.

At breakfast the following day, Harald walked to the living room and stared open-mouthed at the clock with its hands still pointing to 4:20.

Following the haying season, darkness came soon after supper. Rolf and Joey went to bed early, while Harald, a lady's man, dated often.

Once, Rolf and Joey were stirred from sleep at midnight by the sound of something being dragged back and forth under Harald's bed.

Rolf jumped out of bed and turned on the light, and the noises stopped. "Someone's playin' tricks on us." He pulled Harald's bed away from the wall and stared at the bare floor.

When they told Harald about it, he said, "You guys sleep so much, you're going crazy."

When the noise recurred, Joey and Rolf thought of rats and checked the foundation of the building without finding any big enough for a rat to crawl in.

All three men slept undisturbed one night, but, when Harald was out again, the scratching returned even louder. That time, they didn't mention it to him.

Another night, Rolf and Joey lay awake, waiting for Harald to wake up, because the noise under his bed was louder than any time before.

Suddenly, Harald scrambled from his bed, turned on the light, and accused his roommates of playing tricks on him.

"We've told you about the noise," Rolf said, "but you didn't believe us. Do you believe us now?"

"Hell, no!" Harald pulled his bed away from the wall and stared wide-eyed at the floor.

Despite his being present at several mystical occurrences, Harald suggested they create a plan to catch the trickster.

Rolf insisted that since the noise came from under Harald's bed, and they hadn't found any evidence of a trickster, it was useless to try to catch him.

When Harald began dating again, Rolf and Joey slept undisturbed one night, but, when Harald was in bed again, they were awakened by heavy footsteps that stamped up the stairway to the attic, directly over Harald's bed.

They decided it was time to stop the nuisance. They bought flashlights, and Rolf rigged a pulley to the light switch so he could turn it on from his bed. To keep the trickster from getting away, they strung ropes across the attic ten feet inside the stairway at both ends of the building.

Ready for the showdown, they went to bed fully dressed and with their boots on. As soon as footsteps entered the attic, the three men jumped up. Joey ran up the south stair, while Harald entered from the opposite end. Both searched carefully with their flashlights without discovering anything.

Disappointed and suspicious, they returned to bed and lay awake, wondering what happened. Joey was more puzzled than ever about the violin music at Stu Tarn.

Rolf and Joey slept undisturbed for two nights while Harald was away, then, on the third night, with Harald back in bed, they were awakened by staggering footsteps in the stairway. After a moment's silence, something heavy crashed against the attic floor above Rolf's bed, followed by guffaws.

Rolf turned on the light and jumped from bed, shouting, "What the hell's going on here? Let's get him!"

Joey and Harald, barefoot and wearing nothing but underwear, grabbed their flashlights and ran off, but they never saw anyone.

On their way across the yard for breakfast that morning, they met the dairyman in a dark mood.

"I've had enough," he said. "I'm quitting."

"What's the matter?" Rolf asked.

"My wife's afraid of being alone after I go to the barn in the morning, damn it."

"What's she afraid of?"

"You'll find out. I'll be gone in two weeks."

On Thursday, September 13, 1934, Harald went to bed early. Rolf and Joey lay awake, talking softly, trying to understand what was going on.

They finally slept but were awakened by heavy, staggering steps on the stairway. Harald snored loudly in bed, oblivious to the noise.

The footsteps ceased. A few seconds later, something heavy crashed onto the attic floor, followed by loud laughter. Harald woke up.

Sensing a chance to catch the trickster, Rolf turned on the light, but Joey and Harald didn't get out of bed. They knew they wouldn't find anyone.

Harald quit and left. Rolf quit that Saturday and got roaring drunk. Joey went hunting with his dad on Sunday.

Farmhands worked ten-hour days, six days a week. Local farmers pooled their milk deliveries so every sixth day, Rolf delivered milk to the dairy five miles south.

Delivering milk was considered a man's job. The fifty-liter cans were heavy, and the teamster had to be a horseman. With Rolf gone, the responsibility of delivering milk fell to Joey. Even though he had to get up an hour early, he looked forward to it.

One day, Joey was given a list of groceries to pick up for the farmer's wife, as well as getting a crowbar at the hardware store for her husband.

The shopkeeper was busy with another customer, and Joey was browsing for a crowbar, when a young blonde woman approached and asked, "May I help you?"

"I'm looking for a crowbar."

She looked puzzled.

"Do you know what to look for?" Joey outlined one with his hands.

"Of course I do. I carry one in my purse." She smiled.

Joey slept undisturbed in Strutset until the end of September, when he joined a logging crew at Bokkebu, near the Swedish border, fifty miles east-by-north of Oslo, Norway.

Their quarters were a large, one-room log cabin with six bunks. A wide corridor divided it from the adjoining horse barn.

Darkness fell early. The long evenings were spent playing cards or listening to dirty jokes. Occasional entertainment was provided by two men who played accordion and guitar.

Lars, one of the younger men, carved chains from a piece of birch lumber, and Martin was a regular entertainer. His wife made his underwear from flour sacks.

Whenever chubby Martin climbed into his upper bunk, his buttocks read *Made in USA,* and *Weight 100 lbs. Use no hooks.*

On the second Friday in November, ten men with three horses went to the countryside to fetch supplies to last till Christmas. Lars and Joey remained behind to tend the remaining horses.

The crew expected to return Sunday, but a blizzard came Saturday afternoon and roared all night until Sunday afternoon, so Lars and Joey went to bed early.

They were awakened at midnight by horses neighing and stamping their hooves on the floor of their stalls. Soon, they heard horses walking by and stopping in front of the barn.

Lars and Joey got up and dressed quickly, so they could help unload supplies. Lars lit a lantern as they went out, but they found nothing but snow, untouched by men or horses.

Stunned and turning white, Lars asked, "Didn't we hear them coming?"

Joey, remembering the night he and his mother waited up for his father and friends to return from their fox-hunting trip, nodded slowly.

In September, 1941, Joey and two pals, Art and Hans, were hired to cut logs at a remote woodlot south of the city of Hedemora, Sweden. Ingrid, their daughter's employer, drove them to a cabin by a lake. Art and Hans brought bicycles,

"This seems like a nice, cozy place," Art, the lanky one, marveled.

"Maja, my twin sister, loves this place," Ingrid said. "It gives me the quivers."

"Why?"

"The old hermit who owned it was murdered here. The cabin was empty for years before Dad bought it and refurbished it."

Once they unloaded everything, and soft-spoken Ingrid was ready to leave, she said, "Oh. I almost forgot. Maja said to keep the place clean."

The cabin had a twenty-by-twenty-foot front room with cookstove, a kitchen counter under the east window, a table, and four chairs at the west window.

To the south were two bedrooms with bunks, closets, and chairs. What caught Art's eye was a round oak table in the center of the floor.

"Let's move that damn thing out of the way into that corner." He pointed.

Art and Hans placed his hands on the table, but Joey grabbed a long-stemmed crystal dish from the center and walked to the door.

"What do you think you're doing?" Art asked.

"Throwing out these rotten apples."

Art's long arm shot out. "Give 'em to me." He took the dish from Joey and set it on the kitchen counter.

"What's wrong?" Hans was puzzled.

"You guys don't know Maja. She's a real bitch. If we throw out those apples, she'll accuse us of eating them. If someone broke her great-grandmother's dish, she'd eat his heart."

One Saturday, Art and Hans rode their bikes to town to visit friends and see a movie. They promised to be back Sunday evening.

On Sunday, Joey swam in the lake, read, and relaxed. In the evening, he lit a candle on the kitchen table and turned on his battery-operated radio. He was listening to the seven-o'clock Norwegian newscast from BBC, London, when he heard a loud crash behind him that shook the floor.

Joey instantly blew out the candle and sat in the darkness, straining his ears for sounds, but all he heard was silence. Convinced he was alone, he lit the kerosene lamp and stepped in shattered glass from the crystal dish. Art's words about what would happen returned to him.

Awestruck, Joey saw a nasty-looking brown glob of rotten apples on the floor eight feet from where Art set the dish on the kitchen counter. Scattered around were myriads of tiny pieces of light-green crystals. Even the stem had shattered into fragments.

Circumstantial evidence convinced Joey that someone had thrown the dish at the floor. After thinking hard, he left the chips as they were. No one would believe him, anyway, as he found out when he explained to Hans and Art.

"You try to tell that bunk to Maja," Art scoffed.

Hans shook his head in disbelief.

When dark-haired, ill-tempered Maja came to visit, Joey never had a chance to explain. She lashed out at him so vehemently, he walked away.

Early in September, 1942, Joey visited a friend in Stockholm. One Saturday evening, they saw a movie and went to an outdoor restaurant later.

Patrons were entertained by two dark-haired, brilliantly dressed, young Gypsy women who played violin from table to table, playing people's favorite songs on request.

As they reached the table where Joey and his friend sat, they began playing, without request, the same violin tune Joey heard at Stu Tarn thirteen years earlier.

Memories of Three Xmases

Joel Haugland

With only a few guardsmen and some kitchen staff around after the personnel went on Christmas leave, the camp seemed abandoned. Following weeks of rain, mud was everywhere. As I sloshed my way to the battalion office in the morning, mist from dark, overcast skies painted a gloomy picture of my surroundings.

"I thought you'd gone on leave," the sergeant clerk said in greeting.

"Where?" I asked.

"Here." He handed me a letter.

I scrutinized the smudged, light-blue envelope that had been readdressed from another camp.

"From your girlfriend?" he asked out of curiosity.

"It could be Cleopatra the Seventh or Lady Godiva for all I know." I shrugged and left.

Mailed in late November from a place 250 miles due north, the letter was an invitation to spend Christmas with a family I didn't know. I received last-minute leave, telegraphed the host, changed into civilian garb, and called a taxi.

Early evening on December 23, 1943, I was in a group of servicemen in front of a toilet on a crowded, northbound passenger train. A lone civilian among uniformed strangers, I felt out of place and isolated. My thoughts went to Norway, my native country.

On the second day of Christmas, 1940, I went to the railway station to meet my girlfriend in the evening. Leaving the station with her, her sister, and her boyfriend, we found the street blocked by seven drunk Nazi soldiers.

We paused. One soldier approached, stopped at arm's length, and shouted, *"Verschvinden!"*

No one moved.

He drew his bayonet and bellowed, *"Heraus...geschwind!"*

Acting quickly, I aimed a solid kick to the man's knee, sending him down.

"Helf mich, Kameraden!" he shouted. *"Helf mich!"*

My companions vanished into the darkness.

Six drunken killers, shouting battle cries, ran pell-mell down the street with drawn bayonets. Chester...they called him Chester...lay on the ground but managed to trip md in the resulting fracas. Standing on neck and shoulders, I kicked his assailants for all I was worth.

Suddenly grabbed from behind, he was thrown to the ground and held by three soldiers. A flashlight came on. The three assailants knelt with their bayonets raised, ready to kill.

From the corner of my eye, I saw the door of a nearby hotel open, and a soldier appeared on the steps. *"Nein, nein, Kameraden!"*

He fired his pistol into the sky three times, then ran toward the fight, his Luger in his hand. Willy, one of the 1800 German orphans raised in Norway following World War One, recalled to Germany in August, 1938, paid his dues by rescuing the fallen man.

The locomotive chugged on. The loud, monotonous clank of the Pullman car was hypnotic. The only break in the monotony was a long whistle each time they passed through a village or small town. Two short whistles announced a stop that lasted long enough for passengers to disembark or jostle aboard.

Somewhere past midnight, two servicemen came aboard and stood among us. Feeling a tap on my shoulder, I found myself facing a smiling noncom.

"Excuse me," he said. "I might be wrong, but haven't we met somewhere?"

"Give me a clue."

"You played right wing on a Norwegian soccer team against us at Para during the summer of '42."

"That's right."

"You beat us. No hard feelings, though." He smiled and held out his hand. "I'm Aake Nordin."

As we shook hands, I introduced myself, and we engaged in small talk, both deliberately avoiding the war.

Arriving at Sollefteaa at six o'clock the following morning, we ate breakfast together and became better acquainted while waiting for buses.

The road east to the coast of the Baltic Sea followed the Aaengerman River. Nordin told me that river once had so many salmon that the farm hands had the farmers sign a contract not to serve salmon more than twice a week.

We parted at Para, Nordin's stamping ground. After wishing each other Merry Christmas and Happy New Year, we never saw each other again.

At Bjorkaa, farther east, my thoughts went back to Christmas Eve, 1942.

I worked in a bush camp. The foreman and cook were Swedes, the crew were Norwegian refugees, and all were invited to spend Christmas with local families.

Nevertheless, the five men, including Bert, the cook, chose to stay in the camp. The foreman went home to his family and asked me to watch over the camp.

After lunch in December 24, eighteen-year-old Hilmar set off to the country store five miles away to pick up last-minute mail.

Bert, a retired sailor, served a super Christmas dinner in a subdued atmosphere. Hilmar's seat at the table was empty.

I helped Bert do the dishes while the three other guys, who were known as the Three Musketeers, withdrew to their room to celebrate.

Outside, there was over three feet of snow, and the temperature was minus thirty-one degrees Celsius. At eight o'clock on that moonlight night, Hilmar was still missing. From the noise coming from the Musketeers' room, they didn't seem to care if Hilmar returned.

Eighteen hours after leaving camp, I exited a taxi before a large, elaborate, white house. At the center of the circular driveway was a flagpole on a concrete foundation. At the top was a Finnish flag, then came flags for Norway and Sweden. South of the dwelling, a stately red barn dominated the open fields. One end was a horse barn, with dairy cattle in the other and forage between.

Carl and Alice Nymark, my hosts, welcomed me at the door. Inside, I met their children, Alan, Kate, Doreen, Eric, and Hans, who ranged in age from thirteen to four.

At the lunch table, I also met Oscar and Linea Nymark, Carls' parents, Gunnar Hedlund, my foreman from 1942, his wife, Inga, and Pirkko, their eleven-year-old adopted Finnish orphan girl.

After lunch, the men toured the barns, which held eight solid work horses, fifty dairy cattle, some heifers, three dozen well-fed pigs, and a chicken coop with many noisy layers.

In early afternoon, Pirkko's teacher brought the school choir. They sang Christmas carols and surprised us all by singing the national anthems for Finland, Sweden, and Norway flawlessly.

Our Christmas candlelight dinner boasted a beautifully trimmed and lit tree. The table held roast goose, ham, sweet and sour spareribs, and choice of wine for the adults. Children drank milk and juice.

The host wished us Merry Christmas, welcomed us to the *julebord,* and read the Christmas Gospel, Luke 2:1-18. Kate, the eldest daughter, said grace, and we savored a superb meal while soft carols played on the radio.

Doreen said thanks for the delicious food. Leftovers were put away and dishes washed. Children played lively games in the sitting room, the men gathered in the living room, and the women socialized in the kitchen.

Gunnar turned to me. "It was Carl's idea to invite you to make up for the lousy Christmas last year. Things happened so fast when I returned to work, I didn't get to thank you for looking after the camp for me."

"I didn't mind. There was nothing to it, really."

"Don't say that. Hilmar would've froze to death, and the bunkhouse would've burned for sure."

"Tell us about it," Carl urged.

"Please," Gunnar said. "Bert quit, Hilmar wouldn't talk about it, and the Three Musketeers were silent, too. Then you were drafted and left so fast, I got only a vague idea of what happened."

"Well…" I shrugged. "I found Hilmar lying in the snow two miles down the road."

"Drunk, I suppose?" Carl asked.

"He was out cold. Weak pulse and no movement."

"How'd you get him back to camp?"

"First-aid fashion. He was on my neck, right arm over my left shoulder, his right hip at my right shoulder. He was easy enough to carry."

"How'd you revive him?"

"Bert and I put him to bed and heated blankets to cover him."

"What did the Three Musketeers do?" Carl asked.

"The were drunk out of their minds with their boots on, snoring and oblivious."

"What else happened?" Gunnar asked.

"Hilmar stirred, threw up, and fell out of bed. We bedded him down on the floor. Bert went to his room, and I slept with my boots on.

"I was roused after midnight. Bert was hopping in the hall, swinging a fading carbide lamp in circles, singing loudly, 'What shall we do with the drunken sailor?'

"The carbide container came unscrewed. Burning carbide pebbles scattered on the floor. Bert ran to his room and shut the door. Outside was a shovel we used to remove snow from the entrance steps. I shoveled the hot carbide pebbles into the snow."

"Thanks," Gunnar said. "All I knew, I learned at the other camp. Hilmar picked up their mail at the store. When he returned, they offered him a drink, which he refused.

"For that they mocked him, saying, 'Don't walk around pretending to be a man unless you can gulp down six ounces of whiskey without batting an eye.'

"A man handed him a glass and said, 'Here. Show us how much of a man you are.' They said Hilmar took the glass and emptied it quickly, then handed it back to the man and left without saying a word."

"He was a clean-cut teenager," I said. "I don't think he ever tasted whiskey before."

Carl glanced at his wristwatch. "It's past ten. We'd better hit the sack. We have to rise early to get to Mass in time. Because of the gas rationing, the church council decided we should travel by horse and sleigh with lit torches, just like the old days."

Two horses were hitched and ready to go at five-thirty the following morning when Oscar and Linea Nymark arrived to take Gunnar and Inga Hedlund up in their sleigh.

We set out with Carl Nymark leading, Alice at his side and Hans on her lap. Pirkko and I sat in the back seat. Proudly holding the reins, Alan followed with sister Kate beside him. Doreen and Eric were in the back. The senior Nymarks and Hedlunds came in the rear. Each sleigh carried two torches.

Through cracks in the overcast sky, the moon threw a mystical gleam over the snow-covered landscape. Nary a motor vehicle had touched the road ahead of us. The weather was mild, the night calm and peaceful.

Occasionally, ski tracks cut sharp lines in the otherwise-untouched snowy fields. As we entered the woodland, a slap of the reins made the horses break into a trot.

Covered with wolf-skin rugs to our chests, we were quickly comfortable except for flying horsehair and snow from the hooves. The pungent smell of work horses tickled my nostrils, making me sneeze, while glints of moonlight fondled our faces between shadows of hooded conifers across the road until we stopped at the outskirts of the wood.

Carl checked with his family and helped light our torches. I overheard him tell Gunnar, "I hope the minister won't be as long-winded as usual this morning."

We saw the church a couple miles ahead. From a turn in the road, the illuminated building came into full view, situated on meadowland and a little uphill from the river.

Pirkko's face lit up in a radiant smile, and her eyes sparkled with joy. "Look at the nice church!" she said. "Look at this!" She waved her torch. "This is fun!"

Lucky little girl, I thought. *Orphaned in a brutal war, then ending up with nice people like the Hedlunds and Nymarks.*

On the hills on both sides of the river, I saw flickering torches emerge from the woods, moving toward the church.

The predawn scene struck me as a fitting way to celebrate Christmas while simultaneously rekindling the humble but happy ways of our ancestors' way of life.

We threw our torches into a pile that grew to a small bonfire outside the church gate. Horses were unhitched and tied to fence planks, then blanketed and fed hay.

The minister welcomed us to Mass, gave thanks for the filled pews, and elaborated on the Christmas Gospel. The choir and congregation sang hymns.

Toward the end of his sermon, the minister mentioned the war, offered a prayer for the dead, wounded, and men still at the front, and ended with a wish for the next Christmas to be celebrated in peace and harmony among all nations.

While we filed out, the minister stood in the doorway, shaking hands and wishing everyone Merry Christmas and Happy New Year.

People lingered outside for a while, inviting friends and relatives home for a short visit after Mass.

We visited three of the Nymark family's friends and families and were treated with the best of Christmas goodies in a highly social atmosphere.

Out of convenience, the Nymarks, living at the edge of the church district, extended their invitation to an after-lunch get-together the second day of Christmas.

I returned to camp on New Year's Day after a very pleasant and memorable experience. An equally pleasant and happy Christmas would've been spent at home in a free, peaceful country.

Honor Thy Mother

Joel Haugland

I recall Mother holding me so I could watch our penned pigs. I was seventeen months old. One month later, I failed to stir my parents from their sleep.

I couldn't get in bed with them or return to my crib unassisted. During the day, I heard the pigs squealing. At night, I huddled in the cupboard, wearing my flannel nightie.

At noon of the third day, my mother's aunt rescued me. She lost a son and daughter-in-law to the Spanish flu that killed millions in Europe following World War One.

Our small farm nestled against the great wilderness, sixteen miles west of the Swedish-Norwegian border. Three miles west, on the banks of the Glomma River, lay the village of Aarnes.

A great depression gripped Europe. Mom saved wrapping paper, bags, and strings for shopping, because most village shops had signs that read, *No wrapping, no groceries!*

Father worked away from home. Mom tended cows, sheep, chickens, and me. I loved watching her sew. One day, I stuck my forefinger under the needle, and it bit me right through my nail!

The sewing machine stopped. Mom clamped her hand over my

finger and said, "Don't move!" With her free hand, she turned the sewing-machine wheel and pulled out the needle.

I looked at my finger. A tiny red pearl formed on top of the nail. Mom quietly bandaged my finger. I didn't cry, but the incident cured my fascination with sewing machines.

In my third year, Mom gave birth to a little redheaded boy who demanded almost constant attention. On rainy days, she sent me into the attic to play.

The attic of our century-old log home had many old relics, including, discarded household items, long-spiked hemp carders, long-handled waffle irons, old wedding dresses, and more.

Curiosity inspired me to ask what those things were for, so I dragged them down to Mom, who explained and sometimes demonstrated.

One day, I decided to amuse her. With a platinum-blonde wig on my head that hung to my feet and almost tripped me, dragging a raven-black wig behind me, I appeared before her in the kitchen.

"Take that dirty old thing off your head and bring both of those to the woodshed!"

Her word was law. I obeyed, feeling foolish for not amusing her.

Afterward, she washed my hair, face, and hands. "We don't know who wore those old wigs. They could be full of germs."

When Simen was two, Mom gave birth to a girl, and I became Simen's guardian, an unpleasant task. He missed her constant attention and wailed a lot.

To soothe him, Mom made a rag doll and named it Philip. Blue-denim Philip was almost as big as Simen. He had dark, painted-on eyes, a red mouth, a brown nose, and hair made of pink yarn to match his master's.

Simen and Philip became inseparable. He always dragged the doll by an arm or leg while following me around.

I wanted to pick wildflowers for Mom one day. With Simen and Philip in tow, I went into the field. Simen cried constantly.

"What's wrong?" I asked.

He shook his head and increased his volume.

I felt there was trouble and stopped the excursion. Returning home, we found Mom baking cookies.

"Why didn't you bring him in before this had to happen?" she demanded.

Downcast, I went back outside, thinking, *I was all set to pick flowers for her she'd always remember.*

Nevertheless, without any way to cut the stems, I soon pricked my fingers on the thistles, which resisted all attempts to break them.

Sucking blood off my fingers, I discovered that thistles hurt worse than my injured pride. Consequently, I returned to Mom with a handful of field daisies and harebells.

My sister napped. Simen, neat and clean, was also sleeping. Mom, finished with her baking, thanked me for the lovely flowers and rewarded me with milk and cookies. I instantly forgave her.

In the attic was a box of old books and half-used scribblers with neat, hand-printed symbols of the alphabet.

I took the scribblers to Mom.

"Now that's something useful," she said. "Two years from now, you'll start school, so you might as well begin practicing now."

Soon, I sat at the coffee table, scribbler in front of me, pencil in hand, trying to cope with those marvelously neat symbols. I needed help.

Mom guided my pencil-holding hand until my attempts began to resemble the originals.

One heavy, overcast, August afternoon, Mom sat at the kitchen table with a cup of coffee while I played on the floor. Suddenly, a fireball came through a closed window and landed on the table, terrifying Mom.

For a split second, the ball spun at a dizzying speed, emitting a hissing sound and many sparks, then it bounced off the table and landed beside me.

That's fun! I thought, reaching toward the ball.

Mom grabbed me and swept me away from it.

I recall bright summer mornings with lush, green, moist grass and the thrill of skylarks against a blue sky while Mom guided the cows through the gate to their pasture.

On her way back from the chicken coop, she brought an apron filled with eggs. She set a black skillet on the stove, then, with one egg in each hand, cracked them on the rim of the pan into sizzling, hot butter.

A lot of fried and scrambled eggs, pancakes, and omelets came from that large, black skillet over the years, all prepared by Mom.

A raging blizzard sent snow past the windows. Simen and our sister napped. Mom, after washing the lunch dishes, took me on her lap.

"I wish I could've gone to Grandma Abel's funeral today," she said, sighing, "but I couldn't get away. She was my favorite grandma. She taught me a lot about life, and I loved her. Daughter of a priest, she was repudiated for marrying a commoner, but she never looked back."

On the day of my enrollment in School, 24 many proud mothers, dressed in their Sunday best, brought in their children. Among them was Mom. Young, slim, and neat in a light-blue dress and matching hat, she was the most beautiful mother of all to me.

Thanks to her, I began school well prepared. However, since I was also the second-smallest boy in class, with a freckled face and stubby nose, I soon became the butt of class jokes.

"Do you get snow in your nose in winter?" they asked. "Do you cover your nose when it's raining?"

Mom told me to ignore such remarks. "Just show them what you're made of."

As timid as I was, I never raised my hand to answer the teacher's question, but she made up for that by making me write answers on the blackboard.

At the end of the term, the teacher rewarded the best girl and boy student with gifts. When the day came, I watched Emma, who always raised her hand to answer questions, strut up the aisle.

I never expected the teacher to call me, too. She had to say my name twice before I looked up.

"Come forward and stand beside Emma," she said.

She praised us for our work, encouraged us to keep it up, and presented each of us with a framed picture of Christ in Gethsemane.

Mom was elated. It was the fruit of her labors, though to me, the incident added rancor to the comments about my freckles and nose.

School went from eight o'clock in the morning until four in the afternoon, every second day from Monday through Saturday. Arriving home after class, I ate a light meal Mom had waiting, prepared from solid country fare. My favorite dish in winter was Icelandic herring simmered in cream.

Mom sat with me and asked about my day, wanting to know about my homework and when it was due. She also checked my work to make sure I did it correctly and on time, but she never corrected my mistakes.

Her long, dark hair reached to the middle of her calves when it was loose. After shampooing, she threw it over her shoulders to dry, keeping it in place with a belt around her midriff.

Sometimes, she asked us, "How do you like my hairdo? Do you like my new coat?"

She usually set her hair in a long braid, rolled into a bun at the nape of her neck. Sometimes, she made it into two braids and wore one on either side of her head. They looked like Danish pastries.

One day, Mom put a sheet of white paper on the floor and drew a charcoal line down it. "I'll show you how to hypnotize a chicken."

She set a hen down facing the line. The hen stared at the line and didn't move.

"She thinks the black line is a snake," Mom explained.

Toward the end of my second school term, I prayed, *Dear God, please tell Teacher to give the award to someone else.*

That time Esther, the blonde class sweetheart, went up first. When my cousin Jens and I were called together, I thanked God fervently.

Esther received a framed picture of Christ in Gethsemane, while Jens and I received jackknives.

Jens came up with some crazy ideas at times. One day, be brought a spade and said, "Let's dig a tunnel to China. It's right under us." He pointed.

We started in a ditch south of the house, where deep, sandy loam was easy to dig. When Mom called me in for lunch, we were five feet down.

After lunch, I went fishing with two older boys, but a heavy rainstorm chased us home. As I entered the yard, Mom came from the ditch with two-year-old Karla, soaking wet, in her arms.

Mom worked in the kitchen during the storm, while Karla played in the living room. When the storm subsided, Mom noticed Karla was missing and went outside. She saw her wade into the ditch and disappear into our China tunnel.

Our family kept growing. When we were old enough to understand, Mom taught us table manners and how to behave away from home.

"Don't walk across other people's lawns and fields," she said. "Stay on roads and beaten pathways. Don't be nosy.

"Don't badmouth, spit on, or argue with playmates. Treat them as you'd like them to treat you. Don't poke fun or laugh at those who are physically or mentally handicapped. They can't help the way they are."

She also abhorred gossip. "Don't listen to gossipmongers. Shun them. If you convey their tales to others, you become a gossipmonger, too. If you can't find anything good to say about someone, remain silent.

"If you overhear a heated argument, don't try to speak up. Stay neutral. Listen, and you may learn something.

"Don't lend an ear to a slanderer. Be aware that you're listening to Satan.

"When you enter the work force, ignore it when someone badmouths you. They're showing their personality.

"Always behave so that you stand on your own merit. If blamed for wrongdoing, tell the truth. A lie can lead you into great trouble.

"Don't let it go to your head if you manage to climb the social ladder. Be yourself, the way you always were. You might be envied by your fellow workers, but stay away from anyone who belittles you.

"Whatever you do for a living, don't complain. Do your best. Stick to your job until opportunity comes to you.

"Don't shun dirty work. Go home at the end of the day, wash, and change clothes. There's no shame in dirt that can be removed with soap and water."

Every Monday, Mom baked bread for the week. Fall and winter, she carded wool, spun yarn and knit socks and mittens for her family. Afternoons, she filled the coal-oil lamps and cleaned their chimneys with torn pieces of newspaper.

Some evenings, she recited local folklore or fairytales from Grimm's or Asbjornsen and Moe, which she memorized during her school days.

In time, I became the hewer of wood, carrier of water, and Mom's trusted errand boy and confidant.

One of my most vivid memories of her character came from a summer afternoon when I was in my teens.

I was at the woodshed, chopping firewood, when I heard the porch door slam shut. Looking up, I saw Mom running southward. She cleared a barbed-wire fence and headed toward the neighbor's pond, two hundred yards away.

Once there, she ran down a plank pier and jumped into the water. Seeing that, I ran after her.

As I ran, I saw her surface and climb ashore with something in her arms and run toward me. When we met, I saw it was Torbjorn, my four-year-old brother, soaking wet but still alive.

I didn't know how she knew he'd fallen into the pond, though I later realized that we had no window facing that direction.

Mother brought into the world nine children, five sons and four daughters, and cared for all of us without complaint.

During the final eighteen months of World War Two, she was left alone to care for three school-aged boys, six to nine years old. They cherish her memory, like the rest of us do.

Mother died in February, 1980, in her eighty-seventh year. She went to her eternal rest under the first pure-white marble marker beside the church she loved.

The Roberts Collection
Grace E. Gimbel

"If you don't mind my saying so, you're making a grave mistake."

"Gladys, Dear, he's working out all right."

"Don't be too sure. It's not safe. You never should hire just anyone who rings your doorbell and wants a job."

"Yes, I know." Agnes Roberts sighed, her shoulder drooping. "Mack was always so careful about checking references and all that, but I need someone. This place requires a handyman. The grounds have to be kept up."

Roberts Knoll was an acre of land with a Colonial brick house. Azaleas bordered the front entrance, and rhododendrons lined the long driveway. In the rear was a rose garden, a delphinium bed, vegetables, and a raspberry patch.

"There's Elliot's Garden Service," Gladys suggested. "They do all the work for the estates on the hill." She had a reputation for giving advice. Running things for people had become her way of life.

At seventy-seven, Agnes had a mind of her own and felt perfectly capable of managing things her own way. It wasn't likely she'd follow someone else's suggestion. Saddened by the death of her husband the previous year, she felt determined to continue. She overcame the emotional strain of living alone by pursuing her many interests with renewed vigor.

"The garden service is awfully expensive," she explained. "We had them when Mack first took ill. They did a good job with the lawn, but the boy they sent to weed our flowerbed didn't know a dandelion from a chrysanthemum. We lost all our cushion mums."

"Didn't you complain?"

"How could we? He was such a nice young man, earning money for college. They might've deducted something from his paycheck."

Gladys shook her head. "Agnes, you're impossible. What about the one you have now? I saw him as I drove in, and I saw he has long hair tied back in a ponytail. A crew cut would be a lot more comfortable in the summer."

"It's just a fad created by some outrageous rock stars." Agnes brushed back a few wisps of gray hair from her warm, hazel eyes that dominated a pale, lined face.

The living room windows were open. Sitting together on the sofa, the two women heard the snap of the garden shears.

"I told Tony to cut the deadwood out from under the azaleas. They didn't bloom too well this spring."

"Nor did mine," Gladys added. "Do you expect he'll stay?"

"That's one thing I can't be sure of."

"Where's he from?"

"He said he's from the city and was sick of the noise and traffic. He wanted to get out where there was green grass and good air."

"So he drives out here and chooses your house, which can't be seen from the main road? Agnes, I don't like it. You're all alone up here. How can you be sure he isn't an escaped convict?"

"If there's an escaped convict about, I'm sure we would've heard about him."

"I hope you don't let him in the house."

"Oh, occasionally I do. The other day, he got some things out of the attic that I couldn't bring down myself. He's very handy. He put a new roof on the bird feeder. Today, he installed a new lock on the front door."

"My God, a new lock! You let him do that?"

"It works very well now. This morning, the key wouldn't turn. I would've been locked out if Tony hadn't been here. It obviously needed replacing, and he was more than willing to buy a new one and install it. You know how it is with old houses."

A flush of color rose in Gladys' cheeks. "I daresay he's got a key and can walk right in!'"

"You mustn't be so mistrustful. I needed someone, and I always believe the Lord will provide and care for me."

"You can't count on the Lord to be the police. With all these hoodlums running around, you must take precautions."

"So far, I haven't found anything wrong with Tony."

"Have it your way, but whatever you do, don't let him see your diamond collection. I read in the *Register* that you're allowing the jewels to be displayed at the International Gem Convention this weekend."

"Yes. I couldn't refuse. It made quite a hit at the exhibit for the Veteran's Fund at the Hilton. This time, it'll be at the Mountain Lake Hotel. That's nearby. Mack and I spent many summers there. The manager, Ralph Jennings, is a fine man and long-time friend."

Unable to resist, Gladys asked, "I really shouldn't ask, but have you ever considered selling the diamonds?"

"No. Sentimental reasons, I guess." She looked down at the protruding veins on her thin hands. "Although this morning, when I took them out of that dismal bank vault, it seemed a pity that they're locked away so much of the time. I want people to enjoy them. That's what they're for." She got up. "Come and look."

Gladys followed her friend into the dining room. In a silver box on the sideboard were twelve diminutive diamonds, each one exquisitely cut, sparkling brilliantly in the light.

Gladys gasped. "They're priceless! Such beauty is rare in this day and age." She pointed to an open window. "Don't let him see them, and don't let him in the house."

"You needn't worry. There's plenty for Tony to do outside. For the rest of today and tomorrow, I'll be right here, working with them. They have to be remounted, then off they go to the Mountain Lake Hotel."

The grandfather clock in the front hall chimed.

Gladys glanced at her watch. "I must be going. I'm picking up Horace. We're going to that new senior citizen village across the state line. It's lovely. We're considering putting in our names. At our age, it's reassuring to know we'll be taken care of. It would be great for you, too, Agnes."

She shook her head. "No. I've never liked such places. I like to believe I'm still capable and free. Pampering never agreed with me."

Laughing, they embraced. Gladys fumbled in her bag for the car keys and walked down the steps to the driveway.

"Remember, Agnes," she called, "be careful!"

Tony pulled out deadwood from under the bushes. Gladys saw only his back, soiled, torn T-shirt, grimy dungarees, and sneakers. He turned just enough to glimpse her, too, and spat, "So the overinflated balloon in the pink slacks doesn't approve? Too bad."

He overheard every word of their conversation. He couldn't have missed it if he tried.

Gladys didn't drive straight home. She saw Lucy Morgan watering her petunias as she drove by, so Gladys pulled over to the curb.

Ashley Morgan, Lucy's husband, was Warrington's chief of police. Gladys felt it would be wise to let him know what Agnes Roberts was letting herself in for. She was sure Ashley would cooperate. He'd known Mack a long time. Mack was responsible for Ashley's promotion.

That evening, Agnes was surprised to see Ashley at her door. She shook his hand. "Everyone has been so kind and considerate," she said. "To think you'd come personally to offer your help if I should need it. Mack always said you were a dedicated servant of our community."

Slightly embarrassed, Ashley accepted the compliment with a shy smile. A short man, the recent inactivity of deskwork added more unwanted pounds to his already-bulging figure.

At first, she demurred about having the door lock changed. "I wouldn't want to hurt Tony's feelings. He did a good job, and it works well now."

"Please realize he'll never have to know…assuming he's honest."

Reluctantly, she agreed. Ashley quickly replaced the lock and handed Agnes her new keys.

She didn't sleep well that night. She awakened and thought she'd heard someone at the door. She got up and looked out, but no one was there. Moments later, she heard a car engine start, but it was down the road.

Returning to bed, sleep came fitfully. Had she only imagined the doorknob turning?

She was up at dawn, and Tony arrived at nine o'clock in his battered '68 Volkswagen. She sent him to Harvey's Hardware to pick up stakes for her tomato plants.

She worked diligently all morning and afternoon, securing safety clamps to the black velvet background in the diamond box. Each diamond was fastened in place with fastidious care.

Her task completed, she checked each piece, opened the silver box, and placed the gems inside. Suddenly, she noticed how dark it was. Thunder rumbled. It had been a hot, sticky day. If a storm came, it would clear the air.

She realized the clock had chimed five sometime in the past. Was Tony still outside? He usually knocked at the back door before he left at five.

She went into the kitchen and saw him outside, his hands on his hips, staring at the house. Thunder boomed again, so she knew a storm was coming.

"My raspberries!" she gasped. "They'll be ruined if it pours!"

Picking up a basket, she hurried to the garden. "Tony, I need your help. We have to get the berries before it rains."

What's wrong with him? she wondered. *He doesn't seem to hear.*

"Tony, come along!"

He followed her past the rose garden, the delphinium bed, and the rows of vegetables. She didn't even stop to see how he'd staked the tomato plants.

They walked to the high fence where the raspberry bushes were intertwined with each other, their branches loaded with lush berries.

"Oh, Dear," Agnes said. "I should've brought two baskets. Tony, run back for another basket. You'll find one in the pantry. Hurry!"

He ran off. He'd been waiting all day. It would've been easy the previous night if his key fit into the new lock. He thought plugging the old lock with a tiny piece of chewing gum was a clever idea, because it stopped Agnes' key from turning.

It seemed she was clever, too. All along, he thought she trusted him. He rather liked the old lady, even though he would've preferred someone more fussy and forgetful. Under those circumstances, one little diamond wouldn't be missed.

He moved swiftly across the lawn and up the back steps, letting the screen door bang as he raced into the kitchen, through the pantry, and into the dining room. Seeing the silver box on the sideboard, he caught his breath. Lifting the lid with shaking hands, he thought she wouldn't miss just one.

They were securely mounted. When he tried to pry one loose, it wouldn't come out, so he tried again.

With another loud clap of thunder, rain poured down. Agnes would return in a moment. He told himself to work fast. He couldn't afford to fail. He made a promise, and his time was almost up.

Closing the lid, he tucked the box under his shirt and ran from the house to his Volkswagen. It took several attempts to start the engine before he could speed down the driveway and onto the main road.

At the blinking light, the realization of what he'd just done sank in, and he began to panic. Rain splashed ribbons of water on the windshield, slowing his pace. Hail pounded against the roof, playing an obbligato to the beat of his thumping heart. Beads of perspiration dripped from his forehead. His promise to the woman he loved had turned him into a thief.

Dolores would be waiting. She'd have a diamond ring, and they could marry. Then his dream vanished.

He was suddenly wide awake and in serious trouble. He didn't want all those stones. He'd gambled for just one that he could return once he earned enough to replace it.

Dolores worked at the Hilton and saw the Veteran's Fund exhibit. She talked about it with Tony, showing him the brochure that described the jewels. He knew she wanted a diamond, and he promised she'd have one before the summer ended.

Since then, every step led him closer to disaster. Demanding a raise cost him his job. Playing the racetrack and lottery depleted his savings. His pockets were empty. Only the brochure remained. He looked it over carefully and read the note at the bottom, *The Roberts Collection. Twelve miniature diamonds, loaned by Mrs. Agnes Roberts, Roberts Knoll, Warrington, New York.*

Dolores told him that Mrs. Roberts had been at the hotel and seemed like a kind, elderly widow. Tony realized that such women were easy targets, and Warrington wasn't that far away. Telling her he had a temporary job, he kissed Dolores and drove off in her car. She didn't mind, because she could use the subway.

Agnes hurried inside from the storm and set her basket on the kitchen table. Disappointed by its meager contents, she went into the dining room and stopped short.

"My diamonds! They're gone!"

Hearing the sputtering start of a car racing down her driveway left no time for hesitation. She reached for the phone and called the number Ashley gave her.

"Please, Ashley," she begged. "Please do it for Mack's sake."

She hung up and placed another call.

Was he imagining the sound of sirens? No. In the rearview mirror, red lights flashed. The sweat on his face felt like melting ice, and he trembled.

They were coming closer. If he swerved into the giant oaks bordering the road, he'd die. Instead, he had to slam on his brakes as the police cruiser pulled alongside, then in front of his path. Within seconds, two officers approached Tony's car.

The sergeant opened the door and immediately saw the silver box. "Let's see your license."

Ashley Morgan stood nearby, his yellow rain slicker protecting his massive figure.

Tony gulped. When he opened his wallet, the photo of Dolores smiled at him.

"Your erratic driving is doubly dangerous." Ashley warned, "when you're carrying someone else's valuables."

"Take it." Tony pointed at the box.

"Lost your nerve?"

Why hadn't they arrested him? It was torture to have them staring at the proof of his guilt.

"You'll follow the police car," Ashley said. "I'll ride with you. From now on, be careful. You were close to violating the speed limit."

The sergeant handed Tony his license, and the two officers nodded at each other. Ashley squeezed into the front seat beside Tony.

What are they doing? he wondered, following the police cruiser down the road. *The station is two miles behind me in the opposite direction. They can't put me in jail. Not yet, anyway. They won't believe me, but they have to give me a chance to explain.*

They drove past farmhouses and apple orchards. The rain diminished, leaving the road slick and shiny. At a turn, they started up a steep incline until a large, rustic sign came into view, *Mountain Lake Hotel.*

The man at the gate waved them through, and they drove to the main entrance. A tall, gray-haired gentleman on the porch walked down the steps to greet them.

"I've been waiting for you," Ralph Jennings said.

They followed him into the hotel and his office. Tony carried the silver box. Jennings accepted it and placed it on his desk. Lifting the lid, he counted all twelve diamonds.

"Gorgeous," he said. "Each of these is priceless. Thank you for their safe delivery."

Anxious to leave, Ashley said, "Mountain Lake is outside our jurisdiction, so we have to return to Warrington as soon as possible."

The officers shook Jennings hand and left. Once they were gone, Jennings motioned Tony to sit down.

"It was thoughtful of Mrs. Roberts to phone and say you were coming with this valuable collection," he began.

Suddenly dizzy, Tony clutched the arms of the chair and wondered if his presence at the plush hotel was a hallucination. Maybe he'd struck those oak trees after all and was suffering from delirium.

Jennings handed him a piece of paper. "A check from Mrs. Roberts."

As he stood, Tony felt his legs shaking.

"It includes an extra week's pay. You left in such a hurry, she didn't have the chance to explain she won't be needing you anymore. She's closing her house and coming here for the rest of the summer."

Relief, remorse, and gratitude filled Tony. The previous hour had changed his life. Dolores would understand. They'd get married, and he would work until he could buy her a diamond of her choice.

He would continue working, too. Someday, they'd have a house in the country with a rose garden, delphinium bed, a row of vegetables, and maybe a raspberry patch.

Len Gaskell was born in Los Angeles, CA, but grew up in the San Francisco Bay Area. He currently resides in Novato, CA. He avidly enjoys Science Fiction stories and is currently working on an anthology of short stories about life in Marin County.

The anthology will be comprised of stories that have been submitted to the Marin County Fair and he has received ribbons for his works. He is a member of the Marin Rod & Gun Club, loves to fish, do volunteer work for the club, and hates to lose chess games.

The Jogger
Len Gaskell

He was running again.

The fall wasn't too bad that time. Billy quickly picked himself up off the ground, brushed reddish film off his arms, and tried to shake and rub the red dust from his hair, noticing that all around him, the glare in the sky was red, too.

Booming noises sounded in the distance. *More thunder,* he thought.

The light cast a fiery hue onto the gray buildings, making the world look dark and sinister. Windows twinkled as wind and light made them shudder in and out like a small puppy's sporadic breathing. Even the air smelled scorched.

He grimaced. It was like the odor of burning rubber and the smell of a roof being tarred simultaneously.

God, I've got to start running.

Just as he headed toward the next town a quarter mile away, he was violently bumped to the ground again, that time from the side.

Goddamn Crazy Horse, he thought.

He knew it was Crazy Horse. He saw a tall, skinny Indian whose thick, black hair hung long and straight, tied into braids held together at the ends by strands of bright-yellow ribbon.

"Don't you ever watch where you're going?" Billy snapped, picking himself up and repeating the brushing effort without much effect.

"Did you see him?" Crazy Horse asked in a wild, scratchy voice tinged with desperation. "Did you see Golden Hair?" He jumped up and down in place.

"No. I didn't see him, nor have I ever seen him. Don't you ever watch where you're going?"

Crazy Horse turned without apologizing and raced toward the next town, leaving Billy alone and irritated.

As the Indian departed, Billy saw red dust kick up around him. Then he saw his jogging shoes had the same reddish tinge that Crazy Horse's shoes had. It was from the rocks and dirt, probably created from the volcano that erupted two or three days earlier.

How was it that every time Crazy Horse knocked him down or ran into him, it was from behind? Each time they separated, he ran ahead of Billy.

Damn that Indian and his clumsiness, Billy thought.

He jogged toward the next town, but not before noticing that his shoelaces were loose. He looked around quickly to see if any other runners were bumbling around.

Ahead lay a broken tree, its pieces at the bottom of the winding path that led toward the town. It seemed best to jog there to secure his laces. That would be perfect, because from there, he could see ahead and behind, and nothing could surprise him, not even that goddamn Crazy Horse.

Jogging down the path was easy, but, as he did, he heard a rumble like a slow-moving tractor.

Damn it! He knew that sound meant a centipede was coming.

Hurrying to the log, he quickly retied his flailing laces, barely in time. At the top of the hill behind him appeared a group of twenty runners racing toward him. He had to stay ahead of them until he reached the town. Otherwise, he'd end up an unwilling straggler in their group.

They ran like a single unit, though they often traded places within the group without any apparent order, bouncing off each other like bingo balls. It was a wonder that no one fell. Despite their chaotic order, they looked like a single runner.

Frickin' centipedes, he thought.

He was a loner and didn't want to be assimilated into their crowd. He took off at a faster-than-normal pace and headed uphill toward the town.

Once inside the city limits, he felt more secure with the confines of the buildings and the presence of traffic lights. He liked the stop-and-go lights the best. They afforded him the time to look around and plan his strategy, adjust his jogging suit, or retie his shoes.

The town still glowed red from the volcano's eruption. Like all towns, it had an entrance, the necessary stores, and an exit.

He looked for a sporting goods store, because he needed new running gear. While tying his laces, he noticed a tear forming on the side of his right shoe. The tear would quickly develop into a flopping hazard. He didn't want to fall again, especially from inattention to his equipment. That would be unforgivable.

He saw clothing stores, hardware stores. supermarkets, and finally, up ahead, the building he wanted, which had two floors dedicated to sporting goods equipment and clothing. While at a stoplight, he nervously waited for the light to change. The centipede would be entering town by then, and, if they needed shoes, Billy would have to wait until the next town before he dared stop to replace his own. That wasn't a good idea.

The light turned green, and Billy, along with a few joggers who ignored each other, started off slowly. Dashing across the street made no sense. Time wasn't important, though Billy wanted to reach the store first.

He ran inside. Fortunately, only one other person wanted new shoes. Silently, he and Billy ran down the aisles, looking for their sizes. They never looked at each other.

Billy saw the other was truly a runner. His upper body was solid, slightly muscular, while his legs were long and firm. Billy didn't look at his face. They wouldn't be traveling together for long.

They strolled through the aisles, giving each other plenty of room while searching for running shoes. Style and color were meaningless, because no one cared. The fabric and sturdiness, however, were highly important.

Billy found the right size. The fact that the shoes were high cut and relatively modern was an added bonus.

Good, solid running shoes, he thought.

He pulled them from the box, making sure there were laces, and walked toward the door. He'd spent too long in that town, but he was happy to know that he'd face at least five stoplights where he could change shoes before he left town.

As he left, he saw the centipede dash into the store and heard the crash of display stands and the crunch of cardboard boxes. If he'd been a little slower, he would've been caught in that chaotic shopping frenzy.

Two blocks later, he donned his new right shoe and bank-shot his old one into a trash receptacle.

He joined another group of runners. Together, they raced by the town square into a small park. Squirrels and rabbits fled into the bushes as the group of eight approached. Their jogging noises sent all animals for cover.

Just before entering the bushes, the animals stopped, turned, and watched the runners, necks craning up and around. Then they swiftly disappeared into the safety of the shrubbery.

Two blocks later, still in the group, Billy pulled on and laced the other shoe.

These feel good, he thought.

Overhead, the reddish sky darkened, and he thought he heard thunder. *Jeez, another storm.* That meant he'd have wet, cold clothes soon.

Although the town was small, he felt at least four hours had passed since he saw Crazy Horse. The time was relatively peaceful, because he didn't have a run-in with any centipedes, nor did he meet anyone else like Crazy Horse.

The town's border ended with a series of traffic lights, and Billy found himself in the predicament of selecting one of three pathways leading to his next destination. Taking the middle lane, he found he was alone, which was nice. That would enable him to think about the past and work out a plan.

His solitude was short-lived when he heard footsteps pounding behind him.

He was able to get out of Crazy Horse's way as the Indian stumbled from a group of trees, his elbows swinging, his long hair swaying.

"Did he come past here?" Crazy Horse asked, gesturing madly.

"No one came by me. How many times do I have to tell you I haven't seen him? He doesn't exist." *Why do I keep saying that? What good does it do?*

"I'll scalp that blue-coated bastard. I'll scalp him with this knife, then I'll cut out his eyes so he won't escape me again. He'll be mine to torture." He stopped and showed Billy his knife. "I'll be the master!"

It was a very long knife, like a Bowie knife he'd seen in movies. *Where the hell did he get that?* Billy wondered.

To emphasize his sincerity, Crazy Horse made carving motions in the air, making Billy step back fearfully.

"Get away from me, you crazy Indian! I don't know who Golden Hair is, and I don't want to know. Just leave me alone."

"If I catch that bastard…" He ran off. Long after he was out of sight, his chanting carried to Billy.

I'd better watch myself with that one. That was the first time Billy thought Crazy Horse might be dangerous.

Running a little slower than usual, so he wouldn't accidentally catch up to Crazy Horse, Billy daydreamed until he reached a large lake. A path led around it, where Billy saw a group of runners, perhaps another centipede, slowly overtaking a lone jogger. He hoped it was Crazy Horse.

Billy watched almost giddily as the group engulfed the jogger and kept moving forward. The runner went down.

God, I hope it's Crazy Horse.

Much to his disappointment, he saw it was a female. He soon reached the luckless runner, who lay on her back, then slowly sat up on one knee to retie her shoe.

"Bastards," she said. "Knocked me down and didn't even have the courtesy to help me up. Jesus!"

She almost sang her words.

When she stood, Billy saw she was slender without being thin, taller than he without being too tall, and had long, golden hair.

Golden Hair? he wondered.

"Are you OK?"

"OK? What's OK?"

She brushed her short, white shorts and inspected her knees and elbows.

"If you mean this bruised arm and cut on my ankle, yeah, I'm OK. I hurt like hell, but I'm OK."

"Sorry. I was just concerned."

Calming down, she looked at him. Her expression softened, then transformed into that of a gentle, young, college woman.

"Me, too. I'm sorry for snapping. It's just that those freaks must've seen me. They didn't have to bowl me over. Who are they?"

"Those guys? Just another group of runners. They show up at times." He looked at her body. "Usually when you don't expect 'em."

"Well, they're mighty rude."

"You get used to them. There are worse creeps running around here."

She turned toward the distant hill, then she and Billy jogged up the path. Overhead, clouds formed. If it hadn't been for the constant sunset, the land would've been very dark instead of just red. As a wind came up behind them, they increased their pace.

"Just where is here?" she asked.

"Where is here? Why, here is here. Now is now." He hoped he didn't have to explain further. He didn't want to be the one to tell her.

"My name's Billy. Who are you?" he asked, hoping to change the subject.

"You can call me Natalie."

They reached the hilltop. Not far ahead was another town. Before the town were several roads, all occupied by joggers, some in groups, others alone.

"All joggers lead to Rome," she said, chuckling. "Get it? That's a joke."

He smiled, trying to be friendly. He hoped she wasn't one of those babbling broads. A little maturity and sanity would be welcome.

They descended into one of many valleys that preceded the town. For the most part, they were alone, but an occasional runner passed them, or they, in turn, passed a runner or two.

"It would be nice if we could reach the town by nightfall," Billy said.

He didn't like being on the open road at night, though it wasn't any less dangerous than a town. It was just how it felt.

"Is there a place to rest, maybe get something to eat?" Natalie asked.

He saw she was very new, probably on her first race. He tried to remember how many races he'd been in but had long since lost count. He used to keep track of how many times Crazy Horse dumped him, but that got old, too.

How many races has it been? he wondered.

"Yeah," he said. "We'll find a place soon."

It was easier to agree. He remembered the last time he tried to explain it to someone. Their conversation kept going in circles, skirting the real answer. After a while, most people stopped talking about it.

"Let's see if we can enter the town over there." Billy pointed to a path that led into the city through a business district.

Most of the buildings were tall and gray. Smoke poured from a few windows, as if the buildings had been on fire and were still smoldering. That kept most runners from wanting to explore, or so Billy thought. It also stopped the newer runners.

At times, he once toured buildings like that and found that as long as he ran up and down the floors, time passed, and he could stay in the city until daylight. That suited him.

"Are we stopping anywhere?" she asked.

He saw by her expression that she was slowly realizing she was in an extraordinary situation.

She'll understand where she is soon, he thought. *Usually, they turn inward when that happens.*

Instead of aiming for the heart of town, Billy entered a building and found the stairwell. He was pleased when Natalie followed.

After the thirtieth floor, Billy stopped counting. Natalie was puffing hard, but she had a determined look and managed to keep up. He wasn't hurrying, though he maintained a steady pace.

They rose higher and higher inside the building. He didn't know what kind of building it was. Perhaps it was an office building. What kind of business was being run there?

Questions passed through his mind, but he didn't really care. All he wanted was to reach the top.

The end of their ascent was near, because the pattern in the stairwell changed, and they found themselves facing the final set of stairs, which led to a door that had a sign that read *Exit.*

Pushing through the door, they found themselves on a roof.

"Now what?" Natalie asked.

Billy, shrugging, walked to the edge to look down. It was a tall building, and below were streets lined with runners. Looking carefully, he saw more runners on streets that intersected many other streets. Processions led in and out of town.

Beyond them, he saw the edge of town, covered by bushes, trees, and greenery. Beyond those were dark mountains, and beyond that was a sky on fire.

"My," Natalie said in awe, standing so close to Billy their shoulders touched. That startled him, and he instantly feared being pushed off the edge.

"We'd better head down." He turned toward the door.

"Wait. Can't we stay a bit longer and look? It's so, wow, awesome."

She moved toward the door with him. As he opened the door, he gasped at the towering figure of Crazy Horse running past, making Billy stumble.

Crazy Horse grabbed Natalie by the waist and dragged her toward the edge. "Is this your woman?" he asked menacingly, the Bowie knife in his hand.

"Don't hurt her," Billy said. "She's new."

"I asked if this is your woman." Crazy Horse reached the edge of the roof.

"Yeah, so what? She's my woman." He wasn't sure why he said it.

"You have good taste, Wild Bill." Crazy Horse released her.

Natalie rushed to Billy, grasping his arm. "Who the hell is that?"

"Have you seen Golden Hair?" Crazy Horse asked them.

"No, we haven't," Billy said, standing between the Indian and Natalie.

"Who is Golden Hair?" she asked. "Who is this?" She pointed at Crazy Horse while cowering behind Billy.

Crazy Horse looked at the horizon. "I've been tracking Golden Hair for I don't know how long. I have seen traces of him. The general left many signs, but never can I catch him." He lowered his Bowie knife and slowly stepped to the edge of the building. His expression and mood sank with the ever-dimming sun.

"I tire of this chase," he said. "I fear I will never catch him. His shadow is all I can grasp. He is a ghost. I'm so tired." He swam dove from the ledge, pirouetting down toward the street like a broken kite.

Natalie, screaming, moved toward the ledge, but Billy held her before she could follow the Indian.

"We should get going," Billy said.

"What about him?" she asked, her hand over her mouth, tears forming in her eyes.

Billy steered her toward the door. Soon, they retraced their steps downward. The endless stairwell made them dizzy, but it was easier than climbing the stairs. They reached the street, and Billy opened the door. Together, they ran toward the edge of town.

Overhead, clouds angled in, darkening the sky. Loud, thunderous noises sounded, and the ever-ominous specter of rain grew. They continued running.

"Where are we going?" Natalie asked.

She had tied her hair in a ponytail, reminding Billy of a reckless girl he had once known.

"We have to reach the next town before it gets darker." He always told newcomers that to give their running a sense of purpose.

"But I'm tired," she whined. "I think I'm hungry."

Billy knew she was grasping at fading feelings. "Just a little farther."

They jogged in tandem awhile. The road narrowed. On both sides, bushes and trees formed a shrub tunnel. Wind whooshed through the leaves, making Billy and Natalie speed up.

Occasionally, they bypassed a centipede or lone, speeding runner, who they ignored and who ignored them. Even though the road was tight, they were able to pass the others without bumping into anyone. They concentrated on running.

After a series of turns, the road became wider, and Natalie ran alongside Billy. Through splinters of light coming through the trees, he saw tears falling from her face like streaming drops of rain. Slowly, she began to realize it was more than a race.

"I was born in Dixie, Maine," she said. "I went to Robinson High, then graduated from Texas State. I worked for twelve years as a legal secretary. I think I married." She spoke as if reciting from a book.

A blank look came to her face, and Billy realized she'd come to the end of her memories.

"What happened then?" she asked. "I can't seem to recall the rest of my life."

"Don't worry about it," he replied. "It doesn't matter anymore."

"Am I dead?"

Up ahead, they saw a town. Light from the lampposts cast an eerie glow on the streets, which were empty save for the runners who were visible occasionally when the pedestrian lights turned green. Like stiffened, stick figures, they darted in various directions.

"Am I dead?" she repeated.

"No. You aren't dead. You're here, aren't you?"

"Where is here? Is this hell? Am I in hell?"

"Does it look like hell? See any demons? Are people thrashing about in flames?" He stopped and held her shoulders. "You're alive, and you're with me. That's what counts. Hold onto that thought, and maybe you'll get through this." His words ended in a weak whisper.

Ahead, a single jogger moved at a slow pace. When Billy saw him glancing backward frequently, he knew what it meant. A minute later, another lone jogger came up behind the first. He carried a baton, which he swung to and fro. As he reached his partner, he passed the baton flawlessly, and the even-paced jogger took off at a faster gait.

The jogger who carried nothing continued running but went straight for a precipice and disappeared over the side. Natalie's breathing stuttered, but she didn't speak. Her face was expressionless.

Good, Billy thought. *She's coming around.*

They started running again. As they approached the city, they moved toward a street that wasn't as congested with other runners. Billy saw Natalie still wasn't convinced. Her teary expression had been replaced by a frown. She'd reached the second plateau of realization. Next would come anger, though that wouldn't be for a while.

He liked her. She didn't whine, and she had strength. He was tired of carrying people. Natalie was a refreshing comfort. He liked her looks, too. Neither fat nor skinny, she ran like an athlete.

At the next stoplight, he took her hand and looked into her eyes. The warmth that flowed between them was comforting. He was in love again.

"I don't believe a word you're saying," she said. "I'm dead. We're dead. Everybody around us is dead."

"Oh, yeah? Do dead people feel this?" He pinched her neck.

"Ow!" She punched his arm. "That was mean." She smiled at his familiarity. "If we're not dead, we must be dreaming, right? That's it." She smiled. "This is all a dream. I'll wake up soon and be back in Dixie. Yeah. That's where I'm from…Dixie. I had a kid!" Her face brightened at that.

Another stepping stone in reality, he thought. *She's tough. She'll rationalize this to the end.*

That was OK. She was stronger than most women, who usually gave up. *The dream wish,* he thought. *That's a good sign.*

The town was like the others. Taller buildings were located in the center. As the buildings became shorter, the streets grew longer, then they reached the end of the city. Fortunately, both wore newer shoes, so they didn't need to find replacements. As far as running up thirty flights of stairs, Billy assumed they might as well head into the open road.

Thunderous noises, not from the sky, erupted just ahead and out of sight. It sounded as if two cars had collided.

That can't be, Billy thought. *I have to see this.*

Racing to the next block, they peered around it to see what made the noise. Except for joggers, the streets were empty. No cars were visible. More booming noises came from just out of sight, leaving Billy and Natalie feeling frustrated and curious.

What was making those sounds?

Just before they neared the end of the city, a gigantic rigging machine appeared, similar to the ones used to drill for oil in Texas. It moved up and down with a low thumping sound. Occasionally, the loud crunching of metal beating metal came, like two cars meeting head-on.

Runners were all around the machine. Some became trapped in it, disappearing into the mechanism of wheels and hammers. Some skirted the machinery and were left free to dart toward other roads.

"Nothing to see here," Billy said. "Let's move on." He shuddered.

Trotting beyond the city limits, they found the road rising gradually, winding up and around a corner of rock, then down into a gully that would eventually lead to the bottom of a huge mountain. As far as they could see, the road wound up the mountain in endless curves. It would be a long, steady climb, though not impossible.

They were able to run side by side, which pleased Billy. He was able to look at her when they talked.

Up they ran. Overhead, the dim sky turned darker red with streaks of black clouds whizzing by without a sound, adding to the dismal, gloomy atmosphere.

"Where are we going?" she asked.

He didn't answer, because he knew that she knew the answer. She just wanted to hear the sound of her own voice in that quiet, dormant place.

They raced up and around the mountain for a long time. Abruptly, they reached a plateau and couldn't go any higher.

The road ventured near the edge. Ahead was a spiral pathway that led down again.

Although the air was quiet except for the wind, Billy didn't hear the sound of the centipede that caught up to them. He barely had time to grab Natalie to him to prevent her from being pushed into the abyss below.

He didn't have time to save himself, although he heard a war whoop and felt the Indian's unmistakable bump. He never saw him.

Damn him, Billy thought, feeling himself tripping closer and closer to the edge. Natalie reached for him, their fingers touching lightly, but it was too late.

Billy went over the side and plunged down. *One-one thousand, two-one thousand, three-one thousand,* he counted.

Up above, two round, featureless faces watched him fall. Soon, he lost count and concentrated on the mountain rushing past. *Boy, this is going to hurt,* he mused.

The fall continued until he sensed the ground coming up to meet him. As he fell, he felt time slow down. Images of Crazy Horse, the centipedes, and Natalie went through his mind as the mountainside whizzed past.

Damn that crazy Indian, he thought. *Soon. I'll reach bottom soon.* Clenching his fists, he shut his eyes.

As he did, he felt the wind knocked out of him as his back and shoulders hit the ground with a jarring thud. A puff of gray dust rose around him as he lay stunned.

Looking at his feet, he saw he'd landed on a bed of ashen dirt. No hint of green showed nearby. All was gray. Slowly, he rolled over to his side. Pushing from his elbow and forearm, he got to his knees.

A centipede rushed by, almost kicking him. None of them looked at him, their glassy eyes intent on each other as they ran, bouncing off each other. None of them offered to help him.

He stood and brushed gray ash from his jersey. It was torn, which meant he'd have to replace it in the next town. Where had the ash come from? Probably the volcano that had erupted, but when? Two or three days ago?

Looking up, he saw two stick figures at the top of the mountain. One had blonde hair. Light reflected off something the other figure waved in the air. *The Bowie knife?* he wondered.

Then there was one stick figure, then none.

Overhead, the sky turned even darker. He heard thunder in the distance, and the sky glowed intermittently with splinters of lightning. That meant the possibility of rain, which meant wet clothes.

He heard the dull pounding of the distant oilrig, while steam hissed from a nearby river of hot, churning rock.

Shaking his fist at the imaginary being overhead, he shouted, "Damn it! Damn it all! Damn *you* all!"

He was running again.

Some Are Runners, Some Are Eaters

Robert A. Finan

"Boys, we're in the big leagues now. We're knockin' off Santos Restaurant in ten days. It'll be like the old days. if Capone did it, we can do it better."

The tall man heading the oval table smiled triumphantly at his eight listeners. The room rocked with applause as he banged the table for silence.

Frank Ricci, clean-shaven, dapper in a sharkskin suit, strutted around the table, staring at each man as he barked out orders. "We need teamwork, and we need image. Bongi, Ferrotti, ditch that burlap you're wearin' and steal some new threads. Sixty bucks won't kill ya. Nick, Tony, buy a razor. Creep, baby, who's your barber? Jack the Ripper?"

Muffled sounds of laughter and clapping ceased as Frank called for order. If the hoods had any intention of recapturing the old days of mob rule, bootleg booze, and bob-tailed babes, they'd already struck out. There were no tailor-made suits or paneled walls there. They had a big table, hanging lights, and Mafia types with their talking hands, puffing smelly cigars over stained stacks of papers, but there the similarity ended.

The eight haggard faces showed too much stubble and not enough scowl. The table had nicks where there should've been finish, and the floor was bare cement. A few carnations drooped from sixty-dollar suits that sagged off the bodies of scrawny, small-change crooks who still shook from the third-shelf booze they'd been drinking.

"When do we case the joint?" one man shouted.

"When Big Joe says so," Frank snapped.

"Boss…when do we…we…?"

"Spit it out, Creep."

"Do we git real…real guns soon?" Grinning sheepishly, he tossed pistachio shells on the floor.

"We won't need 'em, Nitwit." Frank glared at the confused man.

"Hitting a joint like Santos ain't easy. Restaurants aren't candy stores. Each of you will be assigned a top-notch restaurant to hit. Make Big Joe happy, and you'll soon have all the chicks, bread, and booze you can handle!"

The room exploded in a torrent of whistles and applause as the mob members raised their glasses in a toast to their next heist.

That the comical caucus convened in a cluttered, crack-walled apartment only fifty miles west of the plush suites where Capone and Nitti once reigned made the scene less than credible. It *was* near Chicago, and if that was good enough to recall the Roaring Twenties and Thirties, then the mob was off to a rousing, if dubious, beginning.

Three days later, two detectives hassled over a phone call.

"He said they're hitting Santos Restaurant soon," Sergeant Carns said, turning to the man at the computer.

"You believe it?" Lieutenant Connors asked.

"The caller's a buddy of Ricci's."

"So what? He's probably a stoolie and a damn liar. I'd like a buck for every fink who calls us."

The Detective Bureau was furnished in typical police decor…early Disorder, with olive-drab file cases and antiquated desks littered with butts, cigars, and paper cups in a puzzling ratio to the number of trays available. Teetering stacks of paper towered over the desks that were jammed together, while the phones rang constantly.

Fred Carns wheeled his chair closer to Lieutenant Connors. "Jack, Ricci was a buddy of Frankie Santos, the owner, but they had a falling out. The tipster said that Ricci hand-picked some mugs for a move on the restaurant, and…"

"They're hand-picked? They're about as handpicked as Charlie Manson leading winos into combat. Carns, I know Frank Ricci. Al Capone was his hero, but Capone ran a million-dollar operation, with whores, gambling, booze, and paid-off cops. Frank Ricci couldn't finance a Girl Scout picnic. How much can ya get from parking meters and candy stores?"

An articulate redhead of thirty-five, Fred Carns waved his hands in frustration. "Can't we talk to the owner? He might…"

"Talk about what? Forget that call from some two-bit crook. Try chasing rainbows, Fred. It's a hell of a lot easier."

Wednesday morning, a black limousine purred to a stop in front of Ricci's apartment. Four well-built men carrying briefcases and small white boxes entered the room.

Inside, Big Joe Nimmo, middle-aged and portly, stood rigidly at the long table's head while two of his men placed tiny boxes on the table. He spoke softly, but his dark, piercing eyes commanded attention.

"Gentlemen, I know your names, background, and assignments. Let's get down to business. How 'bout some numbers?"

The eight men nervously shuffled smudged papers and tattered briefcases. In front of each man was a pint-sized bottle of low-grade booze and a four-inch glass.

"Giovanni. Parking meters?"

"Yeah. We raked in a hundred and a half."

Big Joe stared at him. "We're down six percent, Sammy."

"But, well, they double-park more."

"Sure. Rifle through some YMCA lockers this month. Got that? Caminati? Paper boys?"

"Twenty-three bucks, five punchers, three changers, some candy, and five packs of butts."

"That's all, Francis? Can't you handle kids?"

"Dere bigger these days, Boss. They take judo. I got the marks ta prove it."

Joe grinned as the others laughed. "I doubt you could take on an Avon lady. Trivisonno, how are the church collections?"

"Two hunnert and ten beans, Boss."

"Thata boy, Triv. Must be a lotta rich parishes out there. Luciano," Joe said in a hoarse voice. "How'd you do with the drunks?"

"I rolled twenty-eight this month, Sir. Two hundred sixty bucks, fifteen bus tickets, twelve packs of smokes, eighteen keys, four six packs, five watches, and nine packs of rubbers."

"Not bad." Joe smiled. "Try to get 'em on payday."

"Their wives meet 'em, Boss."

"Well, jump the... Never mind. That won't work, either."

The group whistled loudly.

"Let's wrap this up. Creep, how'd the football tickets go?"

Creep lazily shuffled papers, his red, nut-stained hands cracking shells as he worked. "Sixty-five bucks, Boss. Da cops raided us once, and..."

Big Joe's fist slammed against the table as he spewed obscenities. "Screwball, did they get the press?"

"No, Boss. W...we moved it," he stammered, cracking another nut and licking his lips. His full name was Charles Castalanni, but he went by Creep. A short, small-framed man with a mop of curly brown hair nearly covering his eyes, he spoke in a shrill voice. His smile revealed brown-stained teeth.

"Maybe you'd be better off purse snatching, don't you think?"

Another smattering of guffaws erupted. Joe Nimmo responded with a drumbeat of table-rattling salvos. Finally, after a ten-minute recess, he opened two small boxes and dumped two one-inch cockroaches into a bowl.

"Gentlemen," he said, beaming, "we'll knock off Santos and the other restaurants with this."

The men reacted at if they'd been shot.

"Roaches? C'mon. Where's the money in dat?" one man asked.

"I see enough bugs in my own place," Creep whined, cracking one nut in his hands and another between his teeth.

"I'd rather jump Avon ladies," another said.

"Ease up, Boys," Joe pleaded. "These pests, properly placed, will make us tons of bread."

The murmurs continued for twenty minutes while the mob leader answered questions. Joe removed his blue suede jacket, loosened his tie, and explained his plan. His band of bunglers was unimpressed, twirling cheap cigars in their mouths as they pacified themselves with the last bottles of bad booze.

"Joe," Frank said, "you said this was a big-time operation, not crap like this."

"This *is* big time. We've assigned eighty guys in forty cities to plant these bugs in high-class restaurants. When they're released, the men will yell, groan, and fake being sick to get attention. Then they'll sue the restaurant. Other diners will probably join the lawsuit. Lawyers call those things a class-action suit. There'll be millions up for grabs, but we'll benefit the most. Questions?"

Two loud bangs came from the back of the room. All the crooks hit the floor, some drawing guns.

"Tony, Nick, Gino," Joe shouted, "kill the lights. Sammy, guard the door, Frank, Bongi, check the windows."

"Mr. Nimmo?" Creep asked in a squeaky voice. "It's me...Boss. I...I stomped real hard on a bag of nuts, and..."

"What? You stupid idiot! You did what?"

The lights came on, and Joe's burning eyes glared at Creep. "Ricci, educate this moron, or everything we're workin' for will be horse manure."

The accused apologized, his bony body shaking as if he'd stepped on a live electrical wire. The group giggled, then stopped when Joe called for quiet.

"Tomorrow, we test run these babies with time trials," Joe said. "Be at Sam Sporino's house at seven in his downstairs den. Lay off the chicks and the booze for awhile. Pay attention to details. Payday's comin'!"

A crescendo of cheers and whistles signaled the group's change in attitude. Wows had replaced growls. ...except for Frank Ricci. Would Al Capone, gangland's most notorious figure in the thirties, have used cockroaches in a heist? Would he have tolerated a brain-dead mug like Creep? The dilemma clouded his mind. It wasn't something he could learn from a Mafia handbook.

The scene at Sporino's on Thursday night was like an episode from the *Twilight Zone*. A circular, thirty-foot track of eight-inch rubber tubing cut in half lengthwise was securely nailed to the floor. Two trembling men sat at opposite ends of the track with stopwatches, while another man sliced sugar cubes and placed cheese bits and potato chips around the oval. In the far corner, other hoods huddled secretively, structuring odds and taking wagers on the tiny entries.

All that was missing was a tote board, starting gate, some jockeys, and a track announcer. There was one constant...like most racetrack regulars, those misled mugs belonged to the ever-growing membership of Losers Anonymous.

"We record the time for each bug," Joe explained. "The fastest roaches will patrol the restaurant bars. The slower ones roam the tables. We've spilled potato chips, food crumbs, and liquor on the track to simulate restaurant conditions. Certain roaches will perform better than others. Some are runners, some are eaters. Ricci, release the first roach!"

A chocolate-brown roach shot from a small box, scurried diagonally along the track, sloshed through some spillage, teetered near the track's edge, and fell off.

A gallery of groans filled the room.

"Get rid of that loser!" Nimmo yelled. "He reminds me of Creep, goin' nowhere fast."

The mobsters turned toward Creep and whistled their approval. The beleaguered shell-smasher half-smiled as he split nuts with the speed of a revved-up meat slicer.

"A fast roach," Joe continued, "runs a foot in five seconds depending on the temptations. Some bugs drag along and eat everything in sight. The runners zoom forward nonstop."

The second entry slogged cautiously ahead, pausing for edibles and jerking its body left and right, then quickly scaled a plastic cup. It spun around magically, like a circus Wallenda…or a stoned roach.

"Go, Baby, go!" one thug shouted.

As if inspired by the words, the second roach plopped back down to the track, plowing through a mound of food bits and sugar cubes.

Roach number three slid and glided partly upright along the slippery, liquored track, flipping on its back twice and twirling like a figure skater before it skidded to a halt between two potato chips. It scooted to the top of one chip and stood upright in triumph as if it had conquered Everest.

"Bee-u-tee-ful," Ricci said. "What a performer. What poise. Who's his choreographer?"

Joe raised his hands and whistled loudly, urging his cohorts to a frenzy.

The whistles faded when Roach number three, seemingly energized by its sugar-sucking foray, moved closer to the third contestant. The two bugs confronted each other three inches apart, each one flailing its feelers straight ahead. They stood motionless for a minute, like two cowboys in a Dodge City showdown.

The thugs groaned in unison when one roach climbed atop the other.

"They had to do it here?" Joe asked.

"Do what, Boss?" Creep asked, his raised hand scarlet.

"They're doin' what you do in bed, Jackass."

Creep stared in confusion. "Dey weren't sleepin,' Boss." Feet thumping and a serenade of snickers rattled off the stained walls. Joe Nimmo shook his head and glared at his cohort. The man was a moron, a bungling bastard who stumbled through life stupefied, detoured at every turn by his unhinged state of mind.

The travesty continued throughout the night. There were kneeling men and bustling bugs, drunken thugs baiting insects, and cheering misfits looking sillier by the minute as they recorded speed and placed bets on brown blurs cavorting around a boozed-up, buffet-style track.

Finally, the night ended with many of the revelers reeling from too much bad booze. They'd been players in a fruitless farce, backslapping, hugging, singing, and slurring speeches for their well-garbed leader. They staggered home convinced that bugging beat mugging any day, and more bread meant better booze.

At the Detective Bureau, two men weren't celebrating. Sergeant Fred Carns waved a manila folder as he confronted Lieutenant Jack Connors with new information.

"Got something, Jack. It's something we can go on. We've staked out the Sporino place and spotted three goons lugging tubing and different boxes inside. The funny thing is, one box was labeled *Crost's Sugar Cubes*. What's that mean?"

"Maybe they like coffee. Who cares?" Jack pivoted quickly from his computer to prop his feet on the desk. He seemed preoccupied, though he scribbled down Fred's new leads. "Find any ammo?"

"Not really, but..."

"No guns? Nothing? How the hell will they hit Santos? With slingshots?"

"Jack, remember that raid when we found those football tickets?"

"What about it, Sherlock?"

"Well, although they moved the press, we found, well, a mess of shells."

Connors smiled. "Then you *did* find ammo."

"No. We found pistachio shells. There were forty-two of them, and we..."

"You found what?" As Connors yelled, his elbow knocked over a cup, and he gaped at his partner.

"Remember that tail we had on Ricci last month? We talked to his goofy buddy, Creep, and Jack, that guy gobbles those nuts constantly."

Jack's fist hit the desk. "Fred, damn it, there must be ten thousand people who eat pistachios. For Christ's sake, you're the one who's nuts."

"I'm positive that Ricci and Joe Nimmo will rob Santos on Friday. Remember that tip we got?"

Jack vaulted off his chair and trudged to the window, his lean frame rigid as he gazed downward. "I'm still not sold on it, but if you're wrong, you buy the damn doughnuts for six months." He pulled a glazed doughnut from a box, grinned at Carns, and ate it in three gulps.

Fred laughed and pointed. "Watch that waistline. You don't need doughnuts."

Three days later, Frank Ricci and Creep met in a downtown tavern one day before the raid.

"Boss, remember when we started way back, puttin' bugs in beers?" Creep asked.

"Jesus. Forget that. We're big-time now. Those were lean years."

Creep nodded. A frantic gulp from his beer can missed, drenching his shirt and pants.

Frank shook his head and grinned. "Creep, next time we meet, wear a damn bib. Pay attention. Don't slip up tomorrow like you did on the bus."

"When wuzzat, Boss?"

"In '94, Jerk. All you hadda do was fall down when the bus lurched."

"What's lurch mean?"

"It means a sudden movement. We could've sued the bus company if you'd faked bein' hurt."

"Yeah. I remember now. I forgot."

"Lay off those nuts, Ding-Dong. All I hear at our meetings is cracking sounds! It's annoying."

"Sorry, Boss." Creep brushed his soaked pants and shirt, then turned to his friend. "Boss, can I ask a question?"

"Now what?"

He slowly slid the nuts toward Frank. "Want one?"

"Damn it, Asshole, no!" Frank stood quickly and walked toward the exit. "See ya tomorrow at Santos at seven. Wear a tie, Hollow Head."

Friday evening, the lush, exquisite Santos Restaurant was packed with its usual mixture of local sports, media, and businessmen, along with regulars who savored the ultimate in upscale dining. The establishment's gourmet fare had been ranked among Chicago's finest for the past decade.

Adorning the light-blue walls of the posh, chandeliered dining area were two dazzling, three-foot-wide paintings, one of which depicted the grandeur of the Mediterranean coast and the tranquil beauty of a lone fishing boat drifting at sea. The other displayed a stunning panorama of Chicago's famed skyline with crystalline waters reflecting the majesty of lustrous, well-lit skyscrapers.

Through the huge dining room, red-vested waiters darted back and forth serving chic, fashionably dressed women with their suave, Armoni-suited, silk-tied dinner dates.

Frank Ricci and an unusually well-dressed Creep sat slouched at a small table in the rear of the restaurant as a waiter approached.

"May I suggest something from the bar, Gentlemen?" he asked.

"I'll take number five, the Cabernet Sauvignon," Frank said softly.

"And you, Sir?" He named five classic wines.

"Do ya have draft beer?"

Frank, glowering at his companion, leaned forward. "Order wine, Prune Head," he whispered.

"Do ya have Thunderbird? Ya know, the cheap stuff?"

A well-placed kick under the table got Creep's attention.

"Give him Cabernet, too, Waiter," Frank said. "We'll each have the sirloin and spinach soufflé special. Thank you."

When the waiter left, Frank smiled, though his eyes were furious. "Get this straight, Imbecile. You won't live to eat that steak if you can't act human. This is Santos', a top-shelf joint, not a pigpen."

"Sorry, Boss."

There was silence for five minutes. Frank seemed relaxed, dangling a cigarette as he savored his wine. Finally, he smiled politely and asked Creep to lean forward.

"Do you have the roaches?" he whispered.

"Yeah. In my left pocket."

"Good. Give me one under the table. We'll release them midway through the meal. Got it?"

Creep nodded, his quivering left hand massaging his pocket. "They're gettin' frisky in there."

Frank, rolling his eyes, drank more wine.

Halfway through dinner, Frank said, "This is it, Buddy. Let's do it now."

They dumped the bugs from the boxes on the table, grimacing, and began yelling their scripted lines as they feigned illness.

"My God, look!" Frank shoved back his chair as nearby diners stared. "Roaches! Everywhere!"

Creep gasped and flopped to the floor as if sick, pulling the tablecloth and its contents with him. "I'm sick," he moaned, squirming on the floor like a boxer downed by a solid punch.

Patrons screamed and yelled, the noise increasing until the entire dining room was a sea of sobs and shouting. Frenzied waiters and diners scurried about like looters in a windowless Sears.

Some women panicked. Dresses tore. Bracelets and necklaces flew as diners stumbled and fell. Others pushed plates and glasses from their tables. The sound of shattered glass and cracking china drew horrified customers from the bar. The carpeted floor was a morass of spillage and half-eaten food.

Creep and Frank continued their charade. Creep squirmed on the floor, while Frank slumped over the table, pleading for help, pointing as two of the four roaches sloshed through Santos' finest steaks.

Fifteen Chicago policemen with drawn guns poured into the room, diving over upturned tables and fallen bodies, yelling and urging angry diners to calm down.

Two policemen knelt over Creep. "Where'd they get you?"

"Dose bugs made me sick," he gasped, his face contorted.

Three detectives found the screaming cashier atop one of the remaining upright tables.

"How much did they get?" one asked.

"Oh, God," she sobbed. "What do you mean?"

"The robbers. How much did they get?"

"What robbers? Find those scavengers!"

Outside, two ambulances arrived, and eight paramedics rushed in. Creep bulged his eyes and twitched as he panted and moaned. Frank, looking embarrassed, held his stomach but answered the paramedics' questions.

The chaos continued for an hour. The restaurant was a madhouse. Screaming diners dashed for exits, while flustered policemen stumbled and slid past toppled tables, food, and spilled liquids. The restaurant floor, slippery from all the mess, was like a skating rink. Secure footing was as rare as a smiling diner.

Forty minutes after the first scream and smashed plate, frightened diners and bar patrons milled about, searching the floor for lost jewelry.

Frank Ricci confronted the manager and two detectives. "We had roaches for dinner companions," he said.

Soon, an upright Creep joined them. "Dem damn roaches. Dey ate my dinner."

The detectives grinned, realizing Creep's grammar was worse than his acting.

"Santos is an immaculate restaurant," the manager replied. "These men are insane."

"No, we're not, Buddy. Was this your Blue Plate special...roaches on rye?"

"Officers, vermin have never infested this restaurant. Inspect my kitchen if you wish."

A crying woman ran up to them. "I'll never eat here again. My steak was covered with...those things!"

"She's crazy, too!" the manager snapped. "Nothing covers our Supreme Steak but choice mushrooms and onions."

"Look what covered your steaks tonight!" Frank shouted, pointing at a roach rolling through the spinach. "Those roaches turned my steak into a romper room."

The detectives giggled and pulled the manager aside. "Better get a fumigator in here, Sir. They might start a family."

Furious, the manager stalked off.

"Boss, it worked," Creep whispered.

"Shhh! Not so loud."

As the pair walked briskly to the exit, Sergeant Carns and Lieutenant Connors, with eight policemen, blocked the door and pinned the pair against the wall.

"You're under arrest," Connors barked, cuffing them.

"For what?" Frank asked.

"Robbery, Numbskulls. We'll talk more at the station."

One hour later, Carns and Connors circled the two crooks slouched before a long table under hanging lights.

"Boys, two Avon ladies, three paper boys, two parish priests, and a drunk identified both of you," Carns began. "They said one of the robbers had red hands."

"Let's see your palms, Creep," Connors asked.

Creep slowly turned up his hands.

"Nice touch Creep. Early tomato, I'd say."

"We want a lawyer!" Frank blared.

"Perry Mason can't help losers," Carns retorted.

Connors grinned and turned to his partner. "You might say we caught them red-handed." He laughed.

Fred put his arm around Jack's shoulders. "Who buys the doughnuts now?"

They smiled and high-fived each other above the crooks' heads.

Frank nudged his partner. "Thanks, Asshole."

Two days later, the captives were waiting for their attorney. They sat beside each other on a low bench behind bars in a small, gray-walled room thirty feet from the cell block. A long, wooden table had two chairs on opposite sides, and a guard stood just outside the wired structure surrounding the room.

Creep nudged Frank several times to speak.

His partner stared ahead with glazed eyes, his forehead moist in the humid room. They sat there silently for fifteen minutes, shuffling their feet, feeling half-dazed by the turn of events.

Finally, Creep mumbled, "Boss, a lotta guys have red hands. How did...?"

Frank raised his eyes and stared at Creep. "You dumb, stupid, halfwit! Four or five people said a masked gunman had red hands when he reached for their money. The cops found pistachio shells around those parking meters, on the printing press, and in your coat! To top it off, guess what they found at my house?"

"But, Boss..."

"They found pretty, rosy-red shells in my bathroom and basement!"

A teary-eyed, tousled-headed Creep buried his head in his hands. "Boss, how'd the cops...?"

"How? It's bad enough that Nick sang to them and left town, but we're in this craphouse because of you!"

Fifteen minutes passed.

Creep stared at the floor and smiled. "You see what I see, Boss? I'll bet he's an eater."

Frank reluctantly looked where Creep pointed on the cement floor. His eyes widened as a half-inch roach sauntered slowly across the floor, stopping momentarily to munch on a crumb. He gaped at the slow-moving creature, almost admiring its elusive stop-and-go movement.

It scaled Frank's left shoe, then dropped to the ground between his feet. Moving very slowly, Frank raised his right shoe, guiding it in sync with the bug's pace, then flattened it into mush.

"He *was* an eater." The two men clapped.

Creep smiled, and an empty shell fell from his pocket.

Philip C. DiMartino, author of *The Wrong Number*, resides in New Jersey. He is also a published poet.

The Wrong Number
Philip C. DiMartino

Bellevue Hospital
Sunday, November 24, 2001
10:00 AM

"Mr. Baunt, I'm glad to see you again."

"Hello, Lieutenant. How is he?"

"Still in a coma, I'm afraid. Will you accompany me to city hall?"

"I wouldn't miss it for the world. I just wanted to see him first," Baunt said, smiling.

The lieutenant nodded. "Me, too."

Saturday, November 10, 2001
6:00 AM

It was a beautiful autumn dawn, unseasonably warm for so early in the morning. She overdressed for her short walk through the courtyard, so she unbuttoned her leather jacket and exposed her well-defined bosom, caressed in a low-cut, clinging cashmere sweater.

Hundreds of people surrounded her as she walked briskly to her office. They slept in ten-foot concrete cubicles inside four seven-story buildings. She rented to many of those dreaming tenants in the low-income quad. That day, she would fill other vacant apartments with new green-card holders, single mothers, and other down-and-outers like Jayson.

Saturday, 7:30 AM

Oh, do more of that. That's right. Right there. Faster! Harder! Don't stop! Don't stop! Don't...

The phone rang.

Man, what a dream, he thought, waking up. *What time is it? Shit. Who the hell's calling me at seven-thirty AM on Saturday?*

The phone continued ringing.

Whoever it is, he ruined the best wet dream I ever had. I refuse to answer. I'll just go back to sleep and see if I can bring back the dream.

Ring. Ring. Ring.

"Oh, all right! I'm coming!" he shouted, lifting the receiver. "Hello?"

"Hey, Bitch, I got your gun!" a voice said.

"What? Excuse me? What did you say? Who is this?"

"Who is this, Señor? Never mind. Wrong number."

Click.

What the hell was that? Freak me out! No, Jayson. Don't even think that. Just go back to sleep.

Saturday, 9:00 AM

"Want to eat, Sammy? Sure you do. There. Have some of your favorite tropical flakes. Your water's cloudy, so I'll change it later, OK? Let's see what's happening in this concrete village this morning, Sammy.

"I'm so sick of this view, window after window. Did you know there are 2,048 windows in the four buildings? How did I know that? After half a quart of vodka, I spent an evening adding and multiplying. That's how. Yes, Sammy. That's what my life has been reduced to."

Jayson, stepping onto his balcony, looked around. That was his primary entertainment, surpassing TV, because it was depressingly live.

"Shoo, you damn pigeons!" *I gotta clean off this pigeon crap today. If only they paid part of my rent. I'd gladly sublet them the balcony. It would be the first co-op coop in the city.*

Ah. Building C stopped smoldering. I wonder how many apartments were destroyed. Christ, it smells like someone chain-smoked a million cigarettes out here. Where are my binoculars?

Hey, where are you headed with suitcases in hand, my Muslim friends? If you're flying, get ready for a bag and body search. You sure have colorful clothing. If I wore that, I'd be sent to Bellevue. It's hard to imagine what your culture would consider outlandish.

Let's see. Building D, fourth floor, six windows over…there they are…Big Mama and Little Conchita in their bra and panties. The conversation at the breakfast table seems quite heated. They're probably arguing about who had the most johns last night. Oh, no! Scrambled eggs to the kisser! Way to go, Conchita. You'd better run. Here comes Big Mama! Ha!

It seems like everyone is hiding this morning. All the shades are drawn. Even the multiperson, one-bedroom Korean apartment has its beautifully stained bed sheet draping the balcony doorway. Don't these people know I need more stimuli to give me a reason to live in this shithole?

Don't blame them, Jayson. It's your own fault you live here.

Hello, Conscience. I feel another lecture coming.

Well, my boy, you wouldn't be pouting over missed cheap thrills at this peeping-tom theater complex if you hadn't lost your $150,000-a-year job, estranged your children, and divorced your wife…who took all you had. For what? The dream of regaining your first love.

Well put, Mr. C. Enough of that. I've heard it all before, mostly from my ex. What's this in Building A? The police are back. Wait a minute.

That's the city coroner's vehicle. Something really bad happened this time. Oh well, I'll check it out later. Let's see if I recognize the phone number of that weird call. One of my few friends might be playing a joke.

Hmmm. It's a local number, same exchange as mine, but it's not anyone I know. It was no joke.

Saturday, 9:30 AM

"Excuse me, Officer. What happened down here?"

"Who are you, and how'd you get in here?"

"I'm Jayson Noble, and I walked in. I rent here. Oh, God. Is that a body bag?"

"I'll kill Rafferty! Damn it, he was supposed to secure the scene!"

"Who is it?"

"The rental manager was murdered, shot in the head."

"Ms. Calina? Why? Was she raped or robbed? Oh, God, not her."

"That's enough, Sir. Come with me. You have to get out of here without touching anything."

"Who's this?" someone asked.

"Oh, hello, Lieutenant Jameson. This is a tenant, Sir."

"Do you have some information, Sir?" Jameson asked.

"No, Lieutenant." Jayson was visibly upset by the murder.

"Then what the hell's he doing here, Golden?"

"Ah…he got past the tape, Sir."

"You idiots! I can't leave you alone for a minute, and you let this guy contaminate the crime scene!"

"He didn't touch anything, Sir."

"Shut up. I'll deal with you later!"

Man, what a bastard, Jayson thought. *He kinda resembles Peter Faulk's Colombo, only fifty pounds heavier. He wears the same wrinkled raincoat in the same color, and he chews a stubby cigar. This is too weird. Thank God he doesn't have a lazy eye, or I'd swear I just stepped into the Twilight Zone.*

"Are you the lead detective, Lieutenant?" Jayson asked.

"That's right. Now you must leave. No, wait. Did you know the victim?"

"Sure. She rented an apartment to me. I pay...I paid the rent to her in this office each month. She was nice and really sexy. All the men in this complex lined up on the first of the month to pay. That was one chore the married men enjoyed. She always wore a sexy blouse or sweater without a bra on those days. Mind you, she didn't need a bra to hold up those points."

"I get the picture. Is that all you can tell me, Mr. Noble?"

"Well, yes. Can I ask what time the murder took place?"

"The coroner places the time of death between six and eight this morning. Why?"

Should I tell him about the phone call? Could there be a connection? What the hell. It won't hurt, except to ruin my credibility.

Impossible, my boy. You don't have any. Ask your ex.

Very funny, Mr. C.

"Say, Lieutenant..."

Saturday, 10:00 AM

"Sorry, Sammy," Jayson said. "I didn't mean to shake your aquarium by slamming the door so hard, but the lieutenant pissed me off. I told him about the phone call this morning and my theory of a possible connection to the murder, and he laughed at me.

"You haven't heard? Ms. Calina was murdered! Yep. Shot in her office. The cops have no motive, leads, or weapon. I have a creepy feeling that phone call is related to the murder. You know there are no coincidences in life. I'll miss her more than I told the lieutenant.

"I'll never be with her again. How can I fantasize about us anymore? All I'll see in my dreams is that damn body bag. I can't let this go, Sammy. If the cops won't follow this lead, I will. I've got the number listed on my cell phone. Maybe I can track down the owner, get an address, and..."

217

Then what, assuming you get that far, Smart Guy?

I don't know, Mr. C. I'll deal with that when it happens.

That's the first positive thing you've said to me in months. I'll let you proceed with this quest, though I'm not optimistic about it. I don't want to accidentally wipe out your motivation.

Thanks for the backhanded support and forehanded permission. You can leave now. I need to think.

Saturday, Noon

Jayson called a friend who might be able to help him with the phone number. "Hi, Ron. I'm glad I caught you at work. I need a favor."

"Sure, Jayson. How are you?"

"I wake up every morning. For me, that's an accomplishment."

"Sorry, Man. What can I do for you?"

"I remember when I worked part-time at your real-estate office I saw a lot of reference books. We used them to find names or addresses and phone numbers of potential clients."

"We're in the twenty-first century, Jay. That stuff is all computerized now."

"I need to match a number with a name and address. It's important."

"Is it some barfly babe you met and can't remember the name?"

"Nothing like that, Ron. Can you get it and meet me at PJ's at three? I'll flip for shots and beers."

"If it's a listed number, I'll get it for you. It must be important if you're willing to buy drinks. What's the number? Tell me what this is about."

"It's 201-768-6001. I'll tell you when I see you."

Saturday, 3:00 PM

"Ron! It's great to see you! Did you get it?"

"Boy, you look like shit. Are you eating?" Ron asked.

"I'm on a diet. You should try it. It's Dr. Smirnoff's Liquid Diet…a pint a day keeps the blues away. Did you get it?"

"Yeah. What's this about?"

"All right. I'll tell you, but you'd better sit down. You might not believe me. Barkeep! Two Molsons and two tequilas."

Saturday, 4:00 PM

Three rounds of shots and beers later, the two long-time friends stumbled out of PJ's to find their way to Ron's BMW. They met in the ninth grade at PS 103 on the East Side and attended Seton Hall University in Jersey together four years later. Ronald William Baunt became a successful real-estate broker in Manhattan. Jayson Charles Noble became successful, too…for a while. He was the superintendent of the Central Park Recreation Department.

Currently, Jayson didn't even own a car. The two men hadn't seen each other since Jayson's divorce.

"Get in, Jayson," Ron said. "I'll take you home. Where you hanging out these days?"

If he sees where I live, he'll insist I move into his guestroom, but not before giving me a long lecture on how I'm throwing away my life. I get plenty of lectures from Mr. C.

"No way," Jayson said. "I'll take the subway. That Beemer would be car-jacked in my neighborhood. I need time to think, anyway."

Jayson hadn't told Ron that the information Ron gave him was for a man named Ramon Ruiz, who lived in the same slum complex as Jayson. Jayson knew him as the Dominican don of the complex.

Jayson felt certain the call and the murder were connected. There were no coincidences in life.

"OK, Jay," Ron said. "Suit yourself. I warn you, from what you told me, sticking your nose into a murder investigation is crazy, not to mention dangerous. Let's assume this Ramon guy *is* involved in the murder, and you start poking around. When I see you next, it might be in a body bag."

"You sound just like Mr. C."

"Who?"

"Never mind. Don't worry about me, Boo Boo. This Yogi is smarter than the average Hispanic bear."

Stopping at the corner bodega, he bought a pint of his favorite liquid-diet elixir. *No sense letting the afternoon buzz go to waste,* he mused, cracking the seal and swigging from the bagged bottle before descending the steps to the subway.

Saturday, 7:00 PM

Jayson floundered on a park bench in the courtyard of his complex, directly across from apartment 112. He thought playing a local drunk who sipped from a paper bag would be the perfect cover for watching Ruiz' apartment. It was a role Jayson could play from experience, and it helped keep Mr. C in check, too.

He has two goons posted outside his front door, who, for the past hour, have let in some very seedy characters, Jayson thought. *He's dealing. I'd bet my life on that, but exactly what is he dealing? Is it drugs, guns, whores, or porn? All of it? Assuming he has the murder weapon, how'd he get it?*

Maybe he's an accomplice. Maybe he's the shooter. He called me Bitch on the phone. Was he calling a woman, or is everyone a bitch to him? I need to get that gun, which means I need to get inside.

I need to become Ruiz' bitch. Should I go to the police with this, or would Lieutenant Jameson just laugh at me again?

Sunday, November 11
Noon

Straight out of the previous night's hangover, Jayson chugged a half-pint of vodka without bothering with a shower or any other morning hygiene first. He presumed his liquor-induced, disheveled, bad-smelling demeanor would make him look, well, meaner. The liquor would certainly help him feel braver when he confronted the two Hispanic gargoyles posted at Ruiz' door.

His plan, as short-term and illogical as it might be, was to drop Ms. Calina's name as a reference to ask Ruiz if he could buy a gun. Mentioning the dead woman and a gun together should get a response, assuming Ruiz was involved with the murder and still had the gun that was used as the murder weapon.

Beyond that, Jayson expected little good and feared the worst, but it was the best plan his fried brain could muster.

An outside observer, or a very inside one like Mr. C, would question why Jayson was putting himself in such an unpredictable position. Was he finally at the point where he no longer cared for his safety, or was it an act of valor to bolster his self-esteem?

Jayson, enough is enough, Mr. C commented. *I'll admit I'm proud of you for getting this far, but to put it in Mr. Ruiz' language,* "Hombre, estas loco!" *If you get hurt, so do I.*

Mr. C, does C stand for chicken? Either watch my back or bail out, Jayson replied.

Sunday, 12:30 PM

"What you want, *La Punta?*" the smaller of the two Hispanic guards asked.

"Very funny," Jayson replied. "I know a little Spanish. Your mother's a whore, too."

The man grabbed Jayson's shirt with both hands and swung him around, slamming his back against the apartment's steel door. Jayson momentarily lost his breath while struggling to get free of the Dominican apeman.

The door opened, and the guard released Jayson, who sank to his knees as Ramon Ruiz looked down at him.

"Sorry, Boss," the large guard said. "This cockroach was hassling us."

"Mr. Ruiz," Jayson said. "You're just the man I want to see!"

Here goes the last day of the rest of your life.

Shut up, Mr. C.

Jayson's voice slurred slightly as the vodka kicked in. "Ms. Calina referred me to you. She said you, Sir, would be able to provide me with the gun I so desperately need."

"Get him inside fast!" Ruiz shouted.

The goons grabbed Jayson's arms on either side, lifted him off the ground, and rushed him through the door. Behind them, Ruiz angrily slammed the door.

"Hold him tight, Boys," Ruiz said, thrusting his knee into Jayson's stomach.

Jayson gasped, slumping in the men's arms.

"Hold him up."

A left cross split Jayson's lip and spewed blood on the men holding his arms. A right cross to the temple made the world turn black. As consciousness faded, Jayson heard Ruiz say, "I told you never to come back here!'"

The beating continued until there was a loud noise at the door.

"See who it is through the peephole, Chico," Ruiz whispered.

"It's the cops. Two suits and one uniform."

Ruiz thought fast. "Diego, carry this punk outside and put him on the chaise with your hat over his face. Come back in and draw the drapes. Hurry!"

Knock! Knock! Knock!

"Yeah! I'm coming!" Ruiz shouted. "Hold onto your gonads!"

When Jayson was removed from the room, Ruiz said, "OK, Chico. Open the door."

Lieutenant Jameson stepped in. "Ramon Ruiz, I'm Lieutenant Jameson, NYPD. I have some questions for you."

Sunday, 1:30 PM

Ruiz wasn't worried about the police's accusation concerning Ms. Calina's murder. There was no evidence, so they were just checking him due to his reputation.

What really concerned him was knowing the cops would be watching his operation for a while, making it difficult to earn money from his illegal activities. He needed a patsy to divert the police, and they already told him who it should be.

Lieutenant Jameson told Ruiz that someone named Noble walked into the crime scene a few hours after the murder. Jameson claimed the perpetrators with the sickest minds always got a kick from revisiting the site of their latest crime to taunt the police. Jameson boasted, "I'd bet my badge that man works for you."

"Chico," Ruiz said, "bring in Sleeping Beauty."

"What now, Boss?" Diego asked.

"We'll give the suit his killer, someone who'll never give us any trouble. I'll even give Noble the gun he wants, the one I gave you to whack Calina…the one you dropped at the scene, you idiot!"

"Aw, Boss, I was just doing what Al Pacino did in the *Godfather* when he smoked the two guys who shot his father. He was told a hundred times to drop the gun after killing 'em."

"That was a movie, Numskull. I had to risk being seen to retrieve that revolver. I wanted no weapon found and no trace of motive. That bitch was getting a conscience over skimming off the top of everyone's rent. She wanted out and said she loved this loser on the floor. Imagine that. She wanted to start a new life. She even brought him here the night she told me. He was so drunk, I doubt he remembers. I threw them out and told them not to come back."

"I'm sorry, Boss."

"Forget it. Here's what I want you to do. Chico, take the laundry basket to the basement. Diego, stuff Noble in the laundry bag and drop him down the chute in the bedroom. Chico, you catch him as he comes down. The police won't be watching the basement.

"Diego, take a ride in the car awhile and make sure you lose any tail. Come back and park at the basement door. You two put Noble in the trunk and drive to the Colson underpass. Give him one in the right temple with the gun, put the gun in his right hand, stuff the suicide letter in his pocket, and dump him."

"What suicide letter?" Diego asked.

"The one I'm about to write. Noble will confess to Calina's murder, saying he couldn't live with the guilt."

Sunday, 3:30 PM

Wake up, Man. Do it, Jayson. Come on, my boy. For once, listen to Mr. C!

Jayson, opening his eyes, tried to focus. He was cold. Touching his face, he felt double pain trauma, with a sharp spark of pain emanating from his lower lip and a severe headache from the right side of his head. As he closed his eyes again, he heard faint voices and laughter.

No! Shit, Jayson! Oh, my God, we're dead!

Bang!

Friday, November 24
Noon

"Today we honor an ordinary citizen named Jayson Noble, who willingly put his life in jeopardy to help the police catch a murderer and break up a crime ring headquartered in his apartment complex. I, as mayor, am proud to present to Donna Noble and her children, this medal of valor. This honor is usually given to police officers who distinguish themselves in the line of duty. Mr. Noble currently is in a coma in Bellevue Hospital as a result of…"

As the mayor continued speaking, Ron Baunt looked at Lieutenant Jameson with tear-filled eyes. "How'd Jayson end up like this? Why didn't you protect him?"

Jameson, choked up with emotion, cleared his throat. "He came to me with the new information you helped him uncover. I finally listened. The call Jayson received from Ruiz was meant for Diego Torres, Ruiz' hit man. He wanted to tell Torres he retrieved the gun Torres left behind, but Ruiz dialed the wrong number.

"We tried to link Ruiz to the murder from the start, but we had no motive, weapon, or forensics evidence. Jayson volunteered to go in with a recording device, hoping Ruiz would slip and say something we could use against him. Jayson was very brave to do that. I don't know why he agreed, but we sure needed his help."

"I know." Baunt lowered his head, wiping tears from his eyes.

"It was his idea to set himself up as the pigeon by having me confront Ruiz to mark Jayson as part of Ruiz' gang and the possible murderer. We needed to force Ruiz to cover his tracks so we could uncover them.

"The recording device was also a tracking device in case Jayson had to be on the move with Ruiz and his men. We had no idea there was a laundry chute into the basement. The tracking device showed Jayson was still in the building until they removed him to the trunk of a car and drove off.

"We followed the car to Colson underpass. I arrived barely in time to shoot and kill Torres before he could kill Jayson. We didn't know he'd been badly beaten first. I'm very sorry. What we learned from the tape recording is enough to put Ruiz away for the rest of his life."

"Yeah, but what about the rest of Jayson's life?"

Friday, June 25, 2002
3:00 PM

"Jayson, you're doing a great job," the mayor said. "Central Park has never looked better, and that concert in the park you promoted last week was fabulous. You're bringing your beautiful wife to the Mayor's Ball tonight, aren't you? Here, let me help you with the door."

"Thank you, Mayor. Yes, she'll be there," Jayson said, wheeling himself through the door.

Julie Kerr Casper has spent her life exploring and living in the Rocky Mountains of the Western United States. An outdoor sports enthusiast, she loves equestrian sports, hiking, kayaking, canoeing, mountain climbing, and camping. She resides in the mountains of Northern Utah with her husband and four daughters.

She is the author of over a dozen magazine articles and stories. She is also the author of the mystery/adventure novels: *THE SNOW EAGLE: Riddle of the Stone Tablet; THE SNOW EAGLE: Escape Through the Kayawati;* and *THE SNOW EAGLE: Quest for the Shattered Orb.*

She is known for her mystery/adventures with heavy doses of outdoor survival; nonstop action; thrill-seeking, savvy characters; and portrayals of nature in its finest and deadliest forms. Nature enthusiasts love her attention to detail, and she keeps mystery lovers perched on the edges of their seats.

She is a three-time award-winning author in the international Annual Writer's Digest Writing competition; the recipient of the 2004 Zola Literary Award for best fiction; a 2004 Zola Literary Award finalist for young adult novel; a three-time Southwest Writer's Competition winner, and featured in the Marquis Book of Who's Who in 2004. She has also been a presenter at a Society of Children's Book Writers and Illustrators Writing Conference.

She has filled various writing positions throughout her writing career as journalist for the Horizon's newspaper in Salt Lake City, Utah; and as the author/editor of Second Thought's newsletter in Salt Lake City, Utah. She is a member of the Society of Children's Book Writers and Illustrators, Southwest Writer's Association, Mystery Writers of America, The National Writer's Association, and the Pacific Northwest Writer's Association.

She has a Ph.D. in earth science accompanied by a nearly 30-year career with the U. S. Bureau of Land Management in earth science.

Blizzard in August

Julie Casper

They sped along the highway as the first fat raindrops splattered on the windshield. Jenny, flipping on the wipers, anxiously studied the foreboding, roiling skyline.

Airborne grit pelted the windshield like shrapnel. The wind screamed in rage as tree branches whipped the air like frenzied, cavorting dancers. A monstrous clap of thunder shook the car, and the clouds opened up as if the white-hot lightning had slashed their underbellies.

Jenny turned the wipers to high, their staccato clacking almost overpowering the sound of raindrops exploding against the glass and metal.

"No other information?" Sandra asked anxiously. "Just *Mom's been taken to the hospital?*"

"And to hurry," Jenny, her sister, replied.

"I want to get away from here for a while. All this talk about serial killers in town is creeping me out."

"Ditto. Especially because no one knows who to look for. First they say a tall man with brown hair and mustache, then last week, the sheriff said an eyewitness reported a suspicious stocky man with red hair."

Jenny suddenly took an exit off the main highway.

"Where are you going?" Sandra asked.

"I'm taking the route off the mountain pass. That'll shave off at least fifteen minutes." She drove through a rugged stretch of forest.

"But who knows what this storm will bring at higher elevations? The road could be a disaster."

"I've got a SUV. We'll be fine." Jenny's tone allowed no argument.

As the road climbed, the rain transformed into thick slush. The wipers failed to score many points against the deluge.

The road wound through narrow ravines and steep draws. Within minutes, the slushy, beating sleet turned into thick flakes of snow. Jenny alternated looking furtively ahead along the stretch of twisting mountain road and uneasily behind her. There were no other cars in sight.

"We seem to be the only ones out," she said, a nervous twinge clutching her stomach.

"All the campers and hikers probably hightailed out of here when the storm started brewing."

Jenny nodded. In that area, leviathan thunderstorms could develop without much warning. Still, it was unsettling to be alone in a bad storm. Jenny also knew that thoughts of the serial killer were on people's minds. Eleven women were missing. Two were found hacked to pieces just outside town. She suppressed a shiver.

As the road climbed steeply, the snowfall transitioned into a full-fledged blizzard. Visibility dropped by the second, making the hairpin turns leap out at Jenny. Fighting to keep the car under control, she knew she had to hurry. What if their mother died before they arrived?

Unthinkable, Jenny thought, pressing down harder on the accelerator.

She rounded a sharp bend just as a deer bounded onto the roadway. Jenny slammed on the brakes and spun the wheel hard to the left to avoid a collision. The car canted wildly out of control. The low temperature froze the rain that fell previously, creating a deadly patch of black ice.

The car spun mercilessly. Jenny threw all her strength into righting the skidding vehicle. The deer leaped into the swirling snow as the car traced two complete circles diagonally across the roadway.

A huge ponderosa pine loomed in front of her, growing bigger with each rotation of the car. Jenny screamed, closed her eyes, and braced herself.

The car struck the tree head-on, throwing Jenny and Sandra violently forward until their seat belts dug painfully into their shoulders.

All motion and sound ceased. Jenny forced open her eyes and looked at her sister.

"Are you all right?" she asked unsteadily.

Sandra nodded slowly. "I think so."

Shaking, Jenny picked up her cell phone and dialed 911.

Call Failed, appeared on the tiny screen. Only one signal bar was lit, meaning reception was nonexistent. Jenny looked toward a rise off the highway extending through a thick snarl of pine. When she pushed, her door yielded with a shrill protest of metal.

Jenny's mind raced. "We can't wait here. There's so little traffic, we'd freeze to death before someone drives by. If we can reach higher ground, maybe we can get a signal." She thought for a moment. "There's also the ranger station. If we're where I think, we can get there and call for help."

"You want to go out there?" Sandra asked incredulously. "In a blizzard, with a killer on the loose?"

"I don't want to, but one thing's certain. This car won't go anywhere, and we can't stay here and freeze. If we want to find that ranger station, we have to do it before it gets dark, and we lose visibility. It's our only chance."

Sandra groaned, as Jenny rifled through the contents of a box in the back seat.

"No jackets or blankets," she said in disgust. "All I have here are the wallpaper supplies I bought yesterday."

"Who would've suspected a blizzard in August?"

Jenny reached into a plastic bag and took out a retractable razor-blade knife. "This is the only tool I have. Maybe we can use it to get into the ranger station."

She slipped it into her back pocket, closed the door, and walked toward the forest. Sandra followed before the poor visibility erased her sister from view.

They traversed up a hollow between closely spaced trees, mercifully protecting them from the wind howling on the ridge. Snow fell at an alarming rate, collecting in the tree canopies like thick hoards of down stuffing.

As they walked between tree trunks, the wet, heavy snow fell from the branches in clumps like runny mashed potatoes. An eerie silence permeated the air. Sound had a muffled, surreal quality, oddly making Jenny feel as if she were walking through an old, deserted cathedral.

Jenny stopped abruptly, and Sandra nearly collided with her.

"What is it?" Sandra asked.

Jenny pointed at the ground. Despite the falling snow, footprints were visible.

"Someone else is here," Jenny whispered.

"Maybe they can help us," Sandra said hopefully.

"Follow me."

As they rounded a bend, Jenny stopped when she heard a faint chopping sound. A surge of hope went through her. Maybe someone else had been caught by the storm and was cutting wood for a fire, although the sound wasn't quite right. There was a dull, wet thud to it.

The sound was close, and she heard someone grunting with effort from his work. Jenny, slipping around thick brush, slammed to a stop. Bile rose in her throat as her brain registered the horror her eyes saw. She choked back a gag and withdrew behind the bush, dragging Sandra with her.

Jenny fished out her cell phone and dialed 911 again. When nothing happened, she jabbed the numbers again, but the display read, *No Signal.*

Damn, she thought.

"What is it?" Sandra hissed.

"We found the serial killer."

"What?" Sandra instinctively moved toward the edge of the brush.

Jenny pulled her back, then both women peered cautiously around the barrier.

A tall man in a coat and hood was chopping up the remains of one of Jenny's neighbors. No one else had those signature long, green fingernails. He'd already dug a hole and was systematically dropping the wet, oozing pieces into the ground.

He turned sideways slightly, giving Jenny an all-too-clear glimpse of his face and brown mustache. She gasped softly. "Oh, my God! It's the sheriff!"

She stepped back and clamped a hand over Sandra's mouth before she could utter a sound.

"We're getting out of here. Now!" Jenny tried to catch her breath before she hyperventilated and blacked out.

They silently retraced their steps. The blizzard was thickening, reducing visibility to almost nothing. Jenny thought she was moving back toward the car, but she wasn't sure anymore. Everything looked the same, as if she were inside a milkshake.

Snow had already filled their tracks. If they weren't careful, they could circle back on themselves until they were hopelessly lost.

Passing a thick tree trunk, she veered right. The cold, hard business end of a gun jabbed painfully against her neck, making her freeze. Sandra screamed.

"Going somewhere, Ladies?" the sheriff snarled.

Jenny flinched when she heard the safety click off.

"I'd hate to see you come all this way without joining my party. Wouldn't I?" he growled, making Jenny jump.

He dug dirty fingers savagely into the soft flesh above the women's elbows and marched them back to the burial ground like recalcitrant children being led to the principal's office. Jenny's mind raced, trying to find a feasible escape.

He pulled them through a small clearing to a campground, with a circular fire pit ringed by smooth, rounded river rocks.

He pushed them roughly to the ground, kicking Jenny's stomach. She gasped, fighting to breathe.

As Sandra yelled, he backhanded her face, knocking her head against a tree stump.

Mortified, Jenny kicked him, and he rewarded her by slamming the side of her head. White-hot pain exploded behind her eyes, then everything went mercifully black.

When she awoke, her first thought was of cold. She felt frozen. She found herself covered in a layer of thick, wet snow. Her fingers and toes stung so badly, she would've sworn dozens of needles were sticking into them. Coupled with that was a bone-deep, dull ache.

The combination brought tears to her eyes. It hurt to move. Pain exploded in her head like holiday fireworks. Then she remembered. Her eyes snapped opened, and she frantically looked for her sister.

She couldn't move, because her hands were tied behind her back. When she tried to free them, the stiff rope dug into her tender wrists.

She lay on her side. Rotating her head as much as she dared, she tried to assess their situation. Sandra, also bound, sprawled nearby.

White-hot anger threatened to erupt when she saw Sandra's face. She'd been beaten until her face resembled raw steak. Her eyes were swollen shut, the lids a grotesque, bulging, vivid violet.

Jenny's gaze went to Sandra's chest. When she saw it rise and fall, tears came to her eyes. Thank God, Sandra was still alive.

She'd never been so cold in her life. She shivered and gritted her teeth, trying not to shake, but her body had other ideas. She jerked uncontrollably like a jittering skeleton.

Swiveling her head toward the fire pit, she saw the sheriff had collected some tinder and was nursing a small flame.

"It's you," she said dully, finding it difficult to get her sluggish mouth to form words.

He stopped blowing on the flame and faced her. "Did I ever tell you how brilliant you are?" He leered, sarcasm filling his voice.

"All this time we heard conflicting descriptions. You've been tampering with the evidence, misdirecting the investigation, and toying with people's fears. The entire community looked up to you and believed in you."

"What you see isn't always what you get, is it?" he sneered.

Jenny was shocked. "But why? Your daughter was the first victim. You were there every second of the search. You supported your wife after she went through another cancer treatment." She paused to catch her breath as a surge of anger flooded through her. "You animal! The community trusted you."

He laughed, a hollow, psychopathic cackle. "Abigail wasn't my daughter." Spittle flew from his lips. "She was my stepdaughter, and she was nosy, sticking her damn head in where she had no business. She wasn't the first, just the first witness." He gave a mirthless laugh.

"What will you do now?" Jenny fought back panic and the urge to scream. No one would hear her.

He cackled. "I'll build me a little campfire and roast a snack. I'd invite you to join me, but I can't." He stopped, staring into the distance as if receiving a special message. Then his eyes jerked back to Jenny, making her flinch. Staring hard at her as if looking right through her, he added, "Because you're the snack." A spasm of high giggle escaped his lips.

Jenny didn't dare move.

"I'll need a bigger fire to cook both of you at once." He winked at her as if sharing a joke. "Don't go away." Another peal of maniacal laughter broke the silence of the forest, echoing in the distance.

He moved out of sight. Jenny heard branches being snapped from trees. The lower branches would be drier, and they'd probably burn well.

His voice drifted to her from the forest. She thought he was talking to someone else until he began answering his own comments. He was certifiably insane. How long had that been going on in their sleepy, peaceful, little community? She shivered, though it wasn't from the cold.

Trying to shift her shoulders so her hands could reach her back pocket, she almost gasped as pain ricocheted down her arm. One finger wedged into the pocket. She touched the knife, but it was just out of reach.

233

Her body, spasming from uncontrollable shivering, was sluggish and uncoordinated. It wouldn't do what she wanted.

She ground her hip into the snow and twisted, putting pressure on the knife handle. It moved, but not enough. She still couldn't grasp it.

Branches snapped nearby, and the sheriff's giddy whistling grew louder. He was returning. Panicking, Jenny shifted her hips again and pushed the knife a little higher. The tips of her fingers brushed the cold metal, making her flinch.

Using her middle and index fingers like tweezers, she took a precarious grasp of the handle, only to feel it slip away. She tried again, grasping the edge, pulling it out a few centimeters before convulsive shaking broke her grip.

She willed herself to relax and stop shaking. Grasping the knife again, she pulled slowly, coaxing it from her pocket until it finally settled into her spasming, cramped hand.

The sheriff stepped into the clearing beside her. Startled, she cupped the knife in her hand, hopefully out of his view. As he walked by carrying a bundle of wood, he slammed a protruding piece into her head.

She gasped in pain as pinpoints of bright light exploded in front of her eyes. The piece of wood dropped in front of her.

"Oh, I'm sorry." He giggled. "You got in the way."

He dropped the wood beside the fire pit. It clattered as it fell, the sound piercing her tortured brain. He arranged the wood in the pit. It smoldered and then burned, and he honed his knife insistently on a flat stone, humming a tuneless melody.

The small fire slowly grew. Soon, he had a raging bonfire, big enough to cook someone in. As the roaring flames licked the air, she felt the intense heat from where she lay.

He turned, staring intently at her. The wild glint in his eyes made her shrink away in fear. He panted with anticipation.

Jenny's time was running out. As he faced the fire again, she maneuvered the blade handle until her thumb reached the release lever. She slid it up, and the razor blade slowly extended.

She turned it, but, in her haste, she slipped. The blade sliced her palm. She bit her tongue to keep from shrieking. Carefully, she maneuvered the blade between the ropes on her wrist and started sawing. Blood made the handle slippery, and the intense cold made her muscles slow to respond. Her forearms cramped, the pain making her groan inwardly.

She felt tension loosen as some strands separated. Encouraged, she sawed harder. With a soft pop, the tension was gone. Her wrists were free.

She looked at the piece of wood lying in front of her face, then at the sheriff. He honed his knife almost sensually, working himself into a frenzy. When she glanced at Sandra, she saw no movement.

Jenny took a deep breath.

In one swift movement, she leaped up, grabbed the branch, raised it like a club, and swung at the sheriff's back as hard as she could. It struck with a tremendous crack, snapping in half as he pitched forward. Blood ran down his shirt like a river from the large gash she left in his back.

His hands and face plunged into the fire. Screaming, he launched himself backward. Staggering toward Jenny, his eyes partially closed, he had pieces of glowing coals stuck to his eyelashes. He dug frantically at his eyes to clear them.

His blackened face looked like he'd been splashed with acid. His features seemed melted, with his hair and mustache singed black. Flames crept from his wrists to the sleeves of his jacket, filling the air with the smell of melting nylon.

"Bitch!" he shrieked.

Before Jenny could back away, he lunged and grabbed the shoulder of her shirt, slamming her to the ground. He landed roughly on top of her, the stench of burning flesh making her gag. She batted his arms in an effort to keep the flames away, but he wouldn't back off.

She screamed in revulsion. Her flailing fingers brushed the razor knife on the ground. Grabbing it, she slammed the blade into his face, pulling down and out until she sliced his cheek to the bone.

He roared in rage and pulled back his head, but he still clutched

Jenny with superhuman strength. She twisted violently and slashed his arm and hand, repeatedly slicing into his shirt.

He pulled himself off her and stood. As he loomed menacingly over her, blood dripped down his arms in rivulets. Frantic, Jenny rolled to her knees and lunged for a piece of wood he'd left beside the fire pit.

Grabbing a manageable piece, she swung it against his arm hard. A sickening sound filled the air as his humerus snapped. Drawing back the piece of wood like a batter at the plate, she screamed and swung repeatedly, striking his arms and chest.

Expecting him to fall to the ground, she jumped back in horror as he lunged at her again, his ruined arm dangling uselessly. She swung again, clubbing the side of his head with all the force she could muster.

He whirled. Trying to catch himself, he tripped on a rock. Before he could regain his balance, he stumbled into the roaring flames. His bone-chilling shriek turned into a wailing hiss as the flames consumed him. He turned his head to one side and gurgled, blood frothing over his twisted lips.

Jenny drew back and clubbed his head again. Watching in wide-eyed horror, she saw him twitch and go limp. Gasping for air and shaking, she backed away from the fire.

A voice crackled from the snowstorm. Startled, she whirled, seeking the source. The insistent voice lured her to the snow at the base of a nearby tree. Confused, she approached it, knelt, and wiped away snow until she uncovered the sheriff's radio.

She picked it up and keyed the mike after hearing the deputy's voice. After carefully giving him instructions, she sat back and waited as flames danced in the fire pit, melting the contents.

Brush snapped, and the deputy entered the clearing. He stopped in midstride, his eyes going to the charred figure in the fire pit.

"He's the serial killer," Jenny said woodenly. "He killed his daughter."

Raw shock was chiseled on the deputy's face. "This will kill his wife when she finds out, what with all she's been through lately."

"I can show you where he buried Shelly Richards. She was his last one."

He nodded silently, and she led him to the grave. She returned to sit by Sandra as he dug.

"Oh, shit." He began retching violently.

"What is it?" she asked.

"I found more graves…a lot more."

Later that night there was a press release from the sheriff's office. Jenny was there after learning her mother would recover. Sandra was taken to the hospital, where she remained under observation for concussion.

Jenny sat in the audience, bone tired, watching dully. The deputy stood at the podium and cleared his throat.

"The sheriff was found dead today in the campgrounds near Mirror Lake. He appeared to have been brutally attacked. Nothing is conclusive, because most of the evidence was destroyed by fire. All we have to go on is a piece of his shirt, which was totally shredded."

He made brief eye contact with Jenny, and something unspoken passed between them.

"It seems he was attacked by a grizzly bear," the deputy continued. "This happened in the same area he'd been warning people away from for weeks because of sightings of a grizzly. His absence will change our community forever.

"There was a jumble of bones in the fire pit. Based on a strong lead, we believe they are the remains of the serial killer. We're currently investigating that angle."

Gasps came from the crowd.

"Is there anything you'd like to add, Jenny?" He looked at her briefly.

She regarded him in silence for a moment, wanting to say that creatures like grizzlies could become mean and unpredictable when cornered.

Then she slowly shook her head. "No. No comment."

Clyde Braden, a former electronics salesman and technical writer with a BA in Creative Writing, ventures into the interesting world of short story fiction. He makes his home in Princeton Minnesota and travels the western hemisphere in search of his next story.

Kidnapped
Clyde Braden

Colonel John Kenneth Morgan, Retired, better known in Army Special Forces circles as JK, sat at his desk, preparing a proposal to the Illinois Sheriff's Association. They had requested a bid for a series of training sessions in antiterrorist tactics and control. He was putting the finishing touches on the proposal when his computer began beeping frantically, and a pop-up screen flashed an intrusion warning at his home.

A chill went through his body, and his mind raged. His phone chimed with an incoming call from Dell Franklin in company security.

"JK," Dell said, "the intrusion alarm at your home is a broken window in you daughter's bedroom. She arrived home fifteen minutes ago."

"Call the police right now! Give them all you have. I'm on my way home." He slammed down the receiver and bounded across the room to a private stairway leading to the roof. Taking the stairs three at a time, he burst through the rooftop door and scrambled into his waiting helicopter.

As he began the engine starting sequence, he called Chicago

Control and informed them of his emergency flight. By the time he received clearance, the engine was warm enough for a safe lift-off.

The last time this happened, my wife died, he thought. *Now my daughter's home alone. Please, God, don't let anything happen to her.*

Eighteen months earlier, JK's home was broken into, and his wife, Celia, had been brutally raped repeatedly. After the intruder left, Celia showered, set her hair, walked into the bedroom, took a gun from the bedside table, and calmly returned to the bathroom. After inserting the barrel into her mouth, she pulled the trigger. The rapist had never been identified.

After that, JK had his technical staff create an ID chip for his daughter and everyone who worked for his company, Innovative Security. If any of them went missing, he could locate them quickly using GPS and one of the company's communications satellites.

Morgan Manor was forty minutes north of Innovative Security by helicopter. He approached the house fast at treetop level, landing on the lawn instead of his helipad. The highway patrol had two cars there, and he saw the sheriff's department was also on the scene with a deputy.

JK sprinted to the house, where the sheriff waited at the front door.

"There's no one inside," the sheriff announced. "There's evidence of a struggle, including bloodstains on the bed and another unidentified stain with them. You can go in, but please don't touch anything, OK?"

"I understand, Frank. Let an officer come in with me. Do you have the crime lab on its way?"

"Yes. They'll be here in a minute. The state guys are looking for anything outside the house. We'll coordinate with them. I'll try to have something for you in the next few days." He turned to one side and called, "Dave, over here! Go with JK. He wants to look at the scene. Maybe he can spot something that we missed or doesn't fit."

"Sure thing, Frank." Dave walked up. "Anytime you're ready, JK."

"Let's start at the point of entry. Then we'll go in."

They walked to the rear of the house and to the broken window. JK studied the ground. "Have the lab people look at those marks on the lawn. They look like tire marks to me. See if they can identify them. Let's go inside through the patio door."

JK pulled out his PDA and entered a code. Pushing a *Go* button, he watched the door slide open softly.

They walked into Betty's bedroom. Her book bag lay on the desk with a scattering of broken glass across the bag, desk, and floor between the desk and window. JK saw several droplets of blood on the white bedspread, along with a still-wet spot in the middle of the bed.

"Have the lab test that wet spot. Ask them for a DNA test against the one we found when my wife was raped." He looked down and slowly bent over, picking up Betty's underpants.

Not again, he thought. *Please, Lord, don't let it end like Celia.*

"You think it's semen?" Dave asked.

"You bet I do. I'll wager it matches the DNA from the last one. The MO's the same, and he even used the same window to get in."

JK left the bedroom and went to the outside door off the family room. Sure enough, it was open. "There's evidence of a struggle in here. See if the lab people can find anything."

Walking through the rest of the house, they didn't see anything missing or out of place.

"Dave, tell Frank to make sure he does a thorough job collecting the evidence. I'll be at his office by eight o'clock tomorrow morning. I'm going back to the office to see if I can track Betty." Trotting to his helicopter, he quickly became airborne.

As he flew, he hit his cell phone speed dial to call his security chief. "Dell, get two of our field operatives fully equipped for covert operation. Have them in my office by noon tomorrow. I don't care who they are or where you pull them from. Is our comsat tied up with anything important?"

"Not really. Is it that serious?"

"Yes. He's got Betty, and we have to find her fast. Activate a search for her ID chip and let me know if she's still alive. I'll be in the office in thirty-five minutes. Meet me there."

"I'll be there."

JK landed his helicopter on the roof and took the steps three at a time to his office.

"She's still alive, Boss," Dell reported. "The signal has been stationary for the last five minutes."

"That's great." He pressed a button, and his office door opened.

"What do you need, JK?" Lucy, his secretary, asked.

"Have the helicopter refueled and ready within an hour." He turned back to Dell. "Did you find two operatives?"

"Yes. They'll arrive by midnight."

"Great. Equip them for a night assault. No long arms, just side arms and an MP3 for all of us. Give the coordinates to the CIA and FBI. I want some high-resolution prints of the area immediately.

"Please don't tell the police what we're doing. I want to get her back myself, and I don't want the cops involved until later. Understand?"

"Perfectly."

"When the guys arrive, I want us to meet them. I'll make sure I'm back by eleven o'clock. Go get those pictures."

As Dell walked off, Lucy walked in carrying a small paper bag. "The chopper will be ready in five minutes. Dell told me what happened. I figured you'd be leaving again, so I had the lunchroom fix a couple sandwiches and a cold protein drink."

"Thanks. I want to scout the area of these coordinates. I want to make sure we get this guy and Betty back. Call Dr. Chet Winslow for me. As soon as we have Betty, I want her examined."

"I'll give him a heads-up right away. Is there anything else I can do for you?"

"Yeah. As soon as Dell has those pictures, call me on the company frequency. I'll leave my radio on and have a handheld with me. Set up the conference room for midnight tonight. We may not need it, but have it ready, just in case. I want a hot meal for at least four people. That'll do it for now."

Lucy left, and JK opened the top drawer of his desk, taking out a 9mm automatic pistol that fit in his shoulder holster. He dropped a small GPS into his pocket, picked up his map case, and walked to the staircase leading to the roof.

As he came out the roof door, seeing his chopper was ready, he performed a slow walkaround inspection, checking everything. He didn't need any unexpected problems.

He flew twenty miles west of his home around the southern lakes region of Wisconsin. While making a slow pass over the GPS location, he saw a small cabin hidden under the trees three hundred yards from a hard-surfaced road. It looked like there was a narrow dirt road winding through the trees until it ended at the cabin. Thick underbrush surrounded the cabin, which would make it easy to approach undetected.

Three miles away was a small clearing with a nearby farmhouse. He landed in the clearing and turned off his engine, slipping into a light jacket to conceal his gun as he approached the farmhouse.

He knocked on the front door, and a middle-aged woman answered.

"Good morning," JK said. "I'd like to ask you permission to leave my helicopter in that clearing for a few hours. I'm looking at some property nearby and want to see it from the ground. I shouldn't be longer than two hours."

"Whose property are you looking at?" she asked.

"Just west of here a few miles. I don't know who owns it, but my Realtor gave me the location. I flew over it, and it looks like something I'd be interested in."

"That's all right. You can leave it there. My kids are at camp this week, and my husband went to town to pick up some things. No one will bother it."

JK winced as she spoke. "I'm a security specialist. I advise you never to tell such things to a stranger. It leaves you in a very vulnerable position."

She blushed. "Maybe you're right. I'll try to remember that." She closed the door. When he heard the lock click into place, he smiled.

Walking to the blacktop road, he turned toward the cabin's driveway. When he walked a mile, he entered the woods and moved slowly through the underbrush, stopping every two or three hundred yards to check his GPS. When he was within two hundred yards of the cabin, he stopped, crouched behind a bush, and scanned the area with his binoculars.

After a few minutes, he moved to within sight of the cabin and repeated his observation, that time, for twenty minutes. He didn't see or hear anything moving in or around the cabin.

Slowly, he moved away from the cabin and circled to the opposite side. Spotting an old, rusted-out van under a tree ten yards from the back door, he paused. When he didn't see any evidence of a dog, he doubted anything would spook whoever was in the cabin.

It was almost sundown. He decided to see how close he could get to the cabin's rear wall. Perhaps he could hear someone talking inside.

His portable radio vibrated. He moved back into the underbrush, removed the radio from his pocket, slipped the earphone in place, and said softly, "Go."

"I just got your photos," Dell said. "The two operatives have arrived and have been briefed as much as I can."

"Understood. I'll be back in ninety minutes. Have some food ready for us. I'm heading back to the chopper now. Out."

JK began a silent, quick withdrawal. Reaching his helicopter, he took off as quickly as he could. Ninety minutes later, in full dark, he landed gently on the office roof.

Back in his office, he greeted Dell and the two operatives, Bill Justice and Cindy Allan.

"Good to see you both," JK said. "Dell has told you what we're into. As soon as we get some food, I'll tell you what we're up against. This should be a simple rescue."

As they ate, JK described the situation. "I'd like you, Cindy, to take one of our suburban vans and drive to that location." Placing a picture on an overhead projector, he showed her where the driveway was located. "Park on the blacktop road a mile short of the driveway. As soon as Bill and I get Betty out of that cabin, I want you to get in there as fast as you can. We'll load her into the van and have you take her to Dr. Winslow. He'll be expecting you."

"Bill and I will take care of the kidnapper and do clean-up. I don't want the police involved unless I say so. Any questions? OK. Dell, did you get Bill and Cindy equipped?"

"Yes. They've got the things you asked me to get."

"Good. Cindy, it's a two-hour drive. Bill and I will fly up in the chopper. When you arrive, call us on the company frequency. We'll both have portable radios, and the chopper will act as a repeater. Drive carefully. We need you and the van to take Betty to medical attention.

"I didn't see anything at the cabin, but I think both of them are in there, because a van was parked near the back door. Cindy, call as soon as you're in place. It's time to go."

Thirty minutes later, Bill and JK took off from Innovative Security's roof. A little after midnight, they landed in a small clearing a little closer to the cabin.

JK checked his watch. They were twenty minutes early. He turned to Bill, sitting in the left seat, and said, "Let's take five minutes to get you oriented. A mile west of here is the cabin. The front door faces south. I want you to cover the side entrance. I'll go in through the front. I don't think locks will be much of a problem. There may not be any locks at all. It's a remote area, so he might feel safe. Give the handle a try.

"Set your MP3 on a two-shot burst. I don't think we'll need the weapons, but I want to be ready. If we can, we'll take him alive. I have special punishment in mind for him. When we leave the chopper, we'll go directly to the cabin. From then on, no talking. When you're in position, touch the alert button on your comm unit, then move toward the side door. Any questions?"

"None. Let's get this thing started."

Fifteen minutes later, they crouched fifty yards from the cabin. No lights showed inside. JK signaled Bill to take his position, and he melted into the underbrush. JK, listening closely, didn't hear a thing. Even the breeze was still.

Soon, feeling a vibration from his comm unit, he moved toward the front door. When he stepped onto the porch, a board squeaked, and JK froze for several seconds. He turned the doorknob and felt the door open silently.

Stepping inside, he moved to the left and heard the side door squeak as Bill entered the cabin. A moment later, he saw Bill moving in a crouch across the kitchen.

There was no sign of anyone. Two doors were visible on the rear wall. He signaled Bill to enter the room on the left. Bill slowly turned the knob, and quickly pushed the door open and entered low and to the left, while JK came in high and to the right.

It was a bedroom, and someone was sleeping on the bed. With Bill watching, JK moved silently toward the bed. He set his MP3 on the floor and took a package from his combat vest, removing a small piece of cloth. Very carefully, he draped it over the face of the man in the bed, then signaled Bill to move to the next room.

Bill crouched to one side of the door and twisted the knob slowly. He swung the door open and entered the room as before with JK right behind him.

JK walked to the bed and saw his naked daughter tied in a spread-eagled position on the bed, sleeping. He gently touched her shoulder, and her eyes popped open.

"Please, not again," she moaned. "Not now. I can't take anymore." She started crying.

"Betty, it's Dad, Honey. It's Dad!" He grabbed a blanket and covered her with it, then cut off the ropes on her arms and legs.

Watching him, she cried even harder. JK kissed her cheeks and forehead.

"You're safe now, Honey. I'll carry you out to Cindy, and she'll take you to Dr. Chet. Bill, come here."

Bill moved to his side.

"Cindy just signaled that she's in position. I put an ether cloth over the prisoner. Watch him until I return. Tie him down like he did to Betty and take off the ether cloth. Try not to kill him. I'll be right back after I take Betty to Cindy."

JK called Cindy and asked her to drive to the cabin. Lifting Betty off the bed, he carried her outside. Cindy arrived a moment later, and JK placed Betty into the front passenger seat, belting her in. He laid the seat back down and made sure she was covered.

Kissing her, he said, "Close your eyes, Honey. Get some sleep on the trip home. You're safe now. As soon as I finish here, I'll go home. Cindy, take good care of her. Tell Chet I'll be there as fast as I can."

He watched the Suburban maneuver down the narrow driveway, then walked into the cabin.

"Bill, I want you to fly the chopper into the clearing out front. We'll be leaving soon. Right now, I need to talk to the kidnapper."

Bill nodded and left.

JK went to the bed and looked down at the man, who was just waking up from the ether.

"Who the hell are you?" he asked groggily. "Why am I tied up?"

"I'm the father of the young lady you just kidnapped. You made a very big mistake this time. You never should've returned to my house a second time." JK smiled as he pulled up a chair.

"Here's the deal. You're responsible for my wife's death last year, and now you've caused me and my family additional pain by kidnapping, beating, and raping my daughter. To me, you don't deserve to live, but I'll give you a chance to live if you'll write a confession for both crimes and request that the court has you surgically sterilized. After that, you'll devote your life to helping battered women and children. Do you agree?"

"Not in your lifetime, Soldier Boy. Sure, I raped your wife, but I didn't hit her. She took her own life. I just brought her a little pleasure. Your daughter put up too much of a fight. I had to hit her a few times to make her cooperate. Hell, I only did her four times, once at the house, then three times here. If she wasn't so damn good at it, I would've stopped with the one time at the house."

While the man talked, JK removed a small zippered case from the cargo pocket on the back of his left pant leg. Without a word, he filled a syringe with clear liquid.

The man's eyes widened. "What's in the needle? What are you going to do with it?"

"In view of your last statement, I'll be glad to tell you. I intend to inject this liquid into you. What it'll do is a closely guarded secret. I'll tell you after I finish prepping the injection."

When he was ready, he said, "This is a very effective way of taking care of certain situations. A very wise witch doctor, or shaman, in Africa showed this to me and told me how to use it. When I push the plunger, this liquid will circulate through your body in about forty seconds. Within two days, you won't have any bones left. This stuff won't kill you, but you'll sure wish it had. You won't be able to do anything, including eat.

"Eventually, it'll affect your brain. You can't keep your brain in place without your skull. Within a week, you'll be close to death. In another week, you'll be nothing but teeth and spoiled meat."

"You can't do this to me! The police will trace it to you! It's murder!"

A soft smile came to JK's face as he looked down at his captive. "There won't be any trail for them to find. If they find you in time, they'll do an autopsy, but I can assure you they'll never have anything to tie me to this. The only thing they'll find that will make them think your remains are that of a human being will be your teeth. You should note that I'm wearing surgical gloves. There won't be any fingerprints.

"You made a big mistake when you didn't bother checking what I do for a living. I'm a security consultant for the federal government, various police departments, and large corporations.

"In crimes like this, I don't have any faith in our judicial system. With my contacts and inside knowledge, though, no one will question me. I see needle marks on your arms, which mean you're an addict. The doctors who do the autopsy on you will see them, too, and won't bother looking for an extra needle mark. Even if they can identify your remains, they'll just assume you tried some new drug, and it backfired.

"Now, my young friend, your time has come."

The man fought against his bonds. JK pinched a nerve in his shoulder, and he became quiet. He slid up the man's shirtsleeve and exposed the vein on the inside of his elbow. With one sure movement, he slid the needle into the veins and pressed the plunger.

"Damn you!" the man shouted. "You did it! Damn you to hell!'"

"I'm sure I'll meet you there, but not for a while. I'll be back in a few hours to remove the restraints. I don't want anyone thinking you were held against your will. By then, you won't be able to move much."

Three hours later, JK returned to the cabin. "How are things going with you, Young Man? Comfortable?"

"Damn you to hell! I'm burning all over. It hurts like hell."

"I know. I'm afraid it'll get a lot worse, but then, you deserve it." He lifted the man's hand and pinched his fingers and the heel of his hand. He couldn't feel any bones in the fingers, and only the large bones in the hand were still in place.

He placed the man's hand on the mattress and carefully removed all the ropes that tied him down. "I don't advise your getting up or trying to move. If you do, you'll feel a lot of pain before you die. However, that's up to you.

"I have a question to ask. How many women have you raped in the last two years? You don't have to answer. I just thought you'd like to clear your conscience."

"Why not? Over the last two years, maybe forty to forty-five. Maybe more. I lose count after a while. None were badly hurt. Your daughter put up a good fight, but every time I entered her, she climaxed. I hit her only twice. I never wanted to hurt any of them. I just wanted to bring 'em a little pleasure."

JK frowned and stared out the window. "You're very sick, Son. I suppose what I've done to you is cruel and unusual punishment, but I'm not sorry. At least you won't rape any more women in this life.

"I'm leaving now. Take my advice and don't move. It'll be over soon. I'll see you in hell."

JK left the cabin and closed the door.

The Hunter

Clyde Braden

It was mid-November, 1956, an hour and a half before sunrise in the mountains of northwestern Colorado.

Ron Dolan had just returned from Korea for his first deer-hunting trip in four years. He dreamed about making the trip for weeks after he received orders to return to the States. He hoped the Marines would discharge him in time for some hunting, and he was very excited when it happened.

He brought his mother's wind-up alarm clock so he could get up before sunrise, setting it beside the bedding in the back of his father's station wagon. The alarm went off loudly. As he'd done many times during the war, his eyelids popped open, though he didn't move a muscle. Identifying the unwelcome noise, he moved to quiet the clock, dressed, and looked out at the gently falling rain.

"It'll be a cold, wet day. Oh, well. It's not like I haven't been wet before."

He slid several sandwiches his mother made into a jacket pocket, then ate one for breakfast, washing it down with lukewarm coffee from his thermos. Opening the door, he slipped the rifle sling over his shoulder with the barrel pointed down and walked quietly into the darkness.

Rain fell softly. Low, thick clouds closed in on the mountaintops, hiding the sky. Although he carried a flashlight, he was in familiar territory and kept walking without it. Wet leaves and needles muffled his footsteps. The trees stood like silent skeletons, guarding the countryside.

Ron moved carefully and quickly around those silent sentinels. Out of habit, his eyes scanned the trees, underbrush, and hillsides for movement. As he listened intently for a sound, he heard a twig break.

He froze. His rifle came off his shoulder slowly and quietly. Crouching behind a tree trunk, he slipped off the safety as sweat mixed with rain on his face. His eyes strained to penetrate the darkness. Where had the sound come from? What caused it? As far as he could see, nothing moved.

Rain washed his skin and dripped from the brim of his cap. Waiting, he heard another twig snap. His eyes swiveled toward the sound, where he detected slight movement. His heart jumped to his throat, and his mouth was dry. Carefully, he raised the rifle to his shoulder.

Abruptly, he lowered the rifle and slumped against the tree, laughing quietly to himself. *I'm not in the Korean jungle. I'm in Colorado. There aren't any enemies here that I know of.*

When he peeked around the tree, he saw a doe with a yearling spike buck at her side moving slowly away from him.

A shiver went up his spine, and he held his hands in front of his eyes, surprised to see them shaking. Looking toward the heavens, he asked, "What's happening to me?"

After he calmed down a few minutes later, he thumbed on the safety, stood, and slung the rifle over his shoulder as he moved ahead. Force of habit made him constantly scan his surroundings. He moved quickly through the trees, down a ravine, and halfway up the next hill to a tree stand he built three days earlier. Climbing into the stand, he sat on the rain-slicked seat, leaning back against the trunk, and let his breathing and body return to normal.

Slowly, the sky brightened as dawn approached. From his perch high above the ground, he was able to see a long way between the skeletal trees. Nothing moved in the silent woods, and his thoughts returned to Korea. He thought about the war, his two tours or duty, his friends in the Marines, the friends he'd lost, and about killing.

The muscles in his body tightened like the strings of a well-tuned violin until his whole body was shaking. Sobs racked him, and low keening came from his lips while hot tears flooded his eyes. He never noticed when his grip on the rifle relaxed, and it fell to the ground. Burying his face in his hands, he released his rage, fear, and sorrow.

After a time, when the emotional storm passed, and his body was back to normal, he climbed down from the tree stand. Retrieving his fallen rifle, he slung it over his shoulder with the barrel pointed down and walked quietly away. From force of habit, his eyes scanned the trees, underbrush, and hillsides for movement, and his ears listened intently for any hint of sound from the silent mountainside.

The Man on the Corner

Joyce Jackson

Prologue

You don't always know what kind of pictures, activities, and people a child sees walking in a neighborhood. Some things a child sees leave their mark on him the rest of his life. This one marked mine.

Chapter One
Going to Auntie's

Friday I felt good. My chores at home were done, so my foster mother granted me permission for a walk. I never told her where I went. After all, how far could an eight-year-old girl walk before becoming fearful, lost, and running back the way she came?

Perhaps it's best not to know. The moment I left the house, the phone rang.

"Wait a minute, Sarah!" Mom said. "I have an errand for you. That was from my sister, Mrs. Murray. She's been ill for some time and needs food. Will you take her a basket of food?"

I didn't know why she asked. I'd never been to Auntie's house before. She lived at least five miles away. Nevertheless, when Mom or Dad asked me to do something, I did it without talking back. Mom and Dad Miller brought two other foster children and me to visit her sister, but we never walked there. I wasn't sure I could find it alone.

All I remembered about the house was the large yard and living room with a fireplace. Mrs. Murray kept a small space heater on the floor near her recliner chair, which always sat near the fireplace. The last time I saw her, she was in that chair. The space heater was on, and she was wrapped from the neck down in a wrap-around blanket. That was two weeks earlier, the first time I saw a wrap-around blanket. I thought it was wonderful to have one.

"Does the fireplace work?" I asked.

"Oh, yes, but we can't use it until I have my chimney cleaned," she replied.

"Oh."

I thought about what she said and wondered how one cleaned a chimney but didn't ask. I asked if we children could have apples from her tree in the backyard.

"Yes, but only the ones on the ground," she said.

The apples were sour but tasty.

Mrs. Murray once had foster children, too. Rumor had it that her last foster child was a boy. While Auntie slept one evening, he found an old trunk of hers. Inside was her dead husband's Army rifle, and the boy shot himself in the hand. People said she was too old to care for children anymore, and she was negligent, so she wasn't allowed to care for foster children at home anymore.

I realized why she'd been bundled up the last time I saw her. She was ill, but that was two weeks earlier. Two weeks was a long time to be ill.

Mother gave me directions:

Walk on the right of our street to the end. Go around the corner. Remain on that side of the street. Walk one more block until the cemetery, then walk past the cemetery and go one more block before taking a right. After two blocks, cross the street. The street you cross onto will be Martin Street.

"OK," I said, feeling like Little Red Riding Hood taking a basket of goodies to Grandma's house.

I walked past my neighborhood of well-kept homes and apartment houses. The character of the neighborhood changed to old, unkempt, broken-down apartment buildings. Garbage lay in the streets. Once I passed an eerie cemetery and became frightened. I thought I was going in the wrong direction and couldn't remember seeing anything like that before.

Shabbily dressed people stood on the sidewalk near some shops. I needed to reaffirm my directions, but no one I saw looked safe enough to ask. I looked around and saw a man sitting in a chair near the corner, store.

"Do you know where Martin Street is?" I asked.

He looked at me curiously. "Three more blocks across the street. Can you cross the street alone, Little Girl?"

"Yes. Thank you."

I walked past him two more blocks, looked both ways, and crossed the street. I found myself in front of an apartment building where children played in the dirt and on the sidewalk. When I asked which house was Mrs. Murray's, they didn't know.

Soon, a woman came out to call the children inside.

"You'd better go home, Little Girl," she said. "It's getting dark."

"I have to take my basket of food to my auntie's house. I don't have the exact address, just the street name."

"What does the house look like?"

"I don't know. It's a single house with a front and backyard."

"I know that house."

"I know it, too," the boy said. "You'd better stay away from there. That lady's mean. What's in the basket?"

"I don't know. I never looked."

"How come?"

"I don't know."

"Don't you want to see what's in it?"

"Yes."

The boy and I sat on the steps of his apartment building and opened the basket. We found sandwiches, soup mix, coffee, soda, and eight large ginger cookies.

"May I have one of those cookies?" he asked.

"Yes."

We sat on the steps and ate two cookies each.

"There are only three single homes on this street," the woman said. "Only one has a front yard."

I thanked her, said good-bye to the boy, rewrapped the basket, and crossed the street to the only single house on Martin Street with a front yard.

As I approached the house, I saw tall, uncut grass and overgrown hedges. The house looked eerie. The uneven hedges near the door and corners of the house looked spooky. I thought I saw a face in the window as I walked slowly to the door to ring the bell, but no one answered. I was about to leave when Auntie opened the door.

"I saw you out there," she said, "and thought you were one of the neighborhood kids who climb the back fence and the apple tree. Complaining to their mothers doesn't do any good. Their parents want me to cut that tree down. Sometimes, the kids ring my bell and run. They do that all day sometimes. I get mad and throw things at them."

While she talked, I remembered something I did the previous week. I opened the phone book, chose a number, and dialed it. When the person answered, I asked if their house was on a bus line. If they said yes, I'd ask them to move it, because a bus was coming. Sometimes, they won a prize for their answer…a ton of horse manure delivered to their front lawn the following morning. I laughed and hung up.

"Come in and sit down," she said. "Have some cookies."

"Thank you." I handed her the basket.

"Thank you." She carried the basket into the kitchen. When she returned, she said, "I have two spare bedrooms, one beside mine and one at the top of the stairs. You're welcome to spend the night."

"No, thank you. I have to return home."

Suddenly, I saw two cats enter the living room. One was large with huge paws and a big head. The other was smaller.

"Oh, you have cats!" I said. "I never saw cats here before."

"Yes. I have seven cats."

"Where are the others?"

"Somewhere around."

"Who feeds them?"

"I do, but they haven't been fed today. Would you like to feed them?"

I'd never been that close to an animal before. I was frightened, especially of the big one. "No, thank you. I have to return home before dark."

"OK. You'd better run along."

"Good-bye." I left.

As I walked along past the apartment building, nothing looked the same. Crossing the street to the corner store, I found the same man sitting outside.

"Are you still out here, Little Girl?" he asked.

I wondered the same about him.

"It's too dark for you to walk around this neighborhood alone."

"Oh, I'm almost home."

He didn't know how much farther I had to go. I reached the next block, beside the cemetery, and everything from there looked familiar. I had to walk another three blocks down and then go around the corner.

If anyone passes a cemetery at night when the moon is full and the sky is slightly overcast with gray clouds, he knows how the shapes of the gravestones and tree shadows can do things to his imagination. I must've watched too many scary movies about dead people coming from their graves at night. I ran past the cemetery and almost wet my pants.

I arrived home at seven-thirty, and it was almost dark.

"What took you so long?" Mom asked.

"I had trouble finding the house. A man helped me first, then a woman."

"What man and woman? Didn't we tell you not to talk to strangers?"

I explained how different the yard looked at that time of day. Overgrown grass, untrimmed hedges, and no house number made the house difficult to recognize.

"I'm sorry," Mom said. "Did you get the number?"

"I looked for it, but an overgrown tree branch covered the area where the number should be."

"I saved supper for you and called Mrs. Murray, because it was getting dark. She said you were on your way."

I ate and went to bed with a lot to think about.

Chapter Two
Back Again

Several weeks later, I asked Mom if I could go for a walk.

"Yes," she said.

I walked to Mrs. Murray's house without permission. Walking past the cemetery caused no trauma that time. It was daylight, and I walked closer to the street than the cemetery fence, just in case. No dead person would grab me that way.

Around the corner, I saw the man sitting in his chair in front of the corner store again, but I couldn't tell what kind of store it was. The sign needed to be repaired and hung from the side of the building. The painted name was washed or worn off.

The door was different. It resembled a fence gate with a padlock. As dilapidated as that building was, it fit in with the rest of the neighborhood...broken, unpainted, and uncared for. Why would anyone want a store in such a place? Who bought things there, and what did the store have for sale?

I was three feet from the man in the chair when I asked, "What do they sell in this store?"

"What did you say, Little Girl?"

I walked closer. "What do they sell here?"

"Oh, a lot of things. What do you want to buy?"

"Candy."

"I guess we got candy. Go in and see."

I went in and realized it was different from any store I'd ever seen. It looked like someone had taken old, dried wood and cracked boards, nailed them together, and created a store. The smells were good, though…hickory-smoked chicken and ham, collard greens, fish, rice, yams, white potatoes, and other cooked items. Three men were cooking. A few items sat on some boards used for shelves. I saw bread, canned milk, barbecue chips, pork rinds, and cereal, but no candy.

"What do you want?" someone asked.

"Candy."

"We ain't got no candy."

"Do you have gum?"

"Yeah, we got that."

I gave the clerk the nickel he asked for in payment, took my spearmint gum, and left.

"You find any candy in there?" the man in the chair asked.

"No. I bought gum instead."

As I walked by his chair, I saw it was on wheels. *How do they put wheels on chairs?* I wondered. I'd never seen a chair with wheels before. There were two large wheels in back and two smaller ones in front. *Boy, if I were confined to a wheelchair, I'd love to have someone bring me outside. What nice friends he has. Why didn't I notice the wheels before?*

I took one last look and saw other men greeting the sitting one, exchanging words and laughing. One greeter received money from the man, and in return he gave him a slip of paper. It was nice of them to take his grocery list and buy things for him.

I heard about children who had polio who couldn't walk. They had to use wheelchairs, but I never saw them. Perhaps he was a grown-up man who'd been a polio victim. I had to learn to be more observant. How could I miss something as obvious as a wheelchair?

The rest of the walk took me past the apartment house where the children played. I heard them playing inside. Someone cried. I went into the building and saw four apartments, two up and two down. I knocked on the downstairs doors. No one answered the door on the right. On the left, an older boy answered.

"Is your mother home?" I asked.

"She's working."

"May I speak to your father?"

"He's in jail."

"Oh. Who's taking care of you?"

He was just about to answer when a lady from upstairs shouted, "John! Who's that?"

I told her my name. "I'm inviting John to come out and play."

"I don't know," she said. "I'm watching out for him until his mother returns. I don't want him playing on the street."

They don't have a front yard, I thought. *Where else would he play?*

"Are you going to your aunt's house?" John asked.

"Yes, but she isn't expecting me."

"Your aunt has a nice yard." He looked up at the woman. "Can I go out?"

"No. You always run in the street."

John turned to me. "May I play in your aunt's yard?"

I thought that over. "Yes."

Two other children peeked around the woman's legs. One little girl dried her tears, and a boy of five stood opposite her. They wanted to come, too.

I nodded.

"The little girl's too young," the woman said, shaking her head.

Before we left, John's mother returned.

"I spoke with Mrs. Murray yesterday," she said. "We resolved our differences. My son can play in your aunt's yard as long as he has permission and doesn't climb the apple tree."

Both boys came with me to my aunt's yard to play. The little girl stayed home and cried some more.

John, Joe, and I walked across the street to my aunt's yard. *Boy, I'm in trouble now,* I thought. *She doesn't know I'm coming, and she won't expect John and Joe. Besides, I'm not allowed to play with boys.*

What's the difference? Boys are kids, too. People are supposed to share with others, even their yards.

"Can we have some apples?" the boys asked.

"I'll ask my aunt. You have to promise not to climb her apple tree, though."

"OK."

When we arrived, I saw the grass had been mowed. It was a nice yard with plenty of running room. No one answered the door when I rang the bell. To my surprise, I heard a bell ringing inside.

"Maybe she isn't home," I said.

We ran to the backyard and ran around, playing tag and rolling on the grass. It was fun.

I never paid attention to how big her apple tree was. All the large, red apples were in the top branches. One branch extended over the back fence at the corner of the backyard, and the top of the fence was bent.

"John, were you and Joe the ones who bent the fence trying to climb into the apple tree?" I asked.

"I don't know, but climbing onto that branch is the only way I could get any apples. I did most of the climbing, and Joe caught them when I threw them down." He looked around. "You've got a ladder! Want some apples?"

"There are apples on the ground."

Most of those apples were rotten and full of wormholes. I couldn't give rotten apples to my friends. I looked at the tree and wondered how to get apples from it, eyeing the branch hanging over the fence.

"John, are you sure that's the branch you used to climb the tree?" I asked.

"Yeah."

"Did you ever get permission to do that?"

"I rang the doorbell once and was given permission to have some apples, but the ones on the ground were rotten, so I climbed the fence to get to the tree and onto that big limb. Then I picked a few."

"Were they good?"

"Yes, but they were a little sour. The next day, I returned for more apples for Joe and my cousin, Tim. I climbed up without asking. Your aunt came out and asked us to leave. We didn't go, so she threw hot water on us. We left and told our mother."

I climbed the tree.

"You better be careful," John said. "If she comes out, she'll throw hot water on you, too."

"No, she won't. My mother's her sister. That makes her my aunt. If she does that, I'll tell."

Even with a stick, I was able to reach only a few apples.

Suddenly, the back door opened, and Auntie came out, but she didn't recognize me. She carried a pan in her hand, but we didn't know what was in it.

The boys didn't wait to find out. They ran, but instead of running out the way we came in and going past Mrs. Murray, they climbed the fence.

Once my aunt realized who was in the tree, she said, "I didn't know it was you."

"I rang the bell but didn't get an answer."

"Sometimes, it doesn't work."

"It worked today. I heard it."

"That bell hasn't worked for weeks."

"It didn't work the last time I was here, Auntie, but I heard it today."

"You're lying. You never rang that bell. If you did, I would've heard it. I saw you come into the yard. I told those children's parents not to allow them to climb my tree. The last time that bigger boy did, I asked him to leave. When he refused, he said swear words I wouldn't repeat. I threw hot water on him and burned his arm, and he left in a hurry. I didn't see him again until today.

"He walked around for two weeks with a bandage on his arm. His mother called the police, and I told all of them to stay out of my yard. Sometimes, they ring my bell or knock on the door, then hide. One day, they did it all afternoon, and I was tired of the aggravation."

"Auntie, John said you used to have a foster boy here. What happened to him?"

"They took him away."

I didn't know who *they* were. When I thought about it, I realized I didn't know who brought me to my foster home, either. I never asked.

"Why was he taken?" I asked.

"People in the neighborhood were jealous, because I have a nice home with a large yard. Sometimes, when you live in a home like that, people get jealous. They ganged up on me and signed a petition to get me out of here by saying I was crazy."

"Oh."

"Don't play with the children across the street. They're trashy. By the way, Sarah, I don't want you climbing my tree, either. I'll call my sister and tell her. That's too high. All the good apples are on top. You need a long stick to get them down. Last year, I hired a man with a ladder and long apple picker. He didn't get many, either. Now that I'm seventy, I don't bother with that tree. Come in and have lunch before you go home. I want to talk to you."

Before entering the house, I pushed the bell button. "Did you hear that?"

"Maybe it does work," she admitted.

We sat and talked. I said my mother didn't know I was there. I was away from home all day, and I was glad when Auntie called my mother, because that saved me from getting into trouble.

"I used to have foster kids here all the time," Auntie said. "It became too noisy when they and all the neighborhood kids played in my yard. Someone took me to court after his kid fell from the tree and broke his arm. He wanted me to pay the medical costs."

"Did you pay?"

"No. It still cost me the court costs and lawyer's fees."

"Auntie, you have a big yard. This is the only house on Martin Street with a yard. It's bigger than ours."

"How'd you like to spend the night here with me someday? I like you, and I don't think my sister would mind."

"What about school? How would I get there?"

"I'll fix your lunch, and you can walk from here."

"I don't know the way."

"Miller has a car, doesn't he? He can drive you."

Miller was my foster dad.

"He can't come here, pick me up, and drive me to school. He works in the morning."

"Think about it and let me know next week."

"OK."

"Now run along home. My sister's waiting for you."

I left Mrs. Murray's house with a lot on my mind. On the way home, I passed John and Joe's apartment building. His mom sat on the steps outside. I apologized to her for my aunt's behavior and explained that the kids teased her a lot. I added she was very old and couldn't walk very fast.

John's mom told me the same story about the court case, and she said something else.

"Several children used to live with your aunt, and they were taken away."

"Why? Were they her children?"

"I don't know. The little boy got shot in the left hand and was taken away in an ambulance. There was blood all over the place. We never saw him again."

"Mrs. Murray is lonely and wants company. I plan to spend some weekends with her and go to school from her house."

"Be careful, Little Girl. I wouldn't do that if I were you. That woman's crazy."

A man came outside and sat with her.

"This is John's father," she said.

"Hello," I said.

"John can't go there anymore."

I thought John said his father was in jail. Was that man really his father? That gave me another thing to think about.

I walked toward home and reached the corner where the man sat in his wheelchair.

"You back again, Little Girl?"

"Yes. I'm going to spend a few nights with my aunt each week from now on."

"Why anyone would choose to stay in this neighborhood is beyond me. I've been trying to get away from here for years. You'd better stay where you live. It's safer and nicer. Run along now. It's supposed to rain. You don't want to get wet."

It was getting darker. I assumed that meant it was late in the day, but, when I looked up, I saw grayish clouds. The man was right about the rain.

I used the cemetery as my landmark. I couldn't read street signs very well, but I knew that once I was past the cemetery, my street was just around the corner. The gray overcast sky and shadows on the gravestones made me feel eerie again.

A few raindrops touched my ears. As I hurried home, thunder clapped loudly in the sky, and the streetlights went out. I saw, or thought I saw, a large hand come up from behind a gravestone, then I saw other hands behind other stones.

I should've gone to the bathroom before leaving Auntie's house, I thought. I walked faster and stayed closer to the curb to ignore the cemetery.

"It isn't Armageddon yet," I told myself. "Or is it? No one knows when it's coming, or when the dead will be resurrected. Not now, please!"

Another thunderclap startled me, and I began shaking. It rained so hard, I was soaked before I reached the end of the cemetery. That time, I *did* wet my pants. Once I was past the cemetery, I relaxed, though the rain continued.

Mom was just saying good-bye to someone on the phone when I walked in. "Oh. Here she is now."

I hoped she wasn't talking to the police. I knew I'd been away a long time, and I was relieved when she added, "My sister called to see if you arrived safely. Come on. Let's get you out of those wet clothes."

She ran a warm bath for me, then I went to bed.

"I didn't save supper for you, because my sister said she fed you already," Mom said.

Nothing more was said about Mrs. Murray or about my spending the night at her house. I didn't ask about her or sneak over to her apple tree.

I never saw the man on the corner again, either, but I thought about him.

One Sunday after church, Dad took us for a ride to Mrs. Murray's house. We were told to call her that name, not Auntie. On the way, we passed the man in the wheelchair in front of the store. When he saw me, he waved, and I waved back. My family went into an uproar.

"Who's that strange man you waved to?"

"Where'd you meet him?"

"How is it possible for you to know someone like that?" Mom asked.

"What does like that mean?" When they didn't answer, I said, "I don't know him. He gave me directions once."

"To where?" Mom asked.

"To Martin Street the first time I walked to Mrs. Murray's house."

"You didn't need to ask him directions. You've been there before."

"Not walking. It was dark out, and nothing looked the same. I thought I was lost, and he helped me."

"Oh."

Dad didn't say anything.

When we reached Mrs. Murray's house, Mom yelled at her. "I don't want Sandra walking around this neighborhood, talking to strange men and playing with those children across the street. I don't know their parents."

How does she know about John and Joe? I wondered.

Mrs. Murray became angry with Mom. "Why'd you bother coming here?"

"Our visit was to fix your broken fence, clean the rotten apples in the backyard, and trim the hedges."

Mrs. Murray refused the help. "Can Sarah spend a few nights a week with me?"

"Yes," Mom said.

In our house, whatever Mom said usually happened.

As for the man on the corner, I saw him again.

Just before the weather became colder, I took another walk to Martin Street. I reached the corner in early afternoon and saw the wheelchair, but it was empty. It had a very high back made of woven cane and a circular cushion on the seat without a center part. That seemed odd.

I walked closer to the chair and touched one of the small wheels in front. The two large wheels in back had spokes. I heard arguing and loud, angry voices in the store. Soon, I saw the man being carried out.

"There. Are you all right now?" the one carrying the man asked.

I saw why this man needed a wheelchair. Both legs were gone. There was just enough upper leg for him to sit upright. The carrier went back into the store, got a blanket, and covered the man from the waist down. No one could know he was missing his legs.

"Do you have your numbers ready?" the carrier asked.

"Not yet."

"Got a pencil?" He handed one to the man, who wrote something on a piece of paper, and gave it to the carrier. The carrier looked at the paper and said, "OK. You need anything else before I leave?"

"No."

"Did you lose your legs in the war?" I asked.

"Yes, but I don't want to talk about it now."

"How long do you have to sit here?"

"Until someone comes home from work."

"Where do you live?"

Pointing at the stairs in the rear of the store, he said, "Up there on the second floor."

"How do you get up there?"

"My friends carry me."

"Does your wife or children help when you need something? Suppose you have to go to the bathroom? Who helps you?"

"I call, and my cousin inside the store helps me. Otherwise, I just sit here until someone comes. My friends help. There's always someone around. I don't have a wife. Run along, Little Girl, your aunt must be wondering where you are."

As I hurried along, I kept thinking about the man. Suppose there was no one around? He'd have to sit there all day, even if he was tired. What if it rained? He had no raincoat or umbrella. Someone had to make sure he had one.

"You should have an umbrella," I said, walking away.

"You're right," he said.

I went to Mrs. Murray's yard, picked up apples from the ground, turned, and walked toward home. I didn't ring the bell or knock on her door. I didn't want to come in. I just needed proof I'd been there.

Winter came, and I wondered about the man in the wheelchair. On Sunday after church, I asked Dad if he could take us to see Mrs. Murray. When we turned the corner past the cemetery, I looked to see if the man was in front of the store.

"What are you looking for?" Mom asked.

"There used to be a man sitting over there in a wheelchair."

"I know all about that man. My sister told me you've been bothering him with questions, and he doesn't like it."

"Is he related to you? Did you find one of your relatives?"

"No," I said. "At least, I don't think we're related."

Until that time, the possibility of having relatives hadn't occurred to me. I'd been in foster care for as long as I could remember, knowing nothing of my relatives.

On the way home, I asked if we could get some ice cream.

"Where can we get anything in this neighborhood?" Mom asked.

"There's a store on the corner. They might have ice cream. I know they have gum."

"No gum."

We stopped the car, and my two foster sisters and I went into the store. They had no ice cream, but we bought candy, which they had that time.

I asked the clerk what happened to the man in the wheelchair.

"I don't know."

"Are you related to him?" I asked.

"No. His nephew comes over sometimes, to see about him."

"He lives upstairs."

"It's too cold for him to sit outside now."

My sisters and I took our candy back to the car. I was glad the wheelchair man was someplace warm.

"Did you get your ice cream?" Mom asked.

"No. They didn't have any, so we bought candy instead."

Dad drove us home. We were happy.

Chapter Three
The Care

Years went by. I grew up, married, and eventually had teenage daughters of my own. One, like me, was a wanderer. Since I didn't fight in wars, I thought the least contribution I could give was to spend some of my nursing career years working in a VA hospital.

Getting into one as a civilian wasn't easy, but I managed. My husband, who died of cancer, was a veteran of World War Two. Veterans or spouses of veterans were always hired first in most VA hospitals. I went through the orientation program and worked nights, sometimes days, and evenings on a medical ward. I loved my job.

After six months, we had an admission, and I recognized him as the man from the corner.

"I know you," I said. "You sat in a wheelchair outside a store on the corner of Garden and Westland Streets."

"Yes. I done got old. My friends have died. My wife left me a long time ago. After I got back from the war, my nephew moved. Some of my buddies are in jail."

"What for?"

"Running numbers."

"I remember those pieces of paper being passed around had numbers on them."

"Right."

We laughed.

Every night when I arrived at work, I said hello to him. When I left, I said good-bye. In the beginning, men visited him and gave him money, but I never asked who they were. Staff said he had no relatives. No one told me why he was there. I thought he had no one to care for him. That proved true, but there was another reason.

271

One night I arrived at the hospital for my duty and found we were short-staffed. We had one RN, one LPN, and one aide to care for twenty patients. The difficult cases were at one end, while fourteen mostly ambulatory patients were in the short wing.

The aide floated between the two wings, assisting the nurses and the Intensive Care Unit at the end of the short wing...if she had time. I ended up with the short wing of fourteen patients. Three had IVs, six had to be prepped for morning tests, two to be prepped for morning surgery, and two were to be discharged in the morning. There was also one dressing change.

"What's a dressing change doing on this floor?" I asked. "Shouldn't he be on the surgical floor?"

"He needs a private room. We have the only private room available, so he's here."

If I needed help, I could borrow the aide and call the supervisor, too, for the IVs, if the RN was busy. I got a full report on my friend, Mr. Stone, as well as the other patients. Mr. Stone was depressed, unable to get out of bed, poorly nourished, and had a large sore on his butt. It was my job to keep him off his back so the sore could heal and to change his dressing.

I went down the hall with the medicine cart, gave out sleeping pills, checked the IVs, flushed the IV sites of those who needed it, and hung up NPO signs on the beds of all patients receiving tests and surgery. This reminded them not to eat or drink after midnight.

I had no elevated temps to deal with and just two pain pills to dispense. Two vets had finished drinking their Go Litiley. I made sure they had assistance when they needed to go to the bathroom down the hall.

I reached Mr. Stone's room last. As soon as I entered, I smelled an unusual odor and thought he needed cleaning up. He was sleeping on his stomach. This was good, because I wouldn't have to turn him over. Once I turned on the light, though, he woke up.

"I just fell asleep," he said angrily. "I told those nurses not to bother me. Leave me alone."

"I'm sorry. I didn't get that message. They sent me here to clean you and change your dressing."

"I remember you. You were the little girl who asked me all those questions while I sat outside the store in my wheelchair."

"Yes. I work here now. I'm a nurse. I don't usually have this end of the hall, but they sent me here tonight."

"How is it?"

"Not bad. It's my first time here. I'm a little slow. Sorry I didn't get to your room sooner."

I removed the covers as I talked. He'd lost weight. His ribs were visible, and his arms were very thin. His supper tray had barely been touched.

"I see you didn't eat much," I said.

"I wasn't hungry."

"Do you know why you're here?"

"Yes. They're trying to get this sore to heal."

I examined the sore on his coccyx. *Boy, what happened here?* I wondered.

The odor was very bad, and it was not due to feces or urine. I saw serous drainage on the bottom sheet, some new, some old and dried. I offered him a urinal, which he used, and I left the room to empty it, telling him I'd return with a dressing supply pack and change his dressing.

"OK," he said.

When I left, I spoke to the charge nurse about Mr. Stone's condition, explaining the dirty dishes, foul room odor, and large amounts of old drainage on the sheets.

"He doesn't want to be bothered," the male charge nurse replied. "He got angry and swore at the last nurse who tried to care for him, so they left him alone."

"Oh."

Returning to Mr. Stone's room, I told him of my conversation with the charge nurse.

"Can you smell the odor in here?" I asked.

"Yes."

"It's so bad, I can smell it in the hall. Let me get rid of these sheets and give you clean ones."

Pillows went against the bed's side rails. With no legs to assist in turning, he managed, with my help, to rest on his side against the pillows. I draped the top sheet over him, because he wasn't wearing any clothes.

"Where's your Johnny top?" I asked. "Don't you want one?"

Some vets slept naked. As long as they were covered with a sheet, no one made a fuss. Once they were up and about, though, they had to be covered. Occasionally, someone passed me in the hall, heading for the bathroom stark naked. I reminded him of the rules about covering up. We had plenty of pajamas and robes. The men usually apologized and put on a robe or at least pajama bottoms. The hospital might be a vet haven, but it wasn't the Garden of Eden.

"I don't know," he said. "They never gave me one."

It was a good thing I wore gloves. My hands kept slipping and feeling wet. I removed the top sheet to see why, and I understood why he wore no clothing. Running down both sides of his body was serous drainage, oozing from the largest wound I ever saw.

This was no ordinary bedsore. His entire butt was almost gone. The only intact areas were the perineal and a strip of anal tissue. Every time he moved or was moved by someone else, more drainage came.

"How long have you had this?" I asked.

"Off and on for a couple years."

"How long have you been here?"

"Only a few weeks."

"Why didn't you come in sooner?"

"I don't like being confined. Does anyone take people out of here?"

"Sometimes. If you continue to get care here and remain off your back, this might heal. As soon as your doctor says you can get out of bed, I'll take you on the grounds, but now I have to change your dressing."

Once I had the dressing off, I saw the emaciated tissue as well as some bone. "Are you having any pain?"

"No. I don't feel anything back there. Sometimes, I have a headache."

"My medicine cart's right outside the door. I can get you something for your headache as soon as I dress this."

Dressing the wound took time. With all that drainage, some of my dried gauze was wet the moment I applied it. The main problem was getting the old dressing off without disturbing any of the newly healed tissue, as well as trying to keep the new sheets free of drainage. If I ever do his dressing again, I'd dress the wound first and then change the sheets. When the wound was half-dressed, the charge nurse came to help.

"During the day and evenings, they use two people to change Mr. Stone's dressing," he told me.

"Now they tell me," I said.

"By the time you put saline on the old dressing to loosen it enough for safe removal and not have it pull away any of the healed tissue, starting fresh bleeding, everything is wet again."

I wet extra gauze with saline and laid them on top of the old, stuck gauzed areas. Once they were wet, I removed them easily.

Mr. Stone told the charge nurse, "She does a good job. I don't feel sore anymore, and I can sleep again."

"Here are your pills and a drink," I said. "I won't bother you again. Here's your call bell. If you need me, call."

"OK. Thank you."

"I'll stop in before I finish my shift and say good-bye."

He never rang the bell. Each time I passed his room to check the others, I found him sleeping peacefully.

In the morning before I left, I went to his room to talk. We discussed Mrs. Murray. I told him she died.

"All the houses on her side of the street were torn down," he said. "Why?"

"Rats. The whole area was loaded with rats. I got weaker as I got older, and I caught the flu. After that, I couldn't go outside for five years. I spent a lot of time in bed at home alone. Everyone else had to work. There was no one to stay with me. When my sore got bad, I came here. I also ran out of money."

I knew the government would take care of him, because his injury was war-related. His coccyx sore was secondary but also related.

"I have no relatives, and the friends who used to see me years ago moved away. Two died, two others were shot."

"Who shot them?"

"Someone on the street. They were number runners. When the numbers hit, they didn't give the person all he won, so someone shot them."

"That's too bad. Now numbers are legal. You can play every day if you like. Do you still play?"

"Sometimes."

I wondered how, but I didn't ask. After saying good-bye, I left him in good spirits. I had the feeling he'd be all right.

The following night, I arrived for work and learned of Mr. Stone's noncompliant behavior. He was nasty to everyone who came to his room, and he refused to eat. He drank very little liquid.

Deodorizers were put in his room to fight the odor. The coccyx dressings had to be changed twice each shift, but he kept refusing. The order was changed to once a shift. Sometimes, he refused that, too. The chief complaint from everyone was his lying on his back. He was told that his wound would never heal and would continue to drain if he didn't stay off it.

I asked if he was receiving any mood-elevating meds, and was told they just started that day. His doctor asked if I'd speak to Mr. Stone. Perhaps there was something going on we didn't know about.

"He won't talk to us," the doctor said, "but he talks to you."

As a precautionary measure, masks, gowns, and gloves had to be worn by all visitors and caregivers in Mr. Stone's room. As I approached his door, I saw the precaution sign on it. A dressing cart with gowns, gloves, and masks, sat beside the door.

If I were in his position, my life almost over, forced to lie on my stomach all day, and be told every day something different, I'd find it pretty frightening. I remembered how frightened I'd been walking alongside the cemetery.

Mr. Stone was started on a new antibiotic, because the previous two hadn't worked. I stood in the doorway of his room and looked around. There was an IV pole with antibiotics being dripped into his veins. I was glad someone used his left arm. He needed his right arm to turn himself.

I doubted the staff had time to gown and mask every two hours to turn him, so he'd probably use his right arm to turn himself. There was no odor that day. He must've allowed the nurses to care for him and also let housekeeping clean, too. He looked good and had been shaved.

"You smell good," I said. "Is that a new cologne I smell?"

"Yes. I had a visitor."

"Good."

"My granddaughter saw me today."

I looked on his windowsill and saw a picture of a girl. "Is that her?"

"No. That's my great-granddaughter."

"Wow. I have one grandchild. I hope I live long enough to have great-grandchildren."

"Not like this."

I entered the room. "I hope you don't mind if I don't gown up. I'll just wear a mask and gloves. The mask is so you won't catch my germs, and the gloves are in case you want me to hand you a drink or something, you won't have to ring for someone else."

"My sore will never heal. Two years ago, I was in a civilian hospital twice for this, and they couldn't heal it. I can't spend my life on my stomach. As soon as I turn on my side or lie on my back, I start draining again. I'm tired of lying here wet and smelly, waiting for someone to change me."

I felt compassion for him.

"How'd you like it if I spoke to the staff and arranged for two people to give you care? They could change your dressing, your bed, and give you a bath during the shift. That way, you don't have to ring. They'll just come. After all, we're here to care for you. That way, everything is planned ahead of time, and you get all the time you need without anyone feeling rushed or rushing you. You won't feel that because your care takes so much time, you are taking time from others."

He took a large drink of liquids from me, and I held his hand for a little while before going home.

I didn't know why I felt a connection with him. I was ready to help him the way he helped me years earlier. I couldn't take him back to his friends on the corner, but I could be instrumental in setting up his care plan and trying to incorporate his wishes. When I spoke to the staff, they were agreeable and supportive.

Another week passed. Staff complaints about Mr. Stone diminished. My assignment took me away from him, and he saw me only for brief moments, when I said, "Hello," "Good-bye," or "Heard you're doing well." He always waved and greeted me back.

The last time I saw him was Friday. I offered him a drink of soda. While he sipped, he said, "The area on my buttocks is cancerous."

"Does your daughter know?"

"No. I don't want her to know."

He finished the soda, and I left to go home for the weekend.

When I returned Monday night, Mr. Stone wasn't in his room.

"What happened to him?" I asked.

"He died," the charge nurse said. "He had cancer, you know."

"Yes. He told me."

"You had a good rapport with him. All the patients love you. We hope you remain on our floor."

If they only knew the history I had with that World War Two veteran, they would've understood.

I didn't fight in any wars, but I knew they had to be fought. I gave my respect to all who fought so I could have a better life and a chance at success. There are many of us who care about those who shed their blood or gave up their lives for us.

After reading this story, I hope people remember our veterans and the man on the corner.

Larry Parr is the editor of hundreds of published novels and short stories. He is also a nationally known playwright. His plays, beginning with the musical biography of Hattie McDaniel, HI-HAT HATTIE, have been produced in regional theaters all across the United States. HI-HAT HATTIE won Kansas City's Drama Desk Award for Best Musical. Mr. Parr was twice a Florida Individual Artist Recipient, twice the winner of Southern Appalachian Repertory Theater's Annual Play Competition with MY CASTLE'S ROCKIN' and SUNDEW, and a winner of Florida Studio Theatre's Short Play Competition nine years in a row. He won STAGES '93 and the 1994 Porter Fleming Playwriting Competition. In 1995, he became the first white playwright produced in the history of the National Black Theatre Festival with the production of MY CASTLE'S ROCKIN'. A QUESTION OF PRIVACY won the 1999 Gold Coast Players best-play award and The National Arts Club's Playwrights First Award in Manhattan.

In 2000, Florida Studio Theatre presented him with the Barbara Anton Playwriting Award. The American Cinema Foundation awarded him their first prize for his screenplay about Hattie McDaniel, also entitled HI-HAT HATTIE. He is the author of two published novels and the editor of the short-story anthologies, BEST AMERICAN SHORT FICTION, STORIES FROM THE HEART, and STORIES OF THE UNEXPECTED. In 2002, he was chosen as a participant in The Floridian Project with HARRY T. MOORE; THE MOST HATED MAN IN FLORIDA. He teaches playwriting at Florida Studio Theatre.

Printed in the United States
49642LVS00003BA/4